Sam Eastland lives in the US and the UK. He is the grandson of a London police detective.

Further praise for Sam Eastland:

'For those who like their tales told in the John Buchan style, with a shot of vodka downed and a fully loaded Webley at the ready.' *Independent on Sunday*

' A vivid picture of a country still in a state of flux as the storm clouds gather . . . A pageturner of a book with enough neatly resolved twists and turns to keep any thriller fan happy.' *www.shotsmag.co.uk*

' Eastland's weaving of fact and fiction, of real and invented characters, is brilliantly achieved, and Pekkala makes an unusual and captivating hero.' *The Times*

'A brilliantly conceived and perfectly executed mystery, with the requisite deaths, clues, investigation and resolution . . . One can only hope that Eastland has more plans and plots for Inspector Pekkala. This is a series with plenty of promise.' *The Globe and Mail*

' Pekkala is above all a survivor, but also a loveable human . . . As Pekkala emerges from his previous life, I – for one – want to learn more.' *itsacrimetypepad.com*

D1129968

Siberian Red

SAM EASTLAND

faber and faber

First published in this edition in 2012
by Faber and Faber Limited
Bloomsbury House, 74–77 Great Russell Street
London WC1B 3DA

This paperback edition first published in 2012

Typeset by Faber and Faber Ltd

Printed and bound in England by CPI Group (UK) Ltd, Croydon, CR0 4YY

The right of Sam Eastland to be identified as author
of this work has been asserted in accordance with Section 77
of the Copyright, Designs and Patents Act 1988

A CIP record for this book
is available from the British Library

ISBN 978-0-571-26068-3

2 4 6 8 10 9 7 5 3 1

Borodok Labour Camp

Valley of Krasnagolyana

Siberia

September 1939

In a cave, deep underground, lit by the greasy flame of a kerosene lamp, the man knelt in a puddle, his empty hands held out as if to catch drops of water which fell through the cracks in the ceiling. He was badly wounded, with deep cuts across his chest and arms. The home-made knife with which he had attempted to defend himself lay out of reach behind him. Head bowed, he stared with a look of confusion at his own reflection in the puddle, like a man who no longer recognised himself.

Before him stretched the shadow of the killer who had brought him to this place. 'I came here to offer you a reason to go on living,' said the killer, 'and this is how you repay me?'

With fumbling, blood-smeared fingers, the man undid the button on his shirt pocket. He pulled out a crumpled photograph of a group of soldiers on horseback, dense forest in the background. The men leaned forward in their saddles, grinning at the camera. 'They are my reason for living.'

'And now they will be your reason for dying.' Slowly, the way people sometimes move in dreams, the killer stepped behind the man. With movements almost gentle, he grasped the man by his short and filthy hair, pulling his head back so that the tendons stood out in his neck. Then he drew a knife from the folds of his clothing, cut the man's throat and held him like a lover while his heart bled dry.

'Poskrebyshev!' The voice of Joseph Stalin exploded through the wall.

In the adjoining room, Stalin's secretary sprang to his feet. Poskrebyshev was a short, round-faced man, bald except for a fringe of grey which arced around the back of his head and resembled the wreath of a Roman emperor. Like his master, he wore trousers tucked into black calfskin boots and a plain mandarin-collared tunic in precisely the same shade of brownish-green as the rotten apples that two neighbourhood bullies, Ermakov and Schwartz, used to hurl at him from their hiding places along the young Poskrebyshev's route to school.

Since the war had broken out, one month before, there had been many such outbursts from the man Poskrebyshev referred to as Vozhd. The Boss.

On September 1st, 1939, as part of a secret agreement between Germany and Russia, buried in a peace treaty signed between the two countries and known as the Molotov-Ribbentrop Pact, Germany had invaded Poland.

Justification for the invasion had been provided by a staged attack on a German customs house called Hochlinde and on the Gleiwitz radio substation. Thirteen inmates from Oranienburg Concentration camp, believing that they had been chosen to take part in a propaganda film, designed to improve relations between Germans and the Poles, were trucked towards Hochlinde under cover of darkness. All were dressed in Polish Army uniforms. The inmates had been convinced that they were to enact a meeting between German and Polish troops, somewhere in the forest on the border between the two countries.

The plot of the film would be simple. At first both sides, mistrustful of the other, would draw their weapons. For an agonising moment, it would seem as if a gunfight might actually break out. But then the men would recognise their common ground as human beings. The guns would be lowered. Cigarettes would be exchanged. The two patrols would part company and melt back into the forest. Upon completion of the film the inmates had been promised that they would be sent home as free men.

As they neared Hochlinde, the trucks pulled over and the prisoners shared rations with a squad of SS guards accompanying them. Each prisoner was also given what he was told would be a tetanus shot, as a matter of standard procedure. The syringes were not filled with tetanus vaccine, however. Instead, the men were injected with Prussic acid. Within minutes, all of them were dead.

Afterwards, the bodies were loaded back on to the trucks and the convoy continued to the vicinity of Hochlinde, where the corpses were dumped in the woods and shot with German weapons. The bodies would later be exhibited as proof that Polish soldiers had launched an attack on German soil.

Meanwhile, at the Gleiwitz radio station, an officer of the SS named Naujocks, with the help of a Polish-speaking German, interrupted regular radio transmission to announce that Gleiwitz was under attack by Polish troops.

Within hours, German planes were bombing Warsaw. On the following day, German panzers crossed the Polish border.

Two weeks later, in accordance with the secret clauses of the Molotov-Ribbentrop Pact, the Russian army began its own invasion from the east.

Even though the obliteration of Polish forces had been virtually guaranteed from the beginning, the slightest setback – a temporary withdrawal, a mistimed attack, supplies sent to the wrong location – sent Stalin into a rage.

And that rage fell first upon Poskrebyshev.

'Where is he?' Stalin's muffled voice boomed from behind the closed doors of his study. 'Poskrebyshev!'

'Mother of God,' muttered Poskrebyshev, the sweat already beading on his forehead. 'What have I done now?'

The truth was, Poskrebyshev knew exactly what he had done. He had been dreading this moment for a long time and now, it seemed, his crimes had finally caught up with him.

On being made Stalin's personal secretary, the highest appointment a man like Poskrebyshev could ever hope to hold, the first thing he had done was to forge documents of transfer for Comrades Schwartz and Ermakov, the two bullies on whom he had sworn to take vengeance one day. Stamped with a rubber facsimile of Stalin's signature, the documents ordered the immediate dispatch of these two men, one an electrician and the other a roof tiler, from their home town in a cosy suburb of Moscow to the port of Archangel, high in the Soviet Arctic. There, construction had begun to transform the frozen wasteland around the port into a modern military base for Soviet Navy personnel and their families. The construction was expected to take many years. In the meantime, conditions for the workers on this project would be primitive in the extreme.

Why such documents would have emerged from the office of Stalin himself was a question nobody would ever dare to ask. This was the perfect symmetry of Poskrebyshev's revenge, executed more than thirty years after the events which had set it in motion.

In the weeks and months that followed the transfer of Ermakov and Schwartz to the Arctic, Poskrebyshev would often stop in at the Kremlin's meteorological office and inquire about weather in Archangel. Thirty below. Forty below. Even fifty below, on occasion. The worse the conditions, the more convinced Poskrebyshev became that there was indeed justice in the world for people like himself, a thing which had seemed impossible back in those days when the rotten apples, pulpy and reeking of vinegar, had splattered against him by the dozen.

At first his scheme had seemed foolproof, but, as time went by, Poskrebyshev came to realise that there was no such thing. He resigned himself to the fact that, sooner or later, he would be found out.

The double doors flew open and Stalin burst into the outer office.

In this waking nightmare, it seemed to Poskrebyshev as if Stalin, dressed in his brownish-green tunic, had transformed into one of those apples so expertly thrown by Comrades Schwartz and Ermakov.

'Where is he?' screamed Stalin, as he approached Poskrebyshev. 'Where is that black-hearted troll?'

'I am here, Comrade Stalin,' replied Poskrebyshev, his eyes bulging with fear.

Stalin's eyes narrowed. 'What?'

'I am here, Comrade Stalin!' shouted Poskrebyshev, his voice raised to a shout of blind obedience.

'Have you completely lost your mind?' asked Stalin, resting his knuckles on Poskrebyshev's desk and leaning forward until their faces were only a hand's breadth apart. 'I am looking for Pekkala!'

'You have found him,' said a voice.

Poskrebyshev turned. He saw a man standing in the doorway to the outer office. Neither he nor Stalin had heard him enter the room.

Pekkala was tall and broad-shouldered, with a straight nose and strong, white teeth. Streaks of premature grey ran through his short dark hair. His eyes were marked by a strange silvery quality, which people noticed only when he was looking directly at them. He wore a knee-length coat made of black wool, with a mandarin collar and concealed buttons which fastened on the left side of his chest. His ankle-high boots, also black, were double-soled and polished. He stood with his hands tucked behind his back. The shape of a revolver in a shoulder holster was just visible beneath the heavy cloth of his coat.

Stalin's anger dissipated as suddenly as it had appeared. Now a smile crept over his face, narrowing his eyes almost shut. 'Pekkala!' he said, growling out the name. 'I have a job for you.'

As the two men disappeared into Stalin's office and the door closed quietly behind them, the residue of fear in Poskrebyshev's brain was still too powerful to let him feel relief. Later, perhaps, that would come. For now, all he experienced was the luxury of drawing in breath, and an overpowering curiosity to know the weather forecast for Archangel.

Stalin, sitting at his desk in a leather-backed chair, carefully stuffed his pipe with honey-coloured shreds of Balkan tobacco.

There was no chair on the other side of the desk, so Pekkala had to stand while he waited for the man to complete his ritual.

During this time, the only sound in the room was the dry rustle of Stalin's breathing as he held a match over the pipe bowl and coaxed the tobacco to burn. Once this had been accomplished, he waved the match and dropped the smouldering stick into a brass ashtray. The soft, sweet smell of the tobacco drifted about the room. Finally, Stalin spoke. 'I am sending you back to Siberia.'

The words struck Pekkala like a slap in the face. At first, he was too shocked to reply.

'Although not as a prisoner,' continued Stalin. 'Not officially. There has been a murder in your old camp, Borodok.'

'With respect, Comrade Stalin, there must be murders in that place every day of the week.'

'This one has caught my attention.' Stalin seemed preoccupied with the ashtray, moving it from one side of his desk to the other and then back to its original place. 'Do you remember Colonel Kolchak?'

'Of course I remember him!'

Stalin's words threw Pekkala back to a dreary, rain-soaked night in March of 1917, just before the Tsar stepped down from power.

He was woken by the sound of horses passing on the gravel road outside his bedroom window. During his years as Special Investigator for the Tsar, Pekkala had lived in a small cottage on the grounds of the Imperial estate, known as Tsarskoye Selo estate, on the outskirts of St Petersburg. Living near the old Pensioners' Stables, Pekkala was used to the noise of horses moving by, but not at this time of night.

Peering through the curtains, Pekkala glimpsed a shadowy procession of wagons, three in all, and each one weighed down by wooden boxes with rope handles, which resembled ammunition crates. He counted twenty-five boxes on each wagon.

One of these wagons had split a wheel, dumping its cargo. Now soldiers milled about, stacking the heavy boxes at the side of the path. Others were busy trying to remove the wheel so they could rig it with a spare.

Pekkala climbed from his bed, opened the door and stepped out into the dark.

'There you are!' said a voice. 'Sorry to have woken you.'

Pekkala turned to see a man wearing a close-tailored uniform and moving with the slightly bow-legged gait of a cavalry officer. His face was fierce and thin and dominated by a rigidly waxed moustache. Pekkala instantly recognised Colonel Kolchak, a man whose social standing in the ranks of Russian nobility, combined with an utter ruthlessness of character, had won him favour with the Tsar.

Finding Kolchak here, amid all of these boxes, Pekkala suddenly realised what he was looking at. Now that the Revolution had begun, the Tsar's gold was being evacuated to a place of safety. The task had been given to Colonel Kolchak who, in the company of fifty hand-picked men, would transport the treasure to Siberia.

Kolchak's orders, Pekkala knew, were to follow the route of the Trans-Siberian Railroad and link up with his uncle, Alexander Vassileyevich Kolchak, an admiral in the Tsar's Pacific Fleet in Vladivostok, who would then take charge of the gold. The Admiral was forming an army of anti-Bolshevik forces. Rumours were circulating that he planned to declare independence for the whole of Siberia.

The order to begin transporting the gold should have been given weeks, if not months before, but Pekkala had seen for himself that, in spite of all the warning signs that the Revolution would soon overwhelm them, the Romanovs had chosen to believe such a thing was impossible. Now, Revolutionary Guards were in control of St Petersburg. It was only a matter of time before they advanced on Tsarskoye Selo.

'Heading out?' asked Kolchak, as he shook Pekkala's hand.

'Soon,' replied Pekkala. 'All I have to do is pack my bag.'

'Travelling light,' remarked Kolchak. He was trying to sound jovial, but the anger at this delay penetrated his voice.

'Not so for you,' replied Pekkala, as he glanced at the wagons.

'No indeed,' sighed Kolchak. With a sharp command, he sent the two good wagons on ahead, remaining behind to oversee the repair of the third.

Another hour passed before the broken wheel had finally been replaced. As two soldiers heaved the crates back on to the wagon, one of the rope handles broke. The box slipped from their hands, spilling its contents of gold ingots on to the ground.

'Damn you!' Kolchak shouted at the soldiers. Then he turned to Pekkala. 'I am supposed to bring all this to the other side of the country. How can I possibly accomplish my task if these carts can't even make it off the grounds of the Imperial estate?'

'You have much work ahead of you,' agreed Pekkala.

'What you are witnessing,' Kolchak said brusquely, 'is final proof that the world we know is coming to an end. Men like us must now look to our own survival.'

As the last wagon trundled away into the dark, Kolchak climbed back on to his horse. 'We must learn to be patient,' he told Pekkala. 'One day we shall have our vengeance for what these bastards are about to do with everything we love. This fight isn't over, Pekkala.'

'And do you remember what became of the Kolchak Expedition?' asked Stalin.

'I do,' replied Pekkala. 'Almost as soon as the expedition was under way, Kolchak learned that an informant had betrayed him to the Bolsheviks. Guessing that Kolchak would head for the territory held by his uncle, the Bolsheviks sent their own cavalry to intercept the expedition before it reached Siberia. Once Kolchak realised that he was being followed, and since the wagons which transported the gold were slowing down his progress, he decided to leave the gold behind in the city of Kazan as he passed through there on his way to Siberia. The gold was later removed from its hiding place by the anti-Bolshevik forces of the Czechoslovakian Legion, who were also on their way to Vladivostok.'

Stalin nodded. 'Go on.'

'In the winter of 1918, Czech Legion troops under the command of General Gaida had joined with the Admiral's White Russian Army. In the spring of 1919, they launched an offensive against the Reds from their base in Siberia.'

'But the offensive stalled out, didn't it?'

'Yes,' agreed Pekkala, 'and by November of that year, the Admiral was forced to abandon his capital at Omsk. All through that winter, Czech and White Russian troops retreated east towards Vladivostok. There they hoped to board ships which would take them out of the country. They had captured a number of trains, some of them specially armoured, and were travelling along the Trans-Siberian Railroad. By January of 1920, they were still nowhere near the coast. Seeing that his situation was hopeless, Admiral Kolchak stepped down from power. From then on, he was placed under the protection of the 6th Czechoslovakian Rifle Regiment, under General Janin. The Czechs became responsible for the safety of the Admiral as they continued their journey to Vladivostok.

'And what happened then?'

'You know what happened, Comrade Stalin. Why are you asking me now?'

Stalin slowly rolled his hand before his face. 'Humour me, Pekkala. What happened next?'

'Very well,' sighed Pekkala. 'When the Czech train convoy reached the city of Irkutsk, they were stopped by armed members of the Socialist Political Centre, who demanded that they hand over Admiral Kolchak in return for being allowed to pass through.'

'And what else did they want, these socialists?'

'Gold,' replied Pekkala. 'Specifically, the Imperial Reserves which were still being guarded by the Czechs.'

'And what did they do, these Czechs of the 6th Rifle Regiment?'

'They handed the gold over, along with Admiral Kolchak.'

'Why?'

'The Socialist Centre had mined the tunnels around Lake Baikal. If they decided to blow the tunnels, the Czechs would never have gotten through. Handing over Kolchak and the gold was their only hope of reaching Vladivostok.'

'And what became of Admiral Kolchak, the Ruler of Siberia?'

'On January 30th, 1920, the Admiral was executed by the Bolsheviks.'

'And what of his nephew, the Colonel?'

'Red cavalry finally caught up with him. After a fight lasting three days, survivors of the Expedition surrendered. Among the men captured was Colonel Kolchak himself.'

By then, in St Petersburg, on the other side of the country, Pekkala had also been taken prisoner by the Revolutionaries. Both men ended up in the Butyrka prison, although neither was aware of the other's whereabouts at first.

'And, of course,' remarked Stalin, 'you remember what happened at Butyrka?'

'Remember?' spat Pekkala. 'Do you think I could ever forget?'

After months of torture and solitary confinement, prison guards frog-marched Pekkala down the spiral stone steps of the old fortress of Butyrka and into the basement. Knowing that these caverns, which had once boasted one of the world's finest collections of wines, now served as execution chambers for enemies of the state, he fully expected to be murdered there.

Pekkala felt relieved that his time of suffering was almost over. In something approaching a gesture of compassion, some convicts were even shot before they reached the bottom of the stairs, so as to minimise the terror of their execution. Pekkala found himself hoping that he might merit such a speedy end, but when they reached the bottom of the stairs, the guards brought him to a room already occupied by several men who wore the gymnastiorka *tunics, dark blue trousers and knee-length riding boots of State Security Troops.*

There was also a third man, a barely human figure, cowered naked in the corner. The man's body was a mass of electrical burns and bruises.

This man was Colonel Kolchak.

The sentence was read out by Commissar Dzhugashvili, the same man who had been responsible for Pekkala's weeks of interrogation.

In the final seconds of his life, Kolchak called out to Pekkala. 'Inform his majesty the Tsar that I told them nothing.'

Before the last word had left his mouth, the NKVD men opened fire. The concussion of the gunfire was stunning in the confined space of the cell. When the shooting finally stopped, Dzhugashvili stepped forward, stuck the barrel in Kolchak's right eye and put another bullet into Kolchak's head.

It was Dzhugashvili who sat before Pekkala now. Joseph Dzhugashvili, who had changed his name to Stalin – Man of Steel – as was the fashion of the early Bolsheviks.

'You know, Pekkala, memory can be deceiving. Even yours.'

'What do you mean?'

Stalin puffed thoughtfully at his pipe. 'The man you thought was Colonel Kolchak, the man I *also* thought was Kolchak, turns out to have been an imposter.'

Although Pekkala was surprised to hear this, he knew it did not lie beyond the bounds of possibility. The Tsar himself had half a dozen look-alikes, who took his place at times of danger and who, in some cases, paid for that occupation with their lives. For someone as important to the Tsar as Colonel Kolchak, it did not seem unlikely that a double had been found for him as well.

'What does this have to do with the murder at Borodok?'

'The victim was a man named Isaac Ryabov; a former captain in the Imperial Cavalry and one of the last survivors of the Kolchak Expedition still in captivity at Borodok. Ryabov approached the Camp Commandant with an offer to reveal the whereabouts of Colonel Kolchak in exchange for being allowed to go free. But somebody got to him first.'

'Ryabov might well have known where Kolchak was hiding twenty years ago, but the Colonel could have gone anywhere in the world since that time. Do you honestly think Ryabov's information was still accurate?'

'It is a possibility which I cannot afford to overlook.' Stalin removed his pipe and laid it in the ashtray on his desk. Then he sat back and touched his fingertips together. 'Do you suppose Colonel Kolchak has ever forgiven the Czechs for handing over his uncle to be executed?'

'I doubt it. From what I knew of Kolchak, forgiveness did not strike me as being one of his virtues. Personally, I think the Czechs had no choice.'

'I agree,' nodded Stalin. 'But as far as Colonel Kolchak is concerned, the legion's job was to protect his uncle, not to mention the gold. Whether every last one of them died fulfilling that duty would be irrelevant to a man like him.'

'And how do you know what he thinks?'

'I don't. I am only telling you what I would think if I were Colonel Kolchak. And I am also telling you that when a man like Kolchak gets vengeance in his brain, he will set fire to the world before he can be satisfied.'

'Even if Kolchak can be found,' said Pekkala, 'surely he does not pose a threat. He is only one man, after all.'

'I take no comfort in that. One person can still be dangerous. I know, because I am only one man and I am very dangerous. And when I see in another man those qualities which I also recognise within myself, I know that I cannot ignore him. You and I have a strange alliance, Pekkala. In our thinking, we are opposites in almost every way. But the one place where our ideas intersect lies in the struggle for our country to survive. It is the reason you did not die that day in the basement of Butyrka prison. But Kolchak is not like you. And that is why I put him to death, or attempted to, anyway.'

'If this is simply a vendetta against a man you tried and failed to kill, send one of your assassins to find him. I could be put to better use on other cases.'

'You may be right, but if my instincts are correct that Kolchak poses a threat to this country . . .'

'Then I will bring him to justice,' interrupted Pekkala.

'And that is why I'm sending you instead of somebody else.' As Stalin spoke, he slid Ryabov's file across the desk towards Pekkala. Inside that folder would be every scrap of information Soviet Intelligence had managed to accumulate on Ryabov – everything from his blood type to his choice of cigarettes to the books he checked out of the library. 'Your investigation is to be conducted in the utmost secrecy. Once you arrive at Borodok, if word leaks out among the prisoners that you are working for the Bureau of Special Operations, I will lose not only Ryabov's killer but you as well.'

'I may need to involve Major Kirov in this investigation.'

Stalin spread his arms magnanimously. 'Understood, and the Camp Commandant has also been instructed to assist you in any way he can. He is holding the body, as well as the murder weapon, until you arrive at the camp.'

'Who is in charge there now?'

'The same man who was running it when you were there.'

'Klenovkin?' An image surfaced in Pekkala's mind of a gaunt, slope-shouldered man with black hair cut so short that it stood up like porcupine quills from his skull. Pekkala had met him only once, when he first arrived at the camp.

Having summoned Pekkala to his office, Klenovkin did not look up when Pekkala entered the room. All he said was, 'Remove your cap when you are in my presence.' He then busied himself reading Pekkala's prisoner file, carefully turning the large yellow pages, each one with a red diagonal stripe in the upper right-hand corner.

At last, Klenovkin closed the file and raised his head, squinting at Pekkala through rimless spectacles. 'We have all fallen from grace in one way and another,' he said. There was a resonance in his voice as if he were addressing a crowd instead of just one man. 'Having just read your history, convict Pekkala, I see that you have fallen further than most.'

In those first years of the Bolshevik government, so many of the prison inmates were in Borodok on account of their loyalty to Nicholas II, that the presence of a man with Pekkala's reputation as the Tsar's most trusted servant could easily have led to an uprising in the camp. Klenovkin's solution was to place Pekkala as far away as possible from the other inmates.

'You are a disease,' Klenovkin told Pekkala. 'I will not allow you to infect my prisoners. The simplest thing to do would be to have you shot, but unfortunately I am not allowed to do that. Some benefit must be derived from your existence before we consign you to oblivion.'

Pekkala stared at the man. Even during the months of harsh interrogation leading up to his departure for Siberia, he had never felt as helpless as he did at that moment.

'I am sending you out into the wilderness,' continued Klenovkin. 'You will become a tree marker in the Valley of Krasnagolyana, a job no man has held for longer than six months.'

'Why not?'

'Because nobody lives that long.'

Working alone, with no chance of escape and far from any human contact, tree markers died from exposure, starvation, and loneliness. Those who became lost, or who fell and broke a leg, were usually eaten by wolves. Tree marking was the only assignment at Borodok said to be worse than a death sentence.

Provisions were left for him three times a year at the end of a logging road. Kerosene. Cans of meat. Nails. For the rest, he had to fend for himself. His only task, besides surviving, was to mark in red paint those trees ready for cutting by the inmates of the camp. Lacking any brushes, Pekkala stirred his fingers in the scarlet paint and daubed his print upon the trunks. By the time the logging crews arrived, Pekkala would already be gone. The red hand prints became, for most of the convicts, the only trace of him they ever saw.

Only rarely was he spotted by those logging crews who came to cut the timber. What they glimpsed was a creature barely recognisable as a man. With the crust of red paint that spattered his prison clothes and long hair maned about his face, he resembled a beast stripped of its skin and left to die. Wild rumours surrounded him – that he was an eater of human flesh, that he wore a scapula made from the bones of those who had disappeared in the forest, that he carried a club whose end was embedded with human teeth, that he wore scalps laced together as a cap.

They called him the man with bloody hands.

By the time word of his identity leaked out among the prisoners, they assumed he was already dead.

But six months later, to Klenovkin's astonishment, Pekkala was still alive. And he stayed alive.

When a young Lieutenant Kirov arrived to recall him back to duty with the Bureau of Special Operations, Pekkala had been living in the forest for nine years, longer than any other tree marker in the history of the gulag system.

Tucking Ryabov's file into his coat, Pekkala turned to leave.

'One more thing before you go.'

Pekkala turned again. Reaching down beside his chair, Stalin picked up a small shopping bag and held it out towards Pekkala. 'Your clothes for the journey.'

Pekkala glanced inside and saw what at first appeared to be some dirty, pinkish-grey rags. He lifted out the flimsy pyjama-type shirt and recognised a standard prison-issue uniform. A shudder passed through him as he thought back to the last time he had worn garments like this.

At that moment, the door opened and Poskrebyshev walked in. He advanced two paces, stopped and clicked his heels together. 'Comrade Stalin, I beg to report that Poland has surrendered.'

Stalin nodded and said nothing.

'I also beg to inform you that the Katyn Operation has begun,' continued Poskrebyshev.

Stalin's only reply was an angry stare.

'You asked me to tell you . . .'

'Get out,' said Stalin, quietly.

Poskrebyshev's heels smashed together once more, then he turned and left the room, closing the double doors behind him with a barely audible click of the lock.

'The Katyn Operation?' asked Pekkala.

'It would have been better for you not to know,' Stalin replied, 'but since it is too late for that, let me answer your question with a question of my own. Suppose you were an officer in the Polish Army, that you had surrendered and been taken prisoner. Let us say you had been well treated. You had been housed. You had been fed.'

'What is it you want to know, Comrade Stalin?'

'Say I offer you a choice; either a place in the Red Army, or the opportunity to return home as a civilian.'

'They will choose to go home,' said Pekkala.

'Yes,' replied Stalin. 'Most of them did.'

'But they will never arrive, will they?'

'No.'

In his mind, Pekkala could see those officers, bundled in the mysterious brown of their Polish Army greatcoats, hands tied behind their backs with copper wire. One after the other, NKVD troopers shoved them to the edge of a huge pit dug into the orangey-brown soil of a forest in eastern Poland. With the barrels of their guns, the NKVD men tipped off the caps of their prisoners, sending them into the pit below. As each Polish officer was shot in the back of the head, he fell forward into the pit, on to the bodies of those who had been killed before.

How many were there? Pekkala wondered. Hundreds? Thousands?

By nightfall, the pit would be covered up.

Within a few weeks, tiny shoots of grass would rise from the trampled soil.

One thing Pekkala had learned, however. Nothing stays buried forever.

'You have not answered my question,' said Stalin. 'I asked what *you* would do. Not they.'

'I would realise I had no choice,' replied Pekkala.

With a scythe-like sweep of his hand, Stalin brushed aside Pekkala's words. 'But I did give them a choice!'

'No, Comrade Stalin, you did not.'

Stalin smiled. 'That is why you have survived, and why those other men will not.'

As soon as Pekkala had departed, Stalin pushed the intercom button. 'Poskrebyshev!'

'Yes, Comrade Stalin.'

'All messages between Pekkala and Major Kirov are to be intercepted.'

'Of course.'

'Whatever Pekkala has to say, I want to read it before Kirov does. I want no secrets kept from me.'

'No, Comrade Stalin,' said Poskrebyshev, and a fresh coat of sweat slicked his palms.

The intercom button stayed on, whispering static into Stalin's ears. 'Is there anything else, Poskrebyshev?'

'Why do you let Pekkala speak to you that way? So disrespectfully?' Over the years, Poskrebyshev had advanced to the stage where he could occasionally express an unsolicited opinion to the Boss, although only in the most reverent of tones. But the way Pekkala talked to Stalin caused Poskrebyshev's bowels to cramp. Even more amazing to him was the fact that Stalin let Pekkala get away with it. In asking such a question, Poskrebyshev was well aware that he had overstepped his bounds. If the answer to his question was a flood of obscenities from the next room, he knew he would have only himself to blame. Nevertheless he simply had to know.

'The reason I endure his insolence, unlike, for example, yours, Poskrebyshev, is that Pekkala is the only person I know of who would not kill me for the chance to rule this country.'

'Surely that is not true, Comrade Stalin!' protested Poskrebyshev, knowing perfectly well that whether it was true or not, what mattered was that Stalin believed it.

'Ask yourself, Poskrebyshev – what would you do to sit where I am sitting now?'

An image flashed through Poskrebyshev's mind, of himself at Stalin's desk, smoking Stalin's cigarettes and bullying his very own secretary. In that moment, Poskrebyshev knew that, in spite of all his claims of loyalty, he would have gutted Stalin like a fish for the chance to take the leader's place.

*

One hour later, as the last rays of sunset glistened on the ice-sheathed telegraph wires, Pekkala's battered Emka staff car, driven by his assistant, Major Kirov, pulled into a railyard at mile marker 17 on the Moscow Highway. The railyard had no name. It was known simply as V-4, and the only trains departing from this place were convict transports headed for the gulags.

However miserable the journey promised to be, Pekkala knew it was necessary to travel as a convict in order to protect the cover story that he had fallen out of favour with Stalin and received a twenty-year sentence for unspecified crimes against the State.

Major Kirov pulled up behind some empty freight cars, cut the engine and looked out across the railyard where prisoners huddled by the wagons which would soon be taking them away.

'You can still call this off, Inspector.'

'You know that is impossible.'

'They have no right to send you back to that place, even if it is to carry out an investigation.'

'There is no "they", Kirov. The order came directly from Stalin.'

'Then he should at least have given you time to study the relevant files.'

'It wouldn't have made any difference,' answered Pekkala. 'The victim's dossier is incomplete. There was only one page. The rest of it must be lost somewhere in NKVD archives. As a result, I know almost nothing about the man whose death I am being sent to investigate.'

The train whistle blew, and the prisoners began to climb aboard.

'It is time,' said Pekkala, 'but first, there is something I need you to look after while I'm gone.' Into Kirov's hand, Pekkala dropped a heavy gold disc, as wide across as the length of his little finger. Across the centre was a stripe of white enamel inlay, which began at a point, widened until it took up half the disc and narrowed again to a point on the other side. Embedded in the middle of the white enamel was a large, round emerald. Together, the elements formed the unmistakable shape of an eye.

Pekkala had already been working for two years as the Tsar's Special Investigator when the Tsar summoned him one evening to the Alexander Palace, his residence on the Tsarskoye Selo estate.

Entering the Tsar's study, Pekkala found him sitting in a chair by the window. He was relieved that the Tsar did not get up. In Pekkala's experience, if the Tsar remained sitting when he entered the room, the meeting would go well. If the Tsar rose to his feet, however, Pekkala could be sure that the man's temper had already been lost.

Beside the Tsar's chair stood a small table, on which a candle burned. This was the only light source in the room and in that glowing pool, the Tsar seemed to float like a mirage.

With his soft blue eyes, the Tsar regarded Pekkala. 'I have decided that the title of Special Investigator lacks' – he twisted his hand in the air, like the claw of a barnacle sweeping through an ocean current – 'the gravity of your position. There are other special investigators in my police force, but there has never been a position quite like yours before. It was my grandfather who created the Gendarmerie and my father who established the Okhrana. But you are my creation, for which I have also commissioned an appropriate symbol of your rank.'

It was then that the Tsar presented Pekkala with the medallion which would soon earn him the title 'Emerald Eye'.

The Tsar rose from his chair and, taking the badge from its

velvet cushion, pinned it to the cloth beneath the right lapel of Pekkala's jacket. 'As my personal investigator, you will have absolute authority in the fulfilment of your duties. No secrets may be withheld from you. There are no documents you cannot see upon request. There is no door you cannot walk through unannounced. You may requisition any mode of transport on the spot if you deem it necessary. You are free to come and go where you please and when you please. You may arrest anyone whom you suspect is guilty of a crime. Even me.'

'Excellency . . .'

The Tsar held up a hand to silence him. 'There can be no exceptions, Pekkala. Otherwise it is all meaningless. I entrust you with the safety of this country and also with my life and the lives of my family.' The Tsar paused. 'This brings us to the second box.'

From a large, mahogany box beside his chair, the Tsar removed a brass-handled Webley revolver.

'It was given to me by my cousin, George V.'

Pekkala had seen a picture of them together hanging on the wall of the Tsar's study – the King of England and the Tsar of Russia, two of the most powerful men in the world. The two men looked almost identical. Their expressions were the same, the shapes of their heads, their beards, their mouths, noses and ears alike. Only their eyes showed any difference, because the King's looked rounder than those of the Tsar.

'Go on.' The Tsar held out the gun. 'Take it.'

The weapon was heavy, but well-balanced. Its brass grips felt cold against Pekkala's palm. 'It is very fine, Excellency, but you know how I feel about gifts.'

'Who said anything about a gift? That and the badge are the

tools of your trade, Pekkala. I am issuing them to you the same as any soldier in the army is issued what he needs for his work.'

Now Kirov closed his fingers around the badge. 'I will take good care of it until you return, Inspector.'

'The Webley is in my desk drawer,' added Pekkala, 'although I know you are more partial to your Tokarev.'

'Is there nothing more I can do, Inspector?'

'There may well be,' he replied, 'but I won't know until I get to Borodok.'

'How will I stay in contact with you?'

'By telegram through the Camp Commandant, Major Klenovkin. He will make sure I receive any messages.'

The two men shook hands.

'I will see you on the other side,' said Kirov, giving the traditional farewell.

'Indeed you will, Major Kirov.'

As Pekkala made his way across the railyard, heading towards the group of convicts, he was spotted by the train's chief engineer, a man named Filipp Demidov.

Demidov was the brother of Anna Demidova, lady-in-waiting to the Tsarina Alexandra, who had been murdered in July of 1918 by agents of the Bolshevik Secret Service, the Cheka, in the same executions which claimed the lives of the Tsar, his wife and his children.

Several years before her death, Anna Demidova had secured for her brother a post as the Tsar's chauffeur, a job he held until the staff at Tsarskoye Selo was dismissed in March of 1917. Immediately afterwards, Demidov went to work for the State Railways and had been with them ever since.

In his days as a chauffeur, Demidov had often seen Pekkala coming and going from meetings with the Tsar. He had, on occasion, driven Pekkala into the city of St Petersburg in the Tsar's Hispano Suiza Alfonso XIII sedan. Once, by accident, he had even sat down next to Pekkala at the restaurant where the inspector used to take most of his meals; a rough and simple place called the Café Tilsit, where customers ate from earthenware bowls at long, bare wood tables.

Demidov, who had a good memory for faces, had used the occasion to make a careful study of the inspector. Seeing the Emerald Eye among these common criminals overrode all instincts of self-preservation. He climbed down from the engine and strode quickly across to Pekkala.

'Demidov!' he gasped, instantly recognising the former chauffeur.

'Inspector,' replied the Chief Engineer, 'you must come with me at once.'

What Demidov hoped to accomplish with this meeting, Pekkala had no idea, but it was too late now, as the last of the convicts were already climbing on board. There was no way he could join them without drawing attention to himself, so rather than jeopardise his cover, Pekkala followed Demidov into the shadows.

'The prisoners aboard this train are going to their deaths,' Demidov's hoarse whisper cut through the frosty air. 'I can't let that happen to you.'

'I cannot explain to you why,' replied Pekkala, 'but one way or another, I must get aboard that train.'

Demidov's back straightened as he realised his mistake. 'My God, what have I done?'

'Nothing that cannot be fixed.'

'Whatever it takes,' said Demidov, 'consider it done, Inspector.'

By the time ETAP-1889 finally departed, the sun had already set. Pekkala stood with Demidov at the engine controls as the great cyclopic eye of the locomotive's headlight carved out a path through the darkness.

The convoy was more than fifty wagons long. Each had been designed to hold either forty men or eight horses, after the pattern used by the French army during the Great War. The French wagons had occasionally held as many as sixty men, but the wagons of ETAP-1889 now contained eighty men each, which meant that, for the entire ten-day journey to Siberia, everyone would be forced to stand.

'Where is the next station?' Pekkala had to shout to make himself heard above the rumble of the locomotive.

'There's a switching junction called Shatura, about ten kilometres down the line, but we aren't due to stop there.'

'Is there any way you can halt the train at that junction?'

Demidov thought for a moment. 'I could tell them our brakes are overheating. That would require a visual inspection of the wheels. The process would take about twenty minutes.'

'Good,' said Pekkala. 'That is all the time I need.'

*

The master of the V-4 station, Edvard Kasinec, had been informed earlier that day to expect the arrival of a special prisoner for convoy ETAP-1889. The convoy would be passing through Sverdlovsk, Petropavlovsk and Omsk, destined for the Valley of Krasnagolyana, in the furthest reaches of Siberia.

Sometimes, through the frosted windows of his office, Kasinec would study the procession of convicts as they were herded at bayonet point into the wagons, wearing nothing but the flimsy cotton pyjamas issued to them in the prisons of Butyrka and Lubyanka. Kasinec would try to pick out those he imagined might survive the ordeal that lay ahead. A few might even be lucky enough to return home one day. It was a little game he played to pass the time, but he never played it with convoys travelling as far as the Valley of Krasnagolyana. Those men were bound for camps whose names were spoken only in whispers. They were never coming back.

It had saddened him to learn that this special prisoner was none other than Inspector Pekkala of the Bureau of Special Operations. Kasinec was old enough to remember the days when Pekkala had served as personal investigator to the Tsar. To think of that famous detective, packed inside a freezing cattle wagon like a common criminal, was almost more than Kasinec could bear.

There had been so many thousands, tens of thousands, who had passed through here on their way east, and Kasinec had been grateful for the fact that they would only ever be numbers to him. If there had been names, he would have remembered them, and if he had remembered them, the space they would have occupied inside his head might have driven him out of his mind. But he would never forget the name of Pekkala, whose

Emerald Eye had snagged like a fishing lure trolling through his brain.

Kasinec's orders were to wait until Pekkala had boarded the train, and then to communicate by telegram with some man at the Kremlin named Poskrebyshev to confirm that the prisoner had been delivered.

On receiving the instructions from Poskrebyshev, Kasinec protested that he had never actually seen the Emerald Eye before. Few people ever had, since his picture had never been published.

'How will I even know it is him?' he asked.

Poskrebyshev's voice crackled down the phone line. 'His prison number is 4745.'

Kasinec breathed in, ready to explain that the numbers inked on to those flimsy prison clothes were often so blurred as to be illegible, but Poskrebyshev had already hung up. Following his orders Kasinec had notified the guards to keep an eye out for prisoner 4745 and to make sure he was placed aboard wagon no. 6.

Kasinec stood on the platform, studying the number of each convict who boarded the train. But none of these men was Pekkala. He held up the transport as long as he could, until the switching junction in Shatura called and demanded to know what had become of ETAP-1889. Finally, he gave the order for the convoy to proceed. Then, with a quiet satisfaction, Kasinec sent a telegram to Poskrebyshev, informing him that prisoner 4745 was not aboard the train.

Kasinec guessed there would be hell to pay for this and also that he would be the one to pay it, but it comforted him to know that the great inspector had once again found a way to beat the odds.

It crossed Kasinec's mind that the stories he had heard about Pekkala might be true – that he was not even a man but, rather, some kind of phantom, conjured from the spirit world by the likes of Grigori Rasputin, that other supernatural in the service of the Tsar.

*

Once more, the double doors of Stalin's officer flew open and Stalin appeared, his lips twitching with anger, as he waved a flimsy piece of telegram paper. 'This message just arrived from the master of the V-4 station, saying that Pekkala was not aboard the train!'

'Would you like me to try to find him?' Poskrebyshev rose quickly to his feet.

'No! I must handle this myself. Have the car brought around. I will be leaving immediately. Fetch me my coat.'

Poskrebyshev crashed his heels together. 'At once, Comrade Stalin!'

Kasinec was standing on the steps of a flimsy wooden structure grandly named the Central Convict Transport Administration Facility, puffing on a cigarette, when an American-made Packard limousine arrived at the station yard. Its cowlings had been splashed with perfect arches of greyish-black mud as it travelled the unpaved Moscow Highway. To the stationmaster, those muddy arches made the machine appear less like a car than a giant bird of prey, swooping from the evening shadows and intent on tearing him apart.

Kasinec sighed out a lungful of smoke. He had seen this before – desperate people trying to bid one last farewell to friends or family members who had ended up on prison transports. There was nothing Kasinec could do for them. He kept no records of the names of prisoners. By the time convicts arrived at V-4, they had already been transformed into numbers and Kasinec's only job was to see that the tally on his list matched the total of prisoners boarding the train. When the train was full, the list would be handed to the chief guard accompanying the transport and Kasinec never saw them again.

Just then, the air was filled with the loud clatter of the telegraph machine in his office spitting out a message. The people in that car would have to wait. Kasinec flicked his cigarette out over the muddy station yard and walked inside to read the telegram.

Emerging a few moments later, with the telegram still clutched in his fist, Kasinec saw a man in a fur-collared coat climb from the Packard. It took him only a second to realise that this man was none other than Stalin himself.

Immediately, Kasinec's hands began to shake.

Stalin crossed the station yard and climbed the three wooden steps to the balcony where Kasinec was waiting.

Kasinec saluted, fingertips quivering against his temples.

'What happened?' asked Stalin, a halo of breath condensing around his head. 'Why didn't he get aboard the train with all the other prisoners?'

'I don't know,' stammered Kasinec.

'We'll never find him now,' muttered Stalin, more to himself than to the stationmaster.

'Actually, Comrade Stalin, we *have* found Inspector Pekkala.' Kasinec held up the telegram, which had just arrived from the switching junction at Shatura, twenty kilometres to the east.

'Found him? But you just told me he wasn't aboard the train!'

'That's not exactly true, Comrade Stalin. He's just not among the prisoners.'

'Then where the hell is he?'

'According to the message from Shatura, he appears to be driving the train.'

Stalin shuddered, as if an electric current had just travelled through his body. He snatched the telegram from Kasinec's hand, read it through, then crumpled the paper and flung it away into the darkness. Turning away from the stationmaster, Stalin fixed his gaze upon a point in the distance where the rails appeared to converge. 'Pekkala, you son of a bitch!' he roared, his voice like thunder in the still night air.

*

When the train stopped at Shatura, a guard who had climbed down on to the tracks in order to relieve himself was astonished to see a prisoner walking towards him. Instantly, he swung the rifle off his back and aimed it at the convict.

But the prisoner neither raised his hands in a gesture of surrender, nor tried to run away. Instead, he only held a finger to his lips, motioning for the guard to be silent. This so astonished the guard that he actually lowered his gun. 'If you are who I think you are,' he whispered, 'our orders were to put you on wagon number 6, back at the V-4 station.'

'Why does it matter which wagon I get on?'

The guard shook his head. 'Those were the orders from stationmaster Kasinec.'

'Can you get me in there now?'

'Not without making them suspicious. The only time we move people is if a fight has broken out.'

'Will that not do for a reason?'

The guard studied Pekkala uneasily. 'It would, but you don't look as if you've been in a fight.'

Pekkala sighed as he realised what must happen now.

After a moment's hesitation, the guard lifted his rifle, turning the butt end towards Pekkala. 'Travel well, Inspector.'

'Thank you,' said Pekkala, and then everything went black.

He regained consciousness just as the door to wagon no. 6 was slammed shut. His lips were sticky with blood. Tracing his fingertips cautiously along the bridge of his nose, Pekkala was relieved to feel no jagged edge of broken bone.

In those first hours of the journey, the cramped space of the wagon remained silent, leaving each man alone with his thoughts.

As frost began to form across the inside of the wagon walls, Pekkala felt a slow fear creeping into the marrow of his bones. And he knew it would stay there, like the frost, which would not melt until these wagons rolled back empty to the west.

By dawn of the next day, the convoy had reached Sarapaul Station. Through the barbed-wire-laced opening that served as a window, Pekkala saw the platform jammed with soldiers on their way to man the border in the west. In their long, ill-fitting greatcoats, with pointed Budenny caps upon their heads, they boarded wagons no different from the ones in which Pekkala was riding. Blankets, rolled and tied over their shoulders, gave to these soldiers the appearance of hunchbacks. Their long Mosin-Nagant rifles looked more like cripples' canes than guns.

Morning sun sliced through rust holes in the metal roof, flooding the wagon with spears of golden light. As Pekkala raised his head to feel the warmth upon his face, he realised that this simple pleasure had already become a luxury.

*

Kirov sat at his desk, writing a report. The only sound in the room was the rustle of his pen nib across the page.

The sun had just risen above the rooftops of Moscow. Specks of dust, glittering as they drifted lazily about the room, reminded him of the smoke particles he had once seen under a microscope in school, as his teacher explained the phenomenon of Brownian motion.

Suddenly, Kirov paused and raised his head, distracted by a noise from the street below – a jangling of metal against stone.

Kirov smiled. Setting aside his pen, he got up and opened the window. The frigid air snatched his breath away. Just beneath him, hanging from the gutter, icicles as long as his arm glowed like molten copper in the sunlight. Kirov leaned out, five storeys above the street, and craned his neck to get a better view.

Then he saw it – a black Mercedes sedan making its way along the cobbled road. It was in poor repair, with rust-patched cowlings, a cracked headlight and a rear windshield fogged as if by cataracts. The jangling noise emanated from its muffler, which had lost a retaining bracket and clanked against the cobbles, sending out a spray of sparks at every dip in the road.

In the centre of the street lay a huge pothole. Some months ago, a construction crew, whose purpose remained a mystery, had removed some of the cobblestones. The workers never returned, but the pothole remained. There were many such craters in the streets of Moscow. People grumbled about getting them fixed, but the possibility of this actually happening, the mountains of paperwork that would be required to set into motion the appropriate branches of government, stood as a greater obstacle than any of the potholes themselves.

Most people just learned to live with them, but not Colonel Piotr Kubanka of the Ministry of Armaments. He had appealed, to every office he could think of, for the roads to be repaired. Nothing had been done, and his increasingly angry letters were filed away in rooms which served no other purpose than to house such impotently raging documents. Finally, in desperation, Kubanka had decided to take matters into his own hands.

Across the road from Kirov's office stood a tall, peach-coloured building which was the home of the Minister for Public Works, Antonin Tuzinkewitz, a thick-necked man as jowly as a walrus and responsible for, among other things, the filling in of Moscow's potholes. This minister was best known not for his public works but for the facts that he rarely got out of bed before noon and that the primordial roar of his laughter, as he returned in the early hours of the morning from the Bar Radzikov, could be heard more than a block away.

Colonel Kubanka's daily commute to the Ministry of Armaments should not have taken him past Tuzinkewitz's home, but Kubanka made a wide detour to ensure that it did.

The noise, as the front and rear wheels of Kubanka's Mercedes collided with the pothole, was like a double blast of cannon fire. It actually shook the loose panes of glass in Kirov's window. No one could sleep through that, especially not a man like Tuzinkewitz, who still suffered from flashbacks of the war, in which he had been repeatedly shelled by Austrian artillery in the Carpathian Mountains. Tuzinkewitz, rudely jolted from his dreams, would rush to the window, fling back the curtains and glare down into the street, hoping to spot the source of this noise. By then, Kubanka's car had already turned the corner and disappeared and Tuzinkewitz found himself staring down helplessly at the pothole, which returned his stare with a cruel, unblinking gaze.

It was driving Tuzinkewitz mad, slowly but with gathering speed, exactly as Kubanka intended. Kirov saw the proof of this each day in the strain on Tuzinkewitz's meaty face as it loomed into view out of the stuffy darkness of his bedroom.

When this daily ritual had been completed, Kirov turned and smiled towards Pekkala's desk, but the smile froze on his face when he saw the empty seat. He kept forgetting that Pekkala was gone. Even stranger than this, he sometimes swore he could feel the presence of the Inspector in the room.

Although Major Kirov had been raised in a world in which ghosts were not allowed to exist, he understood what it felt like to be haunted, as he was now, by the absence of Inspector Pekkala.

*

Far to the east the freezing, clanking wagons of ETAP-1889 crossed the Ural Mountains and officially entered Siberian territory. From then on, the train stopped once a day to allow the prisoners out.

Before the wagons were opened, the guards would walk along the sides and beat the doors with rifle butts, in hopes of dislodging any corpses that had frozen to the inner walls.

Piling out of the wagons, the prisoners inevitably found themselves on windswept, barren ground, far from any town. Sometimes they stayed out for hours, sometimes for only a few minutes. The intervals did not appear to follow any logic. They never knew how long they would be off the train.

During these breaks, the guards made no attempt to keep track of the prisoners. For anyone who fled into this wilderness, the chances of survival were non-existent. The guards did not even bother to take roll calls when the train whistle sounded

44

for the prisoners to board. By then, most convicts were already huddled by the wagons, shivering and waiting to climb in.

Beside Pekkala stood a round-faced man named Savushkin, who kept trying to make conversation. He had patient, intelligent eyes hidden behind glasses that were looped around his ears with bits of string. He was not a tall man, which put him at a disadvantage when trying to move around the cramped space of the wagon. To remedy this, he would raise his hands above his head, press his palms together, and drive himself like a wedge through the tangled thicket of limbs.

Confronted with Pekkala's stubborn silence, Savushkin had set himself the task of luring Pekkala into conversation. With the faith of an angler tying one kind of bait after another to his line, Savushkin broached every topic that entered his head, trusting that the fish must bite eventually.

Sometimes Pekkala pretended not to hear. Other times, he smiled and looked away. He knew how important it was for his identity to remain secret, and so the less he said, the better.

Savushkin did not take offence at his companion's silence. After each attempt, he would wait a while before trying again to find some chink in Pekkala's armour.

When Pekkala finally spoke, a bright, clear day had warmed the wagons, melting ice which usually jammed the cracks between the walls. While the wheels clanked lazily over the spacers, their sound like a monstrous sharpening of knives, Savushkin hooked his fish at last.

'Do you want to hear the joke that got me fifteen years in prison?' asked Savushkin.

'A joke?' Pekkala was startled at the sound of his own voice after so many days of silence. 'You were sent here because of a joke?'

'That's right,' said Savushkin.

'Well,' said Pekkala, 'it seems to me you've earned the right to tell it twice.'

The others were listening, too. It grew quiet in the wagon as they strained to hear Savushkin's voice.

'Stalin is meeting with a delegation of workers from the Ukraine,' he continued. 'After they leave, the Boss notices that his fake moustache is missing.'

'Are you saying that Stalin has a fake moustache?' asked a man standing beside him.

'Now that you mention it,' another voice chimed in.

Savushkin ignored this.

'You can't tell jokes about Stalin!' someone called from the far end of the wagon. 'Not in here!'

'Are you kidding?' shouted Savushkin. 'This is the *only* place where I can tell a joke about him!' He paused and cleared his throat before continuing. 'Stalin calls in his chief of security. "Go and find the delegation!" says the Boss. "One of the workers has stolen my moustache." The chief of security rushes out to do as he is told. A while later, Stalin realises he has been sitting on his fake moustache, so he calls back his chief of security and tells him, "Never mind. I found my moustache." "It's too late, Comrade Stalin," says the chief. "Half the workers have already signed confessions that they stole it and the other half committed suicide during interrogation."'

For a moment after Savushkin had finished telling the joke, there was silence in the wagon.

Savushkin looked around, amazed. 'Oh, come on. That's a

good joke! If it was a bad one, they would only have given me ten years!'

At that, the men began to laugh. The sound multiplied, echoing off the wooden boards as if the ghosts of those who had been dumped beside the tracks were laughing now as well.

Turning to look through the barbed-wire opening, Pekkala caught sight of a farmer sitting on a stone wall at the edge of a field only a few paces from the tracks. The old man was wearing a sheepskin vest and knee-length felt boots called *valenki*. A horse and cart had been tied to a tree beside the wall, and the back of the cart was filled with turnips scabbed with clumps of frozen earth. The farmer had laid out a red handkerchief on the snow-topped wall and was sitting on it. This gesture, in spite of its uselessness in fending off the damp and cold, struck Pekkala as strangely dignified. In one hand, the man held a small jack-knife and in the other hand he held a piece of cheese. He was chewing away contentedly, eyes narrowed in the rush of wind as railcars clattered past, filling the air with a glittering veil of ice crystals.

Hearing the laughter of the convicts, the farmer's eyes grew wide with astonishment. In that moment he had suddenly realised that the cargo rattling past him was human and not livestock as was painted on the cars, just as the prisoner transport vehicles in Moscow were disguised as delivery vans, complete with advertisements for non-existent brands of beer.

The farmer jumped down from the wall and grabbed an armful of turnips from his cart. He began to jog along the side of the tracks, holding out the turnips.

One of the convicts reached out his hand through the barbed-wire-laced opening and seized one.

More arms appeared, wrists and knuckles traced with blood where the rusty barbs had cut them.

Another hand snatched a turnip from the man's out-stretched hand.

The convicts began to shout, even those who could not see what was happening. The noise took on a life of its own as it spread from wagon to wagon until the roar of their voices drowned out even the sword-clash of the wheels over the tracks. Slowly, the engine pulled ahead.

The old farmer could not keep up.

The turnips spilled from his arms.

The last Pekkala saw of the man, he was standing beside the tracks, hands on his knees, red-faced and puffing milky clouds of breath into the sky.

When the commotion had finally died down, Savushkin made another stab at conversation. 'What class of criminal are you?' he asked Pekkala.

'Fifty-nine,' replied Pekkala, remembering the designation he'd been given as part of his cover.

'Fifty-nine! That means you are a dangerous offender! You don't look like a killer to me.'

'Maybe that's why I'm so dangerous.'

Savushkin gave a nervous laugh, like air squeaking out of a balloon. 'Well, I bet a class 59 has a good tale to tell.'

'Maybe you'll hear it someday,' replied Pekkala.

'I'll tell you his story,' said a man pressed up against the wall, 'as soon as I remember where I've seen him.'

Pekkala glanced at him but said nothing.

The man was shaking with fever. Sweat poured off his face. At some time in his past, he had been cut about the face. Now the white ridges of old scar tissue criss-crossed his cheeks like strands of spider web. These wounds had damaged the nerves, leaving a permanently crooked smile, which seemed to mock not only those around him but also the prisoner himself.

Savushkin turned to the man with the knife-cut face. 'Brother, you look like you could use a holiday,' he said.

The man ignored Savushkin. His focus remained on Pekkala. 'I'm sure I've seen you somewhere before.'

*

The next day, the convict transport pulled into a nameless rail siding in order to let another train pass. This train was heading in the opposite direction. It consisted not of wagons but of numerous flat beds, all of them stacked with large barrels designed to hold diesel fuel, except that the original fuel markings had been overpainted in bright green letters with the word 'Dalstroy'.

Dalstroy was the state-owned company which managed resources coming out of Siberia. These included timber, lead and the highly toxic mineral radium which left Borodok each week in containers painted with skull and crossbones. Another discovery in the Borodok mine was crocoite, also known as Siberian Red due to the colour of its beautiful crimson crystals, which could be refined to make chromium. Exposure to Siberian Red was known to be just as lethal to the miners as radium.

In addition to controlling the resources, Dalstroy also controlled the work force. Ten years before, only 30 per cent had been prison labour. Now it was over 90 per cent. Because Dalstroy only had to pay 10 per cent of its labour force, it had become one of the richest companies in the world.

The convicts, those who could see out, stared at the dreary procession of barrels with the dull, uncomprehending expressions of transported cattle.

But Pekkala knew what they contained, and he shuddered as he watched them going by. In certain camps, particularly those which were not proving to be as profitable as expected, men who died were packed into these barrels. Their corpses were doused with formaldehyde and then exported all over the country, to be sold as medical cadavers.

In Siberia, the prisoners said, even the dead work for Dalstroy.

After the transport had passed by, Pekkala caught the smell of preserving fluid, familiar to him from his father's undertaking business back in Finland, drifting sweet and sickening in the cold air.

The locomotive engine roared as it began to move again, but no sooner were the wagons rolling when there was a great screeching of brakes and the whole convoy lurched to a stop. A few minutes later, the train backed once more into the siding, the wagon doors were opened and the guards ordered everybody out.

The prisoners found themselves in a desolate field of shin-deep snow. The freezing wind cut through their clothes, stirring up white phantoms from beneath their feet.

Some prisoners immediately tried to climb into the wagons again, but the guards held them back.

'What happened?' asked Savushkin.

'The brakes are frozen,' said the guard. 'The wheels are slipping. The whole train could come off the rails.'

'How long will we be here?'

'Could be an hour,' replied the guard. 'Could be more. The last time this happened we were stuck all night.'

'And you won't let us back inside until morning?' Savushkin asked.

'We have to take the weight off the wheel springs, or else they might snap from the cold when the train gets moving.' The guard gestured towards a stand of pine and birch trees in the distance. 'Head over there. The whistle will sound when it's time to go again.'

Pekkala and Savushkin set off towards the woods.

Several others followed, heads bowed against the gusts and arms folded across their chest, but they soon gave up and returned to the train, where men were building walls of snow to shelter from the wind.

Ahead, in the grove of trees, the bony trunks of birch appeared and disappeared like a mirage among the sheets of snow.

'We're all going to freeze to death if they don't let us back on that train by nightfall,' Savushkin had to shout to make himself heard.

Pekkala knew the other prisoner was right. He also knew the guards didn't seem to care how many people died en route to the camps. He stumbled forward, feeling the heat drain from the centre of his body. Already he'd lost sensation in his ears and nose and fingers.

When they finally reached the trees, Pekkala and Savushkin began to dig a hole around the base of a pine tree, where the snow had drifted chest deep. Protected by its spread of lower branches, they would have a place completely sheltered from the wind.

'I'll find some fallen branches to lay out on the ground,' Pekkala told Savushkin. 'You keep digging.'

Savushkin nodded and went back to work. With his hair and eyebrows rimed in frost, he looked as if he'd aged a hundred years since they left the train.

For the next few minutes, Pekkala staggered through the drifts, gathering deadfall. The branches of the white birch, sheathed in ice, clattered above him like a wind chime made of bones. Arriving back at the hollow with nothing more than a handful of rotten twigs, Pekkala stopped to tear some boughs from a nearby pine tree. While he wrestled with the evergreen branches, he did not hear the person approaching from behind.

'I remember you now,' said a voice.

Pekkala spun around.

The knife-cut man stood right in front of him. 'This is the last place on earth I expected to see you, Inspector Pekkala. That's why I couldn't place you at first.'

Pekkala said nothing, but only watched and waited.

'I doubt you remember me, but that is understandable,' said the man, brushing his fingertips over his scars. 'During my stay in the Butyrka prison, the guards left me with a souvenir I will never forget, just as I have never forgotten that you were the one who arrested me.'

'I have arrested many people,' replied Pekkala. 'That is my job.'

The man's cold-reddened nostrils twitched as he breathed in and out. He did not appear to be carrying a weapon, but that did nothing to comfort Pekkala.

'I don't know why you are here,' the man continued. 'Believe me, it is a comfort to know that you and I are going to the same place, but comfort is not enough, not nearly enough to pay the debt you owe for what you've done to me.'

Pekkala dropped the twigs he had been carrying. His frozen hands clenched into fists.

'Do you have any friends, Inspector? Any still alive?' The man was taunting him. 'They're all gone, aren't they, Inspector? They left you here to wander in the wilderness; the last of your kind on this earth.'

It flashed across Pekkala's mind that his whole life had come down to this.

Suddenly, the prisoner threw up his arms and fell backwards. His legs had been pulled out from under him. In the next instant, a creature emerged from the ground. Scuttling like a giant crab out of the earth, Savushkin set upon the man.

With arms flailing, he rained down blows upon the convict, who fought back with equal ferocity, clawing at Savushkin and tearing the shirt from his back, but it did nothing to prevent the hammer strikes of Savushkin's fists.

'Enough!' shouted Pekkala, sickened by the sound of breaking bones and teeth as the man's face caved in.

Savushkin did not seem to hear. In a frenzy, he continued his attack, smashing his torn knuckles against the prisoner's battered face.

'Stop!' Pekkala set his hand upon Savushkin's shoulder.

Savushkin whirled around, teeth bared and his eyes gone wild. For an instant, he did not even seem to recognise Pekkala.

'It's done,' whispered Pekkala.

Savushkin blinked. In that moment, he returned to his senses. He stepped back, wiping the blood from his hands.

The knife-cut man was barely recognisable. He coughed up

a splatter of cherry-red blood, which poured down the sides of his mouth. Seeing the colour of that blood, Pekkala knew the sphenopalatine artery had been severed. There was nothing that could be done for him. His eyes rolled back into his head. A moment later, he shuddered and was gone.

'I think it's time I introduced myself,' said Savushkin. 'And as a friend,' he added.

'You have already proven that,' replied Pekkala.

'Not exactly, Inspector. I am Lieutenant Commissar Savushkin of the Bureau of Special Operations. I would shake your hand but' – he held up his battered fists – 'perhaps some other time.'

'Special Operations?' asked Pekkala. 'I don't understand. Why are you on the train?'

'I was assigned to protect you. Comrade Stalin himself gave the order. No one else knows I am here, not the guards on the train or even the Commandant of Borodok. You almost gave me a heart attack when you didn't show up at the station. I thought I would be travelling all the way to Siberia for nothing. I kept thinking you must be in disguise. Until the moment I set eyes on you, it never occurred to me you would be hiding in plain sight.'

Hearing those words, Pekkala thought back to his days of training with Chief Inspector Vassileyev, head of the Tsar's Secret Police.

Vassileyev drilled into Pekkala's mind the importance of blending into different surroundings in order to carry out an investigation. To train Pekkala in the 'Art of Disappearance', as he called it, Vassileyev constructed a series of elaborate games which he referred to as 'Field Exercises'.

Every Friday morning, while the streets of St Petersburg bustled with people on their way to work, Vassileyev would vanish into the crowds. One hour later, Pekkala himself would set out, with the task of tracking down his mentor. Each week Vassileyev would choose a different part of the city. Sometimes he walked along quiet mansion-lined streets. Other times, he chose one of the bustling markets. His favourite option, however, was the slums that bordered the north-east end of the city.

In the first month of these Field Exercises, Pekkala failed consistently to locate Vassileyev. There were times when the Chief Inspector would be standing almost in front of him and still Pekkala could not see through the disguises. Once, Pekkala hired a droshky to transport him around the district, thinking he would have a better chance of spotting Vassileyev if he moved more quickly through the streets. In desperation, Pekkala explained his predicament to the driver. Caught up in the game, the old man whipped up his horse and Pekkala spent the next two hours clinging to the sides of the open carriage while they careened through the streets in search of Vassileyev. In the end, confounded once again, Pekkala climbed down to pay the driver.

'You have already paid for the ride,' said the old man.

Pekkala, wallet in hand, glanced up to see what the driver meant and only then realised, to his dismay, that the old man was, in fact, Vassileyev.

After these humiliating defeats, the two men would walk back to Okhrana headquarters. Along the way, Vassileyev would explain the tricks of his craft. Considering that Vassileyev had lost part of his right leg to an anarchist bomb years ago, and now stumped about on a wooden prosthesis, Pekkala was amazed at how quickly the man could move.

'Merely throwing on a new set of clothes is not enough,' explained Vassileyev. 'Your disguise must have a narrative, so that people will be lured into the story of your life. Once they become lost in fathoming the details, they will fail to see the magnitude of your illusion.'

'Couldn't I just wear a hat?' asked Pekkala.

'Of course!' replied Vassileyev, oblivious to Pekkala's sarcasm. 'Hats are important. But what kind of hat? No single article of clothing more quickly places you in whatever bracket of society you want to occupy. But hats alone are not enough. First you must find yourself a café.'

'A café?'

'Yes!' insisted Vassileyev. 'Watch the people going past, the people sitting around you. See the clothes they wear. See how they wear them. Pay close attention to their shoes. Gentlemen of the old school will lace their shoes in straight lines across the grommets. The rest will lace diagonally. Once you have chosen your character from among them, do not go out and buy yourself new clothes.

Find yourself a shop or an open-air market where they sell used garments. Every city has one on the weekends. That is the place to choose your second skin.'

'Do people look healthy?' continued Vassileyev. 'Do people look sick? To give the appearance of living an unhealthy life, rub cooking oil on your forehead. Sprinkle the ashes of cheap tobacco in your pockets so that the smell of it will hang about you. Stir a pinch of ash into your tea and drink it. Within a week, your complexion will grow sallow. Dab a piece of raw onion in the corners of your eyes. Put a coat of beeswax on your lips.' As he spoke, he scraped away a crust of grime from the corners of his mouth, which had given the droshky driver the appearance of a man whose days of hard work in the open air should have been behind him, but were not.

'Change your stride!' ordered Vassileyev, cracking Pekkala on the shin with his heavy walking stick.

Pekkala cried out in pain and hopped along beside the Chief Inspector. 'You can't expect me to do that every time I go undercover!'

'No.' Vassileyev held up a one-kopek coin. 'All you need is this. Put the coin inside your shoe, beneath your heel, and it will alter the way you walk. Soon you will not even think about it any more, and that is the whole point. Put too much effort into it, and people will suspect. It must appear natural in its abnormality!'

Vassileyev's lectures were filled with such apparent contradictions that Pekkala began to feel as if he would never master the subtle skills which Vassileyev was trying to teach him.

Then, one day, only minutes after he had arrived in the marketplace chosen for that week's Field Exercise, Pekkala spotted Vassileyev. The old man was wearing a short double-breasted *wool coat and sitting on an upturned barrel with a porter's trolley beside him.*

'How did you do it?' asked Vassileyev, as they sat down to lunch at one of the market restaurants, its floor strewn with sawdust and the tables covered with brown paper.

'I don't know,' Pekkala replied honestly. 'I wasn't even concentrating.'

Vassileyev thumped Pekkala's back. 'Now you understand!'

'I do?'

'Our life's work is to sift through the details,' his mentor explained. 'And yet sometimes we must learn to ignore them, so that the bigger picture comes into focus. Do you see now?'

'I am beginning to,' he answered.

For their final exercise, Vassileyev promised Pekkala his hardest task yet.

That day, as he wandered up and down Morskaya Street, Pekkala studied the faces of everyone he passed, searching for some chink in the armour of their disguises. But he found nothing.

Then, just as he was about to give up, he spotted Vassileyev. The man had been sitting on a bench the whole time. Pekkala had walked past the bench at least a dozen times and never even seen Vassileyev. It was as if he had become invisible.

But the most incredible thing about it was that Vassileyev had not put on any disguise at all. He had simply been himself. And Pekkala, searching for anyone but the man he recognised, had failed to see him.

'Sometimes,' said Vassileyev, 'the most effective place to hide is in plain sight. Only when you have learned to conceal yourself are you ready to see through the disguises of others. The most danger-

ous thing is not the face that remains hidden' – Vassileyev passed a hand before his eyes – 'but what hides behind that face.'

'I didn't think I'd ever need a bodyguard,' said Pekkala.

As Savushkin pulled on his torn shirt, he looked down at the mangled corpse. 'Neither did I, until now.'

'What enemies did you make to draw such a wretched assignment as this?'

Savushkin's face brightened. 'No enemies at all, Inspector. I volunteered for this!'

'Volunteered? But why?'

'For the chance to tell my children I once served beside the Emerald Eye.'

'I'm glad you are here, Savushkin.'

Savushkin grinned, but then his face became serious. 'A word of advice, Inspector. In the days ahead do not place your faith in anyone. Anyone! Do you understand?'

'I think I can trust you, Savushkin. You just saved my life, after all.'

Before Savushkin could reply, the urgent wail of the locomotive's whistle summoned them back to the train.

The two men watched as the wagon doors were slid open and prisoners began to climb aboard.

'Looks like we're not spending the night here after all,' remarked Savushkin, as he kicked a blanket of snow over the body which lay at their feet.

They raced across the field, waving and shouting.

'Why', asked Pekkala, fighting for breath as the cold air raked at his throat, 'did you keep asking me who I was if you already knew?'

'It gave me an excuse to stay close to you,' gasped Savushkin. 'Besides, I knew they were safe questions to ask.'

'And how did you know that?' asked Pekkala.

'Because you'd never have told me, Inspector.'

They climbed aboard just as the train began to move.

The railroad siding slipped away into the grainy air. In the distance the grove of trees seemed to disintegrate, atom by atom, until it too was gone.

If anyone even noticed the absence of the knife-cut man, nobody mentioned it. With a shuffling of feet, the space he had once occupied was filled, as if he'd never been there at all.

As wagon number 6 swayed rhythmically from side to side, with the clatter of its wheels like a heartbeat echoing across the countryside, the atmosphere inside was almost peaceful.

*

'Poskrebyshev!'

'Yes, Comrade Stalin.'

'Have there been any messages from Pekkala?'

'No, Comrade Stalin. He has not yet arrived at the camp.'

'You must keep me informed, Poskrebyshev.'

'Yes, Comrade Stalin.' Poskrebyshev stared at the grey mesh of the intercom speaker. Some of the tiny holes were clogged with dust. There had been a particular tone in Stalin's voice just then; an anxiety almost bordering on fear. I must be mistaken, he thought.

Ten days after its departure from Moscow, ETAP-1889 passed through the town of Verkneudinsk.

This was the last civilian outpost before the train's course diverted from the Trans-Siberian Railroad on to a separate track that would bring it to the Borodok railhead.

Peering through the opening, Pekkala spotted two men standing outside a tavern which adjoined the Verkneudinsk station. Faintly, he heard the men singing. Tiger stripes of lamplight gleamed through bolted window shutters, illuminating the snow which fell around them.

Afterwards, while the train pressed on into a darkness so complete it was as if they'd left the earth and were now hurtling through space, the singing of those two men haunted him.

The following morning, the train arrived at Borodok.

One final time, the prisoners climbed from their wagons, past shouting guards and dogs on choke-chain leashes, and were herded into a lumber yard where thousands of logs had been stacked as high as double-storey houses, waiting to be shipped to the west on the same train which had delivered the prisoners. The air smelled sour from the wood and piles of shredded bark steamed in the cold, melting the snow around them.

In one corner of the yard, behind a wire fence, stood a mountain of metal fuel drums, each one marked with the name 'Dalstroy'.

Pekkala wondered if those drums were already full, with dead men tucked like foetuses inside, or if they had been set aside for the prisoners who stood around him now.

A guard climbed up on top of the log pile. 'There are many rules at Borodok!' he shouted, hands cupped around his mouth. 'You will know what they are when you have broken them.'

The convicts stared at him in silence.

'Now strip!' commanded the guard.

Nobody moved. The convicts continued to stare at the guard, each one convinced that he must have misunderstood. The temperature was below zero and all they had on were the same threadbare pyjamas in which they'd first boarded the train.

Seeing that his words had no effect, the guard drew a pistol from a holster on his belt and fired a shot into the crowd.

The entire group flinched. With the blast still echoing around the lumberyard, prisoners ran their fingers across their faces, down their chests and out along the branches of their arms, searching for the wound which every man felt certain he'd received.

Only then did someone cry out, a sound more of surprise than pain.

The crowd parted around one man, whose hands were clutched against his neck. With wide and pleading eyes, he turned and turned in the space which had been made for him.

Nobody stepped in to help.

Seconds later, the convict dropped to his knees. Slowly and deliberately, he lowered himself on to his side. Then he lay there in the dirty snow, blood pulsing out of his throat.

The guard called out again for everyone to strip. This time, there was no hesitation. Filthy garments slipped to the ground like the sloughed-off husks of metamorphosing insects.

While this was going on, three trucks pulled up at the entrance to the lumber yard.

Following another order shouted by the guard, the naked prisoners formed a line. With shoulders hunched and fists clenched over hearts, they filed past the trucks one by one. From the first vehicle, each man received a black, hip-length jacket called a *telogreika*. Sewn into the jackets were long, sausage-shaped lines padded with raw cotton. From the second truck, prisoners received matching trousers and, from the third, boots made of rubberised canvas. None of the clothing was new, but it had been washed in petrol to kill the lice and strip away some of the dirt.

The guards who threw this clothing from the trucks had no time to think of sizes. Prisoners exchanged garments until they found what fitted them, more or less.

It began to snow. Large flakes, like pieces of eggshell, settled on their hair and shoulders. Before long, a blizzard was falling sideways through the air.

In ranks of three, the convicts set off walking towards the camp, leaving behind the man who had been shot. He lay upon the dirty snow surrounded by a halo of diluted blood.

A short distance away, Borodok's tall stockade fence of sharpened logs loomed from the mist like a row of giant teeth.

The gates were opened, but before the prisoners could enter, a man with a bald head and a jagged-looking tattoo on his hand rode out on a cart piled with emaciated corpses. Wired around the left big toe of each body was a small metal tag. Together, they flickered like sequins on a woman's party dress. The cart was a strange-looking contraption, its wheel spokes twisted like the horns of a mythical beast and its flared wooden sides decorated with red and green painted flowers foreign to Siberia. The horse that pulled this cart wore a white mane of frost and long white lashes jutted from its eyelids like ivory splinters. The tattooed man did not even glance at the convicts as his cart jostled out into the storm.

Then the prisoners marched into the camp.

Once they were inside the stockade fence, the only view of the outside world was the tops of trees in the surrounding forest. Beyond the barracks, administrative building, kitchen and hospital, the camp dead-ended against a wall of stone. There, on rusted iron stakes, snarls of barbed wire fringed the rock where a mineshaft had been cut into the mountain.

The centre of the compound was dominated by the statues of a man and a woman, mounted on a massive concrete platform. The man, stripped to the waist, held a book in one hand and a blacksmith's hammer in the other. The woman clutched a sheaf of wheat against her concrete dress. Both of them were frozen in mid-stride as they headed towards the main gates of the camp.

Engraved into the base were the words: 'Let Us Heal the Sick and Strengthen the Weak!'

The statue had not been there on his last visit to the camp. Pekkala wondered where it had come from and what it was doing there. He wondered, too, what possible comfort a gulag prisoner could draw from such an exhortation.

Like giants bound upon some journey without relevance to man, the statues appeared to stride past the barracks huts, whose tar-paper roof tiles winked like fish scales in the sunset.

The prisoners were ordered straight to their barracks, which were large, single-room buildings with bunk beds fitted one arm's length apart. Bare wooden planks made up the floors and ceiling. The heating in the barracks came from two wood stoves, one at either end. Prisoners measured their seniority in how close they slept to those stoves. The room smelled of smoke and sweat and faintly of the bleach used to wash down the floors once a month. The barracks was guarded at night by an old soldier named Larchenko, who sat on a chair by the door reading a children's book of fairy tales.

Having eaten his rations, which consisted of a scrap of dried fish wedged between two slices of black bread, Pekkala found himself in a bunk near the centre of the main barracks block.

After the long journey, the convicts were too exhausted to talk. Within minutes, most of them were asleep.

Some time in the night, Pekkala woke to see a figure shuffling about between the rows of beds which lined the walls.

It was the guard, Larchenko.

At first, Pekkala thought he must be looking for something, the way the soldier moved so carefully across the splintery wooden boards. One of Larchenko's arms was held out crookedly, as if it had been broken and then anchored in a cast. Blinking the sleep from his eyes, Pekkala lifted his head to get a better view.

In the darkness of the barracks, Larchenko was still nothing more than a silhouette, turning and turning like a clockwork ballerina in a jewellery box.

Then suddenly Pekkala understood. The man was dancing. His crooked arm was held about the waist of an imaginary partner. In that instant, the clumsy, swaying movements translated themselves into a waltz. Pekkala wondered who she was, this ghost of past acquaintance, and which orchestra's music echoed in the ballroom of his skull.

A memory, shrouded until now in darkness, came hurtling like a meteor into the forefront of Pekkala's mind.

The door of his cottage flew open.

It was the middle of the night.

By the time the Imperial Guard's eyes had accustomed themselves to the dark, he was already looking down the blue-eyed barrel of Pekkala's Webley revolver.

'What do you want?' demanded Pekkala.

'Inspector!' The guard had been running. He gasped for breath as he spoke. 'The Emperor has sent for you.'

Pekkala lowered the gun.

A few minutes later, buttoning his coat as he ran, Pekkala followed the Guard along the gravel path which led to the Alexander Palace. Moonlight turned the lawns of the Tsarskoye Selo estate into vast slabs of lapis lazuli.

The two men raced up the wide stone steps and into the front hall of the palace.

The building echoed with shouts and whispered voices.

A maid of the Imperial Household, in her uniform of black dress and white apron, drifted past them like an albatross, one hand held against her mouth to stifle the sound of her crying.

Then Pekkala saw the Empress. Still in her mauve silk nightdress, she darted out of the Imperial bedroom. On slippered feet, the Empress glided towards Pekkala. 'You must go to the Emperor at once!'

On her breath, Pekkala smelled the sickly odour of the opium-laced medicine, without which Alexandra Romanov could no longer find her way into the catacombs of sleep. 'What has happened, Majesty?'

'It is the nightmare,' she hissed.

A moment later, Pekkala stood in the doorway to the Tsar's bedroom.

The Tsar lay spreadeagled on his bed. The sheets had been kicked off. Sweat darkened his nightshirt.

Two nervous doctors hovered in the shadows.

'Pekkala!' groaned the Tsar. 'Is that you?'

'I am here, Majesty.'

'Get these butchers out of the room.' Feebly he gestured towards the doctors. 'All they want to do is turn me into a morphine addict.'

The two men, sombre as herons, filed out of the room without even glancing at Pekkala.

'Shut the door on your way out!' the Tsar commanded.

The doctors did as they were told.

Slowly, the Tsar sat up in bed. He was a picture of complete exhaustion. With twitching hands, he reached for the cigarette case which lay beside his bed. It had been fashioned out of solid gold by Michael Perchin, one of the workmasters at the Fabergé factory. The case had been engraved with gentle S-shaped curves, which reminded Pekkala of patterns he had seen as a child, in windblown sand down by the water's edge at his family's summer cottage on the Finnish island of Korpo.

From this case, the Tsar removed a cigarette. Each one contained a blend of tobacco prepared for him alone by Hajenius of Amsterdam. The frail rolling papers were emblazoned with a tiny silver double-headed eagle, the crest of the Romanov family.

As Pekkala stared at these objects, flinching momentarily when the Tsar struck fire from a jewel-encrusted lighter, it occurred to him how little they mattered to their owner at that moment. The Romanovs had built a wall of silver, gold and platinum to keep the world away from them. But the world still found its way in. Like water filtering through cracks in a stone, it would ultimately shatter their existence.

'The Empress mentioned a nightmare,' said Pekkala.

The Tsar nodded, picking a fleck of tobacco off his tongue. He muttered a single word. 'Khodynka.'

Then Pekkala understood.

On May 26th, 1896, the day of Nicholas's and Alexandra's coronation, the Tsar and Tsarina had undergone a gruelling five-hour service at the Assumption Cathedral in the Kremlin. Four days later, as dictated by tradition, the newly crowned couple would proceed to Khodynka Field. There, they would greet the thousands, perhaps even tens of thousands, of spectators who had come to wish them well. These spectators would be fed and gifts marking the occasion would be distributed. The Imperial couple would then proceed to the French Embassy, where a celebration of unparalleled extravagance had been prepared. This included more than 100,000 fresh roses, which had been brought by express train from France.

The festivities began at Khodynka long before the Imperial couple were due to arrive. At one point, reacting to a rumour that the food tents were running out of beer, the crowd stampeded. More than a thousand people were crushed to death, many of them falling into shallow drainage ditches dug in lines across the field.

As the royal procession began its journey to Khodynka, the dead and dying were loaded on to carts and transported from the field, forming a macabre procession of their own. In the confusion, cartloads of disfigured corpses ended up amongst the lines of ornate coaches bearing the jewel-encrusted guests who had been invited to the coronation ceremony.

To make matters worse, the Imperial couple were persuaded to continue with their schedule and attend the French Embassy gathering.

Although guests at the party remarked on the obvious distress of the Emperor and his bride, the image of them waltzing, surrounded by thousands of bouquets of roses, remained in the minds of the Russian people. The royal couple had danced while their subjects were dying. And for a couple who were every bit as superstitious as the people whom they ruled, the omen seemed clear from the start.

'In my dream,' the Tsar told Pekkala, 'it is after the coronation. I am at the French Embassy, greeting the guests. But there are no ambassadors, no heads of state, no cousins who are kings. Instead, it is the dead from the Khodynka Field. They trail their blood into the hall and the orchestra plays and they cling to each other with their mangled fingers and dance on their shattered limbs, staring into each others' faces with their bulging eyes.'

'The dead are dancing?'

'All around me. The music never stops.' The Tsar inhaled on his cigarette. A moment later, two grey jets of smoke streamed from his nose. 'And they are laughing.'

'But why?'

'Because they don't know they are dead.' The Tsar swung his legs down from the bed and walked over to the window. Drawing back the curtains, he stared out at the velvet sky.

'Why did you send for me?' asked Pekkala. 'You know I can't protect you from your dreams.'

'That may be true,' replied the Tsar, 'but with all that Finnish witchcraft in your blood, I thought perhaps you might be able to tell me what it means.'

He already knows, thought Pekkala, only he cannot bring himself to say the words. That is why the dream comes back to him and why he will run from it for the rest of his life, scattering gold and jewels in its path in the hope of distracting the beast which is pursuing him. But the beast does not care about his treasure, and it will hunt him down and kill him in the end.

'Four-seven-four-five!'

Pekkala's heart lurched as the barracks door flew open and a guard walked in, calling out Pekkala's prison number.

It was still the middle of the night.

Awakened from his waltzing trance, Larchenko tottered back to his chair by the door.

'Four-seven-four-five!' the guard called out again.

Pekkala climbed out of his bunk and stood to attention, bare feet cringing against the cold floorboards.

The guard's flashlight sliced through the musty air of the bunkhouse, until it finally settled upon Pekkala. 'Put your boots on. Come with me.'

Pekkala wedged his feet into the wooden-soled boots he had been issued and clumped after the guard. As he emerged into the Siberian night, the first breath felt like pepper in his lungs.

He followed the guard across the compound until they reached the Commandant's office.

'In there,' said the soldier and, without another word, he trudged back to the guard house.

*

While Pekkala was being marched across the compound, Commandant Klenovkin had been watching.

Ever since Klenovkin had learned that Pekkala would be handling the investigation, he'd been dreading this meeting with his former prisoner.

When Klenovkin had mentioned the murder of Ryabov in his weekly report, he'd had no idea that Stalin would come to hear about it, much less put Pekkala on the case. Nothing good can come of this, he thought, as anxiety twisted in his guts. One way or another, those White Russians of the Kolchak Expedition had been the source of all his troubles. As soon as they arrived, they had formed themselves into a gang which virtually took over the camp and even though most of them had died from the usual effects of overwork, malnutrition and despair, the few who remained continued to exert a powerful influence.

Klenovkin blamed the White Russians for the fact that he had never received the recognition he deserved. All the commandants who had started out at the same time as he did were senior executives now. They lived in comfort in the great cities – Moscow, Leningrad, Stalingrad. They ate their lunches in fine restaurants. They took their holidays at resorts on the Black Sea. Klenovkin had none of these luxuries. The nearest restaurant, a rail station café serving kvass and smoked caribou meat, was more than 800 kilometres away.

The only sign Klenovkin had ever received from Dalstroy that they appreciated him at all was an ashtray, made of pinkish-white onyx, which he had been awarded for fifteen years of service to the company. And he did not even smoke.

The way Klenovkin saw it, he had been left here to rot among these Siberians – 'Chaldons' as they called themselves. To Klenovkin, they were all the same – a dirty and suspicious people. They trusted nobody except their own kind. I could live a dozen lifetimes here, thought Klenovkin, and I would still be a stranger to them. Every time he heard that train departing from the Borodok railhead, it was all he could do not to run down there and jump aboard.

But it was impossible. What held him back were not the guards and the stockade fence but paperwork, quotas and fear. As far as Klenovkin was concerned, he was as much a prisoner as any convict in the camp.

But now, perhaps, all that was going to change.

As much as he had hoped never to set eyes on Pekkala again, Klenovkin knew that if anyone could get to the bottom of Ryabov's murder, it would be the Emerald Eye.

So Klenovkin had made up his mind to endure the presence of the unearthly Finn, who had somehow survived in a place where death had been a virtual certainty.

However, thought Klenovkin, addressing the voices in his head, which had been clamouring at him ever since he'd learned that Pekkala was on his way, I am not simply going to grovel at the feet of a man who was once my prisoner. I must maintain some shred of dignity. I will remind him, in no uncertain terms, that I command at Borodok. The Emerald Eye can do his job, but only as my subordinate. I will be in charge.

The Commandant looked out at the statues in the compound, hoping to match the seriousness on the faces of those workers with a steely expression of his own.

When the concrete sculpture had arrived, six years ago, Klenovkin assumed that he was at last being recognised for his years of loyal service to Dalstroy. No other camp had statues like this, and even if the motto did not seem entirely relevant to men imprisoned at a gulag, nevertheless it was a sign to Klenovkin that he had not been forgotten.

Klenovkin had the statues installed in the centre of the compound. The work had barely been completed when he received an inquiry from the University of Sverdlovsk, asking if he had by any chance seen a statue of a man and a woman which had been commissioned as the centrepiece of the university's new Centre for Medical Studies. Apparently, the statues had been placed on the wrong train and nobody seemed to know where they were.

Klenovkin never answered the letter. He tore it up and threw it in the metal garbage can beside his desk. Then, overcome with paranoia, he set the contents of the garbage can on fire.

In the years which followed, Klenovkin had often found inspiration in the determined faces of that nameless man and woman.

Today, however, the hoped-for inspiration was not there. Wind-blown snow swirled through the compound, filling the eye sockets of the half-naked figures so that they seemed to stagger blindly forward into the storm.

Klenovkin was snatched from his daydream by the sound of the outer door creaking open. Hurriedly, he returned to his desk, sat down and tried to look busy.

*

Pekkala stepped into the warm, still air of the Commandant's waiting room. A lamp was burning on a table. In the corner, a potbellied iron stove sighed as the logs crumbled inside it. Beside the stove, another guard, wearing a heavy knee-length coat sat on a rickety chair with his boots up on the windowsill. Pekkala recognised this man as the same one who had opened fire on the prisoners when they first arrived at the Borodok railhead. The guard stared sleepily at Pekkala, his eyes as red in the lamplight as the sun on a Japanese flag.

'Send him in!' Klenovkin's muffled voice reached through the door.

The guard did not bother to get up. He merely nodded toward the Commandant's office and then went back to staring at the lamp.

Crossing the bare floor, Pekkala knocked on Klenovkin's door, his knuckles barely touching the wood.

'Enter!' came a muffled voice.

Inside Klenovkin's office, Pekkala breathed the smell of soapy water, which had been used to clean the room. In the coppery light of a lantern, he could make out the streaks of a cleaning rag on the glass panes, like mare's-tail clouds in a windy sky.

Klenovkin was sitting at his desk, sharpening pencils.

'Camp Commandant,' said Pekkala, as he quietly closed the door.

'I am busy!' Klenovkin turned the pencils in the tiny metal sharpener, letting the papery curls fall into his ashtray. When, at last, he had finished this task, he brushed the shavings into his hand with a precision that reminded Pekkala of a croupier at a roulette wheel, hoeing in chips across the green felt table. Not until Klenovkin was satisfied that every fleck of dirt had been removed did he finally raise his head and look Pekkala in the eye.

Even though Pekkala had not seen Klenovkin in many years,

the Commandant's features had been etched into Pekkala's brain. Time had rounded the edges of Klenovkin's once-gaunt face. The dark hair Pekkala remembered had turned a greyish-white. Only the man's gaze, menacing and squinty, had not changed. 'Prisoners must remove their caps when they are in my presence.'

'I am no longer your prisoner.'

Klenovkin smiled humourlessly. 'That is only partly true, Inspector. You may be running this investigation, but I am running this camp. As long as you are wearing the clothes of an inmate, that is how you will be treated. We wouldn't want that guard out in the waiting room to become suspicious, would we?'

Slowly, Pekkala reached up to his cap and slid it off his head.

'Good.' Klenovkin nodded, satisfied. 'I must admit, Pekkala, I do find this meeting somewhat ironic. After all, following our last meeting, I did my best to kill you.'

'And failed.'

'Indeed, and thus the irony that I am now expected to assist you in whatever way I can. Bear in mind, however, that I may be the only help you get. As for that gang of White Russians, of which Captain Ryabov was a member, I wouldn't expect much from them.'

'And why is that?'

'Because they have gone mad. The years at Borodok have worn away their minds as well as their bodies. Now they speak of a day when they will be rescued from this place and sent to live like kings in some faraway land.' Klenovkin rolled his eyes in mocking pity. 'They really believe this! They are fanatics, tattooing their bodies with the symbols of their loyalty to a cause that no longer exists. These men have nothing left but hope, for which they no longer require proof or logic or even reason to support their beliefs. They even have a name for the dwindling ranks of their disciples. They call themselves Comitati – whatever that means.' Then he laughed. 'It is a word that has no meaning for men who serve no purpose.'

But that word did have a meaning, and the mention of it made Pekkala's blood run cold. The Comitatus was an ancient pact between warriors and their leader, in which men swore never to leave the battlefield before their leader, and the leader swore in return, never to abandon those who followed him. As each swore allegiance, the man and the oath became one and the same. Together, those who had made the pact formed a band known as the Comitati. Now Pekkala knew why these men had never given up the fight. They were waiting for Kolchak to return and fulfil the oath he had taken.

'In a way,' continued Klenovkin, 'they have already been rescued. Their minds escaped from this camp long ago. The only sane thing left for them is to surrender to their madness. The one man among them who had any grip on reality was Ryabov, and that, I think you will find, is the reason he is dead.'

'How many of these Comitati were originally sent to Borodok?'

'There were about seventy of them in the beginning.'

'And how many remain?'

'Three,' replied Klenovkin. 'There is a former lieutenant named Tarnowski, and two others, Sedov and Lavrenov. In spite of how many have died over the years, Ryabov was the first to be murdered.'

'Has his body been preserved?'

'Of course.'

'I need to see the remains,' said Pekkala. 'Preferably now.'

'By all means,' replied Klenovkin, rising to his feet. 'The sooner you can deliver to Stalin whatever it is that he wants from these men, the quicker I can be rid of them. And of you as well, Inspector.'

Heaving on a canvas coat, thickly lined with coarse and shaggy goat fur, Klenovkin led Pekkala out of the office.

Shivering in his prison jacket, Pekkala followed the Commandant to the camp kitchen, which had been closed down for the night.

Inside, at the back of the building, stood a large walk-in freezer, its door fastened shut with a bronze padlock as big as a man's clenched fist.

Removing a key from his pocket, Klenovkin unfastened the padlock and the two men stepped inside.

Klenovkin turned on an electric light. One bare bulb glimmered weakly from the low ceiling. Frost which had coated the thin glass shell of the bulb immediately melted away. By the time the droplets reached the floor, they had frozen again and crackled on the ground like grains of unboiled rice.

On one side of the freezer, pig carcasses dangled from iron hooks. On the other stood glass jars of pickles, slabs of pasty white beef fat and stacks of vegetables which had been boiled, mashed and pressed into bricks.

A wall of splintery wooden crates lined the back of the freezer. The crates were filled with bottles, each one marked with a yellow paper triangle, indicating Soviet Army issue vodka.

On the floor, behind the barricade of vodka crates, lay a dirty, brown tarpaulin.

'There he is,' said Klenovkin.

Pekkala knelt down. Pulling aside the brittle cloth, he stared at the man whose death had brought him to Siberia.

Ryabov's skin had turned a purplish-grey. A dark redness filled the lips and nostrils and the dead man's open eyes had sunk back into his skull. His open mouth revealed a set of teeth rotted by years of neglect.

Ryabov's throat had been cut back to his spine, almost as if the murderer had wanted not simply to kill him, but to remove his head as well.

The huge amount of blood which had flowed from Ryabov's severed jugular had formed a black and brittle crust over the dead man's chest.

At least it had been quick, Pekkala noted. From a wound like that, Ryabov would have bled out in less than thirty seconds.

The hands of the dead man had been wrapped in strips of rag, a common practice among prisoners to protect against the cold. Pekkala peeled back the layers of filthy cloth. It was not easy. Ice had bonded the strips so solidly together that Pekkala's fingernails tore as he prised away the layers. At last the skin was exposed, revealing the image of a pine tree which had been crudely etched on the tops of Ryabov's hands using a razor blade and soot.

'The mark of the Comitati,' answered Klenovkin.

Pekkala set his fingertips against the edges of the wound in the dead man's neck. The skin was curved back on itself, a sign that the blade used to kill Ryabov had been extremely sharp.

Now Pekkala turned his attention to the man's clothes. The padded coat and trousers had been washed so many times that the original black colour had been bleached to the same dirty white shade as the snow which piled up on street corners in Moscow at the end of winter. The buttons had been replaced with pieces of wood hand-carved into toggles, and there were many repairs in the cloth, each one meticulously stitched with whatever fabric had been available. Searching the pockets of Ryabov's jacket, Pekkala found nothing but black crumbs of Machorka tobacco, the only kind available to gulag prisoners. It was made from the stems as well as the leaves of the plant and produced a thick, eye-stinging cloud that could be inhaled only by the most desperate and hardened smoker.

'Where was the body found?' Pekkala asked.

'At the entrance to the mine. I discovered it myself when I went there to speak with him.'

'Why were you there and not in your office?'

'When he first came to me, saying he knew where to find Colonel Kolchak, I told Ryabov I didn't believe it. Kolchak is dead, I told him. But he insisted he had proof that the Colonel was still alive, and he was so convincing that I thought I should at least hear what he had to say.'

'And what did Ryabov want in exchange for this information?'

'He didn't say. He refused to talk in my office, because he didn't want to risk being overheard, so we set up the meeting for that night in one of the mine tunnels. It's not difficult for the prisoners to sneak out of their barracks at night. The entrance to the mineshaft is not guarded and the tunnels are not patrolled at night. We had set a time, just after midnight. By the time I got there, Ryabov had already been killed.'

'I was told you'd found the murder weapon.'

Without removing his hands from the warmth of his pockets, Klenovkin nodded towards an object lying on a nearby crate.

Pekkala saw it now – a crude, home-made stiletto, whose finger-length blade had been fashioned from a piece of iron railing. The handle was a split piece of white birch, into which the railing had been inserted and string wrapped tightly around the wood to hold it in place. The tight coils of string were coated with a lacquer of dried blood. 'This was made by a prisoner,' said Pekkala.

'It was lying right next to the body,' explained Klenovkin. 'There's no doubt this was the murder weapon.'

Pekkala said nothing, but he knew that the weapon which had killed Ryabov was no prison-made contraption. One glance at the blade told him that.

Prison knives were fashioned to be small, so that they could be easily concealed. He had seen lethal weapons constructed from pieces of tin can no larger than a thumbnail and fitted into the handle of a toothbrush. The weapon Klenovkin claimed he had found beside the body was a type used for stabbing, not cutting.

The blade which had cleaved Ryabov's throat was wide and sharp enough to sever the jugular with one stroke. This was evident in the clean edge of the wound, showing that the killer had not required multiple strokes of the blade to accomplish his task.

'It proves the Comitati were involved,' continued Klenovkin.

'And how have you reached that conclusion?'

Only now did Klenovkin remove a hand from its fur-lined cocoon. One finger uncurled towards the dead man. 'The

Comitati did this, because no one else would have dared to lay a hand on Ryabov.'

'But why do you think they were the ones who murdered him?'

'I have considered this, Inspector, and there is only one possible answer. I first assumed that he was trying to secure the release of his men along with himself. What else is there to bargain for? But the more I thought about it, the clearer it became. Ryabov had no intention of escaping with the others. The only freedom Ryabov desired was for himself. He had finally seen the Comitati for what they really are – a clan of painted madmen clinging to a prophecy which becomes more and more improbable with every passing year. Ryabov had at last reached the correct conclusion; that unless he did something to help himself, he would die here in the camp.'

'Why do you think he would come to you now, after all these years of silence?'

'I believe their tight-knit group had been whittled away until those few who remained had finally begun to crack. Of those, one was prepared to give up his old loyalties. The others were not. If you want to find the man who killed Ryabov, you need look no further than the men he used to call his comrades.'

After Klenovkin locked the freezer, the two men walked out of the kitchen.

Under the glare of the camp's perimeter lights, sheets of newly formed ice glistened in the compound yard. Beyond the tall stockade fence, the saw-tooth line of pine trees stood out against the velvet blue night sky.

'If he was so desperate to escape,' asked Pekkala, 'then why did he not simply attempt to leave on his own? He had learned to survive in the camp. He could have found a way out and then, surely, he could have endured conditions in the forest long enough to make it across the border into China, which is less than a hundred kilometres from here.'

'The answer to that, Inspector, is the same as why you never escaped, in spite of the fact that you lived beyond the gates of this camp, with no guards to oversee your every move. Even if Ryabov could have made it through the forest on his own, he would never have got past the Ostyaks.'

'Do you mean to say they are still out there?' Pekkala asked Klenovkin. 'I thought you would have driven them away by now.'

'On the contrary,' remarked the Commandant. 'They are more powerful than ever.'

Beyond the gates of Borodok lay the country of the Ostyaks, a nomadic Asiatic tribe whose territory extended for hundreds of kilometres around the camp.

At the time of the foundation of Borodok and its sister camp, Mamlin 3, on the other side of the valley of Krasnagolyana, an uneasy truce had been established between these nomads and the gulag authorities. The valley would belong to the gulags, and the taiga – that maze of rivers, forests and tundra which made up so much of Siberia – would remain off limits. The camp's perimeter fence had been built as much to keep the Ostyaks out as to keep the prisoners in.

The Ostyaks butchered any convict found upon the taiga. The corpse was then delivered to the camp. Pekkala had heard rumours of bodies returned only after their palms and cheeks had been cut away and eaten.

So violent were these Ostyaks in tracking down those who

85

sought to trespass on their land, and so difficult was the terrain, that during Pekkala's years as a convict, not a single successful escape had ever been recorded in the history of the two camps.

On their visits to Borodok, the Ostyaks traded with the guards, exchanging the pelts of ermine, mink and arctic fox for tobacco. As a result, some men wore greatcoats lined with furs more precious than anything that ever trimmed the robes of kings and queens.

Occasionally, in winter, a time when his work as a tree marker would bring him to the outer fringes of the valley, Pekkala had seen the Ostyaks slaloming between the trees on sledges whose iron runners hissed like snakes across the snow. Other times, they seemed to be invisible, and all he heard were the clicking hooves of the lightning-antlered caribou which hauled their sleds, and the sinister metallic chant of harness bells.

Up close, Pekkala had only ever seen them once.

Halfway through his first year as a tree marker, two men appeared one day outside his cabin. They were on their way to Borodok with a sledge carrying some men who had escaped from the camp. Whether the Ostyaks had killed them or simply found their frozen bodies out on the taiga, Pekkala could not tell. The rigid naked corpses lay heaped upon the sledge, seeming to claw the air like men snatched from their lives in the midst of grand-mal seizures.

At first, Pekkala thought these Ostyaks meant to add him to their pile of dead, but all they did was stare at him in silence. Then they turned abruptly and continued their journey.

They never came near him again.

'Those heathens are more useful to me than any of the guards in this camp,' continued Klenovkin. 'Over the years, there have been many escape attempts from Borodok, but no one has ever got past the Ostyaks, for one very simple reason, I pay them. In bread. In salt. In bullets. I reward them well for every corpse they bring me.'

'But couldn't Ryabov have bribed them?'

Klenovkin laughed. 'With what? The Ostyaks may be savages, but they are also crafty businessmen. They deliberately miscount those bodies they bring me, hoping I am too genteel to stand out in the cold and count the dead. Then, when I catch them in their deception, they grin like imbeciles, throw up their hands and act like schoolchildren. They have no respect for Soviet authority. As far as the Ostyaks are concerned, the only difference between me and the frozen bodies they bring in is that I have something to trade, and those dead men did not. Otherwise, they would never set foot in the Valley of Krasnagolyana, because they say those woods are haunted.'

'By what?'

Klenovkin smiled. 'By you, Inspector! Back in the days when you lived out in the forest, they came to believe that you were some kind of monster. And who can blame them? What was it the loggers used to call you – the man with bloody hands? After Stalin recalled you to Moscow, I had a hard time convincing the Ostyaks that you had actually gone. They still believe your spirit haunts this valley. I told you, Inspector, they are a primitive and vicious people.'

'They are just trying to make sense of the things we have brought to their world,' said Pekkala, 'and when I see men with their throats cut like the one lying in front of me, I have trouble making sense of it myself.'

'But you will make sense of it,' Klenovkin replied. 'That's why Stalin gave you the job.'

'I may not be able to complete the task alone,' said Pekkala. 'I will need to keep in touch with my colleague in Moscow.'

'Of course. That has all been arranged. I have placed you in a job which will allow us to meet on a regular basis without arousing the suspicion of the inmates.'

'What job is that?'

'You will be working in the kitchen. From now on, you will bring me my breakfast each morning. At that time, we can discuss any developments in your investigation.'

'I am to be your servant?'

'Try to set aside your dignity, Pekkala, at least if you want to stay alive. And remember to keep your mouth shut when you're around the head cook,' added Klenovkin. 'His name is Melekov and he's the worst gossip at Borodok. Whatever you say to him will find its way into the ears of every convict in this camp.'

By now, the first eel-green glimmer of dawn showed in the sky.

'Good luck, Inspector,' said Klenovkin, as he turned to leave. 'Good luck, for both our sakes.'

*

Back in Moscow, Kirov woke with a start.

He had fallen asleep at his desk. Blearily, he stared at the earthenware pots arranged upon the windowsills. His plants – herbs and cherry tomatoes and a beloved kumquat tree – dappled the darkness with their leaves.

Groaning as he rose to his feet, Kirov stepped over to the wall and flipped on the lights. Then he strolled around the room, hands in pockets, while the last veils of sleep were lifted from his mind. He paused to admire Pekkala's desk, on which the file belonging to the dead captain Ryabov was neatly flanked by pens, a ruler and a pencil sharpener. It did not usually look so tidy. Normally, the arrangement of Pekkala's possessions seemed to follow some path of logic known only to himself. And yet somehow, in defiance of reason, Pekkala always seemed to know where everything was. Unlike Kirov, Pekkala never had to hunt about for his keys, or his wallet or his gun.

The day before, in a moment of fastidiousness, Kirov had tidied Pekkala's desk. Now it looked smart. Efficient. And completely wrong. Kirov wished he hadn't touched anything, and he looked forward to the day when Pekkala would return and rearrange everything to its naturally shambolic state.

Kirov wondered how long it would be before Pekkala sent a telegram, asking for assistance. He hoped it would be soon. Ever since the Inspector had gone away, Kirov's life had become a dreary procession of paperwork, solitary meals and doubts about his own abilities to function in the absence of Pekkala.

Kirov sat down in Pekkala's chair. Like a mischievous schoolboy sitting at the teacher's place, he knew he was trespassing but, also like a mischievous schoolboy, he did it anyway. Then he stared at the phone on Pekkala's desk. 'Ring, damn you,' he said.

*

The intercom clicked on.

'Poskrebyshev!'

'Yes, Comrade Stalin.'

'Any word from Pekkala?'

'Nothing yet, Comrade Stalin.'

'Are you certain that all transmissions have been intercepted?'

'Comrade Stalin, there have been no transmissions between Kirov and Major Pekkala.'

'Doesn't that seem strange to you, Poskrebyshev?'

'I am sure he will communicate with Major Kirov when he has something to report. He only just arrived at the camp.'

'I may have been wrong to put my faith in him.'

'In Pekkala? Surely not . . .'

Without another word, the intercom clicked off.

There is that tone again, thought Poskrebyshev. What can be worrying him? A sense of foreboding clouded Poskrebyshev's mind. This was not the first time he had witnessed Stalin's moods as they began to swing erratically. In the past, bouts of good humour would be suddenly and inexplicably replaced by fury, frustration and paranoia. And the results had always been deadly. In 1936, when Stalin had become convinced that officers in the Soviet army were about to overthrow him, and he had initiated a policy of arrests and executions which wiped out most of the officer corps, leaving the Red Army virtually stripped of its High Command. These purges, which had begun before and continued long after Stalin's attack on the army, caused a death toll that ran into the hundreds of thousands.

Nervously, he glanced towards Stalin's office. A storm is

brewing, Poskrebyshev decided, and when it hits, it's going to come right through those doors.

*

The sun had just risen above the tree line as the new prisoners of Borodok assembled in the compound to receive their work assignments.

Some convicts were assigned to logging operations, but most, including Savushkin, went directly to work in the mines which harvested crystals of Siberian Red, as well as the radium used to illuminate the hands of military watches, compasses and aircraft dials.

As Klenovkin had promised, Pekkala found himself detailed to the camp kitchen, which had, until that moment, been run entirely by one man. His name was Melekov. He had short grey hair and skin as pale as a plucked chicken.

There was no time for introductions, and Pekkala went immediately to work handing out breakfast rations to men who had lined up outside the kitchen window. Each received one fist-sized loaf of bread known as a *paika* and a cup of black tea, served from one of three huge metal tubs. The cups were chained to these tubs, so the men had to drink the tea quickly before handing the mug to the next in line.

In spite of the cold outside, the kitchen grew so hot from the bread oven that Melekov stripped down to his shorts and a filthy undershirt. In this unofficial uniform, together with a pair of army boots which were missing their laces, he stamped about the kitchen barking orders.

'Rejoice!' commanded Melekov. 'Rejoice that you are working here with me. I control the food, and food is the currency of Borodok. The value of everything which can be bought or sold is measured in those rations of bread you are handing out. And the source of all rations', he jabbed a thumb against his chest, 'is me!'

As these words filtered into his brain, Pekkala stood in the kitchen doorway, reaching mechanically into burlap sacks containing *paika* rations and pressing the loaves into the workers' outstretched hands. He had to look carefully at those hands, because Melekov had instructed him to give two rations of *paika* to the three remaining Comitati, all of whom were identifiable by the pine trees tattooed on their hands.

'Those men are dangerous,' explained Melekov, leaning over Pekkala's shoulder. 'Do not speak to them. Do not even look at them.'

'But there are only three of these men in the whole camp. Why is everyone so afraid of them?'

'Let me explain it this way,' replied Melekov. 'If you beat a man to the ground in order to teach him a lesson and all he does is get back on his feet and keep on fighting, what does that tell you about this man?'

'That you have not taught him anything.'

'Exactly!'

'But what lesson would you be trying to teach with such a beating?'

'That the only way to survive in this camp is to live by its rules. There are the rules of the Dalstroy Company, the rules of the Commandant, the rules of the guards and the rules of the prisoners. All of them must be obeyed if you want to go on breathing in Borodok, but the Comitati have never learned to obey. That is why, out of the dozens who were sent to this camp, so few of them are left. But those few are not ordinary men.'

'What do you mean?'

'No one can find a way to kill them! That is why the Comitati always get an extra bread ration, and if there's anything else they want, just give it to them and keep your mouth shut. And stay out of the freezer!' Melekov added as an afterthought. 'If I catch you in there, stealing food meant for Klenovkin or the guards, I'll hand you over to them. Then you'll learn what pain is all about.'

As Pekkala handed out bread to the shadows of men filing past, he failed to notice the pine-tree tattoo of a huge bald man, whom he immediately recognised as the driver of the cart loaded with bodies which had passed them on their way into the camp. The bald man grabbed Pekkala by the wrist, almost crushing the bones in his grip, until Pekkala handed over an extra ration.

The man let go, grunted angrily and stepped away.

'Didn't you listen to a word I said?' asked Melekov, who had been watching. 'That is Tarnowski, the worst of all the Comitati and the last man you want to upset, especially on your first day in the camp!'

Next in line was Savushkin. 'How are they treating you?' he whispered.

'Well enough so far,' replied Pekkala, quickly pressing an extra *paika* ration into Savushkin's outstretched hands.

'They have made it difficult for me to keep an eye on you,' continued Savushkin, 'but not impossible. You might not see me, but I will try to be there when you need my help.'

Before Pekkala could thank Savushkin, the next man in line took his place.

When he had finished handing out the rations, Pekkala, who had not yet been given any food for himself, swiped his wetted thumb around the inside of the large aluminium bowl which had contained the bread. Dabbing up the crumbs, he popped them in his mouth and crunched the brittle flakes.

Although this yielded barely a mouthful, Pekkala knew that, from now on, he would have to take food wherever he could find it.

He already knew the grim equation of the quota system at these camps. If a man completed his daily workload, he would receive 100 per cent of his food ration. But if he failed to meet this quota, he received only half of his food. The following day, he would be too weak to carry out his tasks, and so his ration would be short again. Inevitably, the man would starve to death. The only sure means of survival was to break the rules and avoid getting caught. Prisoners referred to this as 'walking like a cat'.

After the rations had been distributed, Pekkala and Melekov sat down at the little table in the corner to eat their own breakfasts. Pekkala was permitted to take a single *paika* ration, while Melekov, still wearing only shorts and undershirt, devoured a bowl of boiled rye mixed with dried apples and pine nuts.

While Pekkala ate, he paused to watch an old man dragging a sledgehammer out across the camp. The man came to the edge of a sheet of ice which had formed in the yard. He raised the hammer, and brought it smashing down, slowly breaking up the ice.

Two guards approached the old man. Laughing, they bowed

to him and crossed themselves. Pekkala recognised the taller of the two guards as the man he had seen in Klenovkin's office, the same one who had shot the prisoner dead when they first arrived at the railhead.

'That big one is Sergeant Gramotin,' explained Melekov. 'During the Revolution, he was involved in battles against the Whites and the Czech Legion up and down the Trans-Siberian Railroad. People say he lost his sanity somewhere out there on those tracks. That's another person you should do your best to avoid.' As he spoke, Melekov wolfed down his breakfast, his face only a hand's breadth above the wooden bowl. 'Most of the guards in this camp are sadists and even they think Gramotin is cruel. Lately, he's been worse than ever, on account of the fact that six prisoners escaped last month. Some of them were found by the Ostyaks . . .'

'Dead?'

'Of course they were dead! And lucky for the convicts that they froze to death before the Ostyaks found them. But a few of those prisoners are still missing and Gramotin will take the blame if they can't be accounted for.'

'Do you think they got away?'

'No,' growled Melekov. 'They're lying out there somewhere in the valley, frozen solid as those statues in the compound.'

'If they're dead, then what is Gramotin worried about?'

'Dalstroy wants those bodies. They make good money selling corpses, provided the wolves or the Ostyaks haven't eaten too much of them by the time they get back to camp.'

'Who's the other guard?' asked Pekkala.

'His name is Platov. He's Gramotin's puppet. He does whatever Gramotin does. Gramotin doesn't even have to

95

prompt him. If Gramotin whistles the first notes of a song, Platov will finish it for him.'

It was true. When Gramotin bowed, Platov immediately did the same. When Gramotin laughed, Platov's laughter was only a second behind.

'And the old man they are tormenting?'

'That is Sedov, another Comitati. But you don't have to worry about him. He won't cause you any trouble. They call Sedov the Old Believer because, even though religion has been banned in the camps, he refuses to give up his faith.'

First Gramotin, and then Platov, unshouldered their Mosin-Nagant rifles and began to prod the convict with fixed bayonets.

'Dance for us!' shouted Gramotin.

'Dance! Dance!' echoed Platov.

'Dancing is a sin in the eyes of God!' Sedov shouted at them.

'Didn't anyone tell you?' shouted Gramotin. 'God has been abolished!'

Platov cackled, jabbing Sedov so violently that if the man had not stepped backwards, the bayonet would have run him through.

'You may have abolished God,' replied Sedov, 'but one day he will abolish you as well.'

Melekov shook his head, a look of pity on his face. 'Sedov has forgotten the difference between this life and the next one. Gramotin will kill him one of these days, just like he killed Captain Ryabov, that man we've got lying in the freezer.'

'Gramotin killed Ryabov?'

'Sure!' Melekov said confidently. 'Ryabov thought it was his job to look after the other Comitati, since he was the highest ranking officer among them, but it proved to be a hopeless task. One after the other, most of them died. There was nothing he could do. That's just the way things are in these camps. People say it pushed Ryabov over the edge, not being able to save them. The rumour is that he finally just snapped.'

'And did what?' asked Pekkala.

'He went up against Gramotin one too many times. That's how you end up in the freezer, while Klenovkin tries to figure out whether anyone will buy a body whose head is practically cut off.'

*

Swathed in the hand-me-down clothes of a dead prisoner, and with a beard quickly darkening his cheeks, Pekkala had become invisible among the similarly filthy inhabitants of Borodok.

But he knew this couldn't last. If he was to solve the murder of Ryabov, he would have to learn, from the Comitati themselves, everything they knew about the killing. Pekkala's only chance was to win their confidence. But he would have to move carefully. If the Comitati learned of his true purpose, or even if they became suspicious, he would never leave Borodok alive.

While he waited for the right moment to break cover, Pekkala studied them from a distance.

Lavrenov was a tall, thin man with feverishly glowing eyes and cheeks hollowed out by years of gulag life. 'That one deals in everything,' Melekov told Pekkala. 'From tobacco, to razor blades, to matchsticks, Lavrenov can get his hands on whatever you want, as long as you can pay for it. And, somehow, he can still keep out of trouble.'

Sedov, the Old Believer, could not. He was small, wiry and muscular, with the scars and crumpled cheekbones of a man who had been beaten many times. Most prisoners kept their hair short, as a precaution against lice, but Sedov's was long and pleated with dirt, as was his unkempt beard. A broken, slightly upturned nose and twisted lips had given him a permanent expression of bemusement, as if recalling some private joke. This, in combination with a stubborn, almost suicidal refusal to conceal his religious faith made him a perfect target for Gramotin. Daily, the sergeant sent the old man skittering across the ice-patched compound, while he taunted the convict, chanting scraps of outlawed prayers.

But the man Pekkala watched most closely was Lieutenant Tarnowski. Now the highest ranking member of the Comitati, Tarnowski enforced its violent reputation. At those rare times when words alone proved unsuccessful, Tarnowski carried out his threats with a relish that seemed to rival even that of the guards.

On Pekkala's fifth day at the camp, after the rations had been distributed, he sat down as usual with Melekov at the little table in the corner to eat breakfast.

On the floor beside Melekov's chair was a battered metal tool box, which he used to carry out repairs around the camp. Whenever anything mechanical broke down – phones, alarms, clocks – the guards would send for Melekov.

'What is it this time?' Pekkala nodded towards the tool box.

'Guard tower phones are down again.' As Melekov spoke, he removed a hardboiled egg from the jumble of pickled beets, cheese, bread and scraps of cold meat which filled his bowl. Gently, he rolled the egg between his palms, until the shell was mosaicked with cracks. 'The batteries that power the ringers keep freezing. I hate going up and down those ladders. They shouldn't make me do it. I'm a wounded veteran, you know.' He pointed to his thigh, where an X-shaped scar was visible just below the tattered edge of his shorts. 'I'll tell you how I got it.' Melekov breathed in deeply, ready to begin his story.

In that moment, Pekkala saw his chance. 'Instead of telling me how you received that wound, how about I tell you?'

'You tell *me*?' Melekov's breath trailed out.

Pekkala nodded. 'I'll tell you what it is and where you got it and what you used to do before you came to Borodok.'

'What are you,' grunted Melekov, 'some kind of fortune teller?'

'Let's find out,' replied Pekkala, 'and if I'm right, you can give me that egg you were about to eat.'

Eyeing Pekkala suspiciously, Melekov laid the egg down on the table.

As Pekkala reached out to take it, Melekov's hand slapped down on top of his.

'Not yet! First, you can tell me my fortune.'

'Very well,' said Pekkala.

Cautiously, Melekov removed his hand.

'That scar was made by a bayonet,' began Pekkala.

'Perhaps.'

'To be specific, it was the cruciform bayonet of a Mosin-Nagant rifle, the standard issue for a Russian soldier.'

'Who told you?' demanded Melekov.

'Nobody.'

The two men stared at each other for a moment, waiting for the other to flinch.

Slowly, Melekov folded his arms across his chest. 'All right, convict, but where was I when I received the wound?'

'The branches of the X are longer at the lower edges of the scar,' Pekkala went on, 'which means that the bayonet thrust was made from below you, not above or at the same level, which would be more usual. This means you were either standing on a staircase when it happened . . .'

Melekov smiled.

'Or on the top of a trench.'

The smile broadened, baring Melekov's teeth.

'Or,' said Pekkala, 'you were riding a horse at the time.'

The smile dissolved. 'Bastard,' whispered Melekov.

'I haven't finished yet,' said Pekkala. 'You are a Siberian.'

'Born and bred here,' Melekov interrupted. 'I've never been anywhere else.'

'Your accent puts you east of the Urals, probably in the vicinity of Perm. You are old enough to have fought in the war and from the cut of your hair,' he nodded towards Melekov's flat-topped stand of grey bristles, in the style known as *en brosse*, 'I am guessing that you did.'

'Yes, that's all true, but . . .'

'So you were a Russian soldier and yet you have been wounded by a Russian bayonet. Therefore, you were wounded by one of your own countrymen.' Pekkala paused, studying the emotions on Melekov's face, which passed like the shadows of clouds over a field as the cook relived his past. 'You did not receive your wound during the war, but rather in the Revolution which followed it.'

'Very good, convict, but which side was I fighting for?'

'You were not with the Whites, Melekov.'

Melekov turned his head and spat on the floor. 'You've got that right.'

'If you were,' said Pekkala, 'you would more likely be a prisoner here than someone who is on the payroll. And I have not seen you speaking to the Comitati, which you would do if you were one of them.'

Melekov held out his fists, knuckles pointing upwards. 'No pine-tree tattoos.'

'Exactly, which means you fought for the Bolsheviks, and because you were a horseman, I believe you were in the Red Cavalry.'

'The 10th Brigade . . .'

'You were injured in an attack against infantry, during which one of the enemy was able to stab you with a bayonet as you rode past. A wound like that is very serious.'

'I almost died,' muttered Melekov. 'It was a year before I could even walk again. I could not even leave the hospital because the leg kept getting infected.'

'And since you've already told me that you've never left Siberia that must be where you were injured. I believe you must have been fighting against the forces of Generals Semenov or Rozanov, the White Cossacks, who waged their campaigns in this part of the world.' When Pekkala had finished, he slumped in his chair, feeling the tingle of sweat against his back. If even one detail was wrong, the minutes he had spent unravelling the mystery of Melekov's crucifix scar would do more harm than good.

For a long time, Melekov was silent, his face inscrutable. Then suddenly he stood. His chair fell over backwards and landed with a clatter on the floor. 'Every last word of what you've said is true!' he shouted. 'But there is one more thing I'd like to know.'

'Yes?'

'I would like to know who the hell you *really* are, convict.'

This was the moment Pekkala had been waiting for. If Klen-ovkin had been right that Melekov was the worst gossip in the camp, all Pekkala had to do was speak his name, and it would not be long before the Comitati knew that he was here.

'I was known as the Emerald Eye.'

Melekov's eyes opened wide. 'Do you mean to tell me you are the tree marker who lasted all those years and then suddenly disappeared? But I thought you were dead!'

'Many people do.' Pekkala's fingers inched forward, reaching like the tentacles of an octopus until they closed around the egg.

This time, Melekov did nothing to prevent him.

The cracked shell seemed to sigh in Pekkala's grip. Hunched over the table, he plucked away the tiny fragments, which fell to the table like confetti. He sank his teeth through the slick rubbery white and bit into the hardboiled yolk.

*

At sunrise the next day, the gates of Borodok swung open and a band of heavily armed men entered the compound. They were short and swathed in furs, their wide Asiatic faces burned brick-red by the wind.

The men brought with them a sledge pulled by reindeer, on which lay half a dozen bodies, each one solid as stone.

Melekov and Pekkala stood in the doorway of the kitchen, handing out rations.

'Ostyaks,' whispered Pekkala.

'That must be the last of the prisoners who tried to escape before you arrived at the camp. Gramotin will be happy now. Or at least less miserable than usual.'

One of the fur-clad men set aside his antiquated flintlock rifle and stepped into Klenovkin's office. The others glanced warily at the camp inmates who had paused in the breadline to witness the spectacle. A minute later, the Ostyak emerged from Klenovkin's hut, carrying two burlap sacks stuffed full as pillows.

The bodies were dumped off the sledge. Borodok guards opened the gates and the Ostyaks departed as suddenly as they had arrived, leaving behind the grotesquely frozen corpses.

'Come on, Tarnowski!' Gramotin shouted at the convicts. 'You know what to do. Find your men and put these carcasses beside the generators. I want them thawed out by the end of the day.'

Taking hold of frozen limbs as if they were the branches of a fallen tree, the Comitati carried the corpses over to a building where the electrical generators were housed.

'Why does he force the Comitati to do that job?' Pekkala asked Melekov.

'Force them?' Melekov laughed. 'That job is a privilege. The Comitati fought for it until no one else would dare take it from them, not even Gramotin.'

'But why?'

'Because the generator room is the warmest place in this

camp. They take their time laying out those bodies, believe me, and thaw themselves out a little as well.'

'What's the reason for thawing out the bodies?'

'It's the only way they can get them into the barrels.'

By the time the Comitati reappeared, the breadline had begun to move again, but no sooner had Pekkala begun distributing the rations than a fight broke out among the prisoners.

Pekkala had been so focused on handing out the bread that he did not see who started it.

Those convicts not involved fell back from the commotion, leaving an old man, whom Pekkala immediately recognised as Sedov, down on one knee and wiping a bright smear of blood from his nose.

Above him stood Tarnowski. With fists clenched, he circled the old man like a boxer, waiting for his opponent to raise himself up before knocking him down once more.

Pekkala remembered what Klenovkin had said about the Comitati turning against each other. From what he could see, it appeared to be the truth.

Sedov climbed shakily to his feet. He was upright for only a second before Tarnowski smashed him again in the face. Sedov spun as he tumbled, his teeth limned in red, but no sooner was he down than he began to get up again.

'Stay down,' muttered Pekkala.

Melekov grunted in agreement. 'They never learn. I told you.'

As he watched the Old Believer struggle to his feet, Pekkala could stand it no longer. He walked towards the door which led out to the compound.

'What are you doing?' barked Melekov.

'Tarnowski's going to kill him.'

'So what if he does? He'll kill you as well if you get in his way.'

Pekkala did not reply. Opening the flimsy door, he strode into the compound and pushed his way into the circle where the fight was taking place.

Tarnowski was just about to strike the old man another blow when he caught sight of Pekkala. 'Get out of the way, kitchen boy.'

Pekkala ignored him. Turning to help the injured man, he was astonished to see that the place where Sedov had been lying was now empty. The only thing remaining was some splashes of blood in the snow. The Old Believer seemed to have vanished into the crowd.

'Look out!' shouted a voice in the crowd.

Glancing at the blur of dirty faces, Pekkala caught sight of Savushkin.

Too late, Pekkala spun around to meet Tarnowski.

That was the last thing he remembered.

*

On the other side of the country, Poskrebyshev had just arrived for work.

As he did every day, he entered the Kremlin through the unmarked door that led directly to an elevator, which was also unmarked. This elevator had only two buttons, *up* or *down*, and brought him directly to the floor on which Stalin's office was located.

Poskrebyshev prided himself on following exactly the same

path to work, even down to where he placed his feet, this side or that side of cracks in the pavement.

From the moment Poskrebyshev left the small apartment, which he had shared with his mother until the year before, up to the instant he sat down at his desk, Poskrebyshev found himself in a pleasant haze of predictability. He liked things to be in their place. It was a trait Poskrebyshev shared with Stalin, whose insistence on finding things just as he had left them was even more acute than his own.

Entering his large, high-ceilinged chamber, Poskrebyshev hung up his overcoat, placed his paper-wrapped lunch on the windowsill and sat down at his desk.

He noticed, from the tiny green light on the intercom, that the Boss had already arrived. It was not unusual for him to come in early. Stalin often could not sleep and sometimes spent the whole night in his office or wandering the secret passageways that ran between the walls of the Kremlin.

Poskrebyshev's first task was always to fill in his personal logbook with the time he had arrived. In all the years he'd worked for Comrade Stalin, he had never been absent or late. Even on the day he discovered that his mother had died in her sleep, he left her lying in her bed, made his lunch, and went to work. He did not call the funeral home until he arrived at the Kremlin.

With a movement so practised it was practically unconscious, he slid open the drawer to retrieve his logbook.

What took place next caught him so completely by surprise that at first he had no idea what was happening. The desk seemed to shudder, as if the Kremlin, perhaps the whole city of Moscow, had been seized in the grip of an earthquake. Then the desk began to move. It slid forward, the sturdy oak legs buckling, and crashed to the ground. Documents, stacked and ready for filing, slid across the floor in a cascade of lavender-coloured telegrams, grey departmental reports and pink requisition slips.

When everything finally stopped moving, Poskrebyshev was still sitting in his chair, still holding on to the drawer.

Then, from somewhere in the rubble of his collapsed desk, the intercom crackled. It was Stalin. 'Pos . . .' he began, but he was laughing so hard that he could barely speak. 'Poskrebyshev, what have you done?'

Then Poskrebyshev realised he had fallen victim to another of Stalin's cruel jokes. The boss must have come in early and sawed the legs of his desk completely through, so that even the slightest movement would bring the whole thing crashing down.

'Poskrebyshev!' Stalin snorted through the intercom. 'You are such a clumsy little man!'

Poskrebyshev did not reply. Setting aside the drawer, he retrieved his phone from the floor and called maintenance. 'I need a new desk,' he said.

There was another howl of laughter from the other room.

'He did it again?' asked the voice from maintenance.

This was, in fact, the third time Stalin had sabotaged Poskrebyshev's desk.

The first time, Stalin had sawed off the legs completely, so that when Poskrebyshev arrived for work, he found that the desk only came up to his knees. The second time, Poskrebyshev walked into his office and saw only his chair. The desk appeared to have vanished until, one month later, he received a letter from the regional commissar of Urga, Mongolia, thanking him for the unusual and generous gift.

'Just get me a new desk,' Poskrebyshev growled into the phone.

When Stalin's voice crackled once again over the intercom, his laughter had vanished. This sudden disappearance of good humour was another of Stalin's traits which Poskrebyshev had learned to endure. 'What is the news from Pekkala?' Stalin demanded.

With the toe of his boot, Poskrebyshev pressed down on the intercom button. 'None, Comrade Stalin. No word has come from Borodok.'

*

Pekkala woke up on a stone floor. He was freezing. As he looked around, he realised he was in a small hut, with a low roof made of rough planks and a wooden door which fitted poorly in its frame. Wind moaned around cracks in the door, which was fastened with a wooden block set across two iron bars. In the corner stood a metal bucket. Otherwise, the room was empty.

He realised he must be in one of the camp's solitary confinement cells, which were perched up on high ground at the edge of the camp, where they were exposed to a relentless, freezing wind.

Pekkala climbed stiffly to his feet. His jaw ached where he'd been hit by Tarnowski. With one hand against the wall to steady himself, he walked over to the door.

Peering through the gaps in the wooden planks, Pekkala

saw only bare ground scattered with twigs, broken branches, and yellow blooms of lichen like scabs upon the stones. Below, down a narrow, meandering path lay the tar-paper rooftops of the camp.

He was hungry. By now the shuddering emptiness Pekkala felt in his gut seemed to be permanent. Thinking about food made him remember it was Friday, the day Kirov used to prepare a meal for him before they both left the office for the weekend.

Prior to his instatement as a Commissar in the Red Army, and his subsequent appointment as Pekkala's assistant, Kirov had trained as a chef at the prestigious Moscow Culinary Institute. If the Institute had not been closed down and its buildings taken over by the Factory Apprentice Technical Facility, Kirov's life might have turned out very differently. But he had never lost his love of cooking, and Pekkala's office became a menagerie of earthenware pots and vases, in which grew rosemary, sage, mint, cherry tomatoes and the crooked branches of what might have been the only kumquat tree in Moscow.

The meals Kirov cooked for him were the only decent food Pekkala ate. The rest of the time, he boiled potatoes in a battered aluminium pan, fried sausages and ate baked beans out of the can. For variety, he wandered across the street to the smoke-filled Café Tilsit and ordered whatever they were serving that day.

Pekkala hadn't always been this way. Before the Revolution, he had loved the restaurants in St Petersburg, and was once a discerning shopper at the fruit and vegetable stalls in the great covered market of Gostiny Dvor. But his years in the Siberian wilderness had taken from him any pleasure in food. To him it had simply become the fuel that kept him alive.

All that changed on Friday afternoons, when their office filled with the smells of roast 'tetereva' woodpigeon served with warm Smetana cream, Anton apples stewed in brandy, or 'tsiplyata' chicken in ripe gooseberry sauce, which Kirov cooked on the stove in the corner of the room. Pekkala's senses would be overwhelmed by cream cognac sauce, the barely describable complexity of truffles, or the electric sourness of Kirov's beloved kumquats.

Now Pekkala realised he had almost done what, in retrospect, seemed unforgivable, which was to take for granted the tiny miracles which Kirov had laid before him every Friday afternoon. Pekkala swore to himself that, if he was lucky enough to get out of this camp in one piece, he would never again make such a mistake.

He noticed a solitary figure making its way up from the camp. A moment later, the wooden post which locked the door slid back and the man walked into the cell.

It was Sedov.

He carried a blanket rolled up under his arm and a bundle of twigs clutched in his other hand. With a smile, he tossed the blanket to Pekkala and dropped the bundle of twigs in the corner.

'How did you get up here without being stopped?' asked Pekkala, as he unravelled the blanket, a coarse thing made from old Tsarist army wool, and immediately wrapped it around his trembling shoulders.

'Tarnowski persuaded one of the guards to let me go.'

'Persuaded?'

Sedov shrugged. 'Bribed or threatened. It's always one or the other.' Removing several flimsy matches from his trouser pocket, Sedov tossed them on the ground before Pekkala. 'You will need these as well,' said the old man. 'They are a gift from Lavrenov.'

'How long am I in for?'

'A week. The usual punishment for brawling.'

'You were the ones who were brawling.'

'But you were the one who got caught.'

'What about Tarnowski?' asked Pekkala.

'When the guards arrived, he told them you had started it. Somebody had to be punished. It just happened to be you.'

'What was the fight about?'

In answer to this, Sedov only smiled. 'All in good time, Inspector Pekkala.'

They know who I am, thought Pekkala. Klenovkin had been right about Melekov. The cook had not waited long to share his latest scrap of information.

'I have brought you a message from Tarnowski. He says you should try not to freeze to death before tomorrow night.'

'Why should Tarnowski care?'

'Because he is coming to see you.'

'What about?'

'Your fate,' replied Sedov. Without another word, he turned and left.

Pekkala listened to the wooden bolt sliding into place, and after that the old man's footsteps in the snow as he made his way back to the camp.

Worry twisted in Pekkala's gut. Whether he lived or died depended entirely on whether the Comitati believed his cover story. Alone in this cell, weak from lack of food and sleep, he would be no match for Tarnowski if the man decided to kill him.

He had no way of knowing how his fate would be decided. All he could do was to try and stay alive until they had made up their minds.

Gathering the matches that the Old Believer had thrown before him, Pekkala undid the bundle of firewood and arranged the twigs in a pyramid. Beneath them, he laid out shreds of papery white birch bark, peeled from the branches with his fingernails.

Of the four matches, one had already lost its head and was nothing more than a splintery toothpick. The next two, Pekkala tried to strike against the stone slab of the floor. One flared but died before he had a chance to touch it to the bark. The second refused to light at all.

As Pekkala knelt over the wood with the last match in his hand, a feeling of panic rose up inside him, knowing that the threadbare blanket would not be enough to get him through this night.

When the match flared, he crouched down and gently blew on the embers. The birch bark smouldered. Then a tiny flame blossomed through the smoke. He cupped his hands around it, feeding the fire with broken sticks until it had grown big enough to burn on its own. Sitting cross-legged, as close to the heat as he could, Pekkala slowly began to feel warmth spreading through his body.

By the following evening, he had used up the last carefully rationed splinters of his fuel supply.

As he huddled by the glimmering embers of his fire, he heard piano music down in the guard house. Although it was poorly played and the piano was badly out of tune, he could still make out the haunting tune of Sorokin's 'Fires on the Distant Plain'.

The door rattled suddenly, startling Pekkala. He had not heard anyone approach. Then the wooden bolt slid back, and Tarnowski entered the cell.

The air seemed to crackle with menace. Pekkala felt it all around him, as if an electric current were passing through his body. If the Comitati had got wind of his true purpose here at Borodok, the odds of surviving this meeting would be zero.

Tarnowski reached into his jacket.

Pekkala thought he might be going for a knife, but when the Lieutenant removed his hand, he was not holding a weapon. Instead, it was another small bundle of twigs, which he dumped beside the dwindling sparks of Pekkala's fire.

At the sight of that kindling, the knot of fear in Pekkala's stomach began to subside. Pekkala knew he wasn't in the clear yet, but at least he wasn't fighting for his life.

'I apologise for the unusual way in which I brought you here,' said Tarnowski.

'Brought me here? I am in this place because I tried to break up your fight with Sedov.'

'That is what you and the guards were supposed to think.'

'You mean it was staged?'

'After Melekov informed me of your identity, he mentioned that you didn't like the way Sergeant Gramotin was treating our Old Believer. I guessed you wouldn't stand to see him beaten right before your eyes, especially by the likes of me.'

'You have a crude way of getting things done,' said Pekkala.

'Crude, perhaps, but efficient. This is the only place where we could talk without being observed by the authorities. We used to hold meetings in the mine after dark, but after what happened to Captain Ryabov, the guards have been watching the entrance at night.'

'You damn near broke my jaw,' said Pekkala.

'That is something we might have avoided if you'd identified yourself to us when you arrived at the camp.'

'I didn't know who I could trust.'

'We felt the same way about you, Inspector, when we first learned you were here.'

'And what do you think now?' Pekkala settled a few of the twigs on the fire.

'The fact that you are still alive should tell you all you need to know,' Tarnowski replied.

Soon the wood began to burn. Flames cast their flickering light across the bare stone walls.

'We were surprised to see you back at Borodok.'

'Not as surprised as I was,' answered Pekkala.

'We almost crossed paths here, you know,' Tarnowski continued. 'The last survivors of the Kolchak Expedition reached Borodok not long after you did, but by that time you had already been sent into the forest. For a long time, we heard that you were still alive, even though no one had actually seen you. But when a new tree marker was sent out to take your place, we became convinced you had died. Then new prisoners started showing up at the camp, saying you had been recalled to duty in Moscow. They said you were working for the Bureau of Special Operations, under the direction of Stalin himself. At first, we didn't believe it. Why would the Emerald Eye put himself at the disposal of a beast like Stalin? But when these rumours persisted, we began to suspect that the stories might be true.'

'The stories are true,' Pekkala admitted. 'I was recalled to Moscow in order to investigate the murder of the Tsar. After that, I was given a choice. Either I could come back here to die or I could go back to the job I had been trained to do.'

'Not much of a choice.'

'Stalin is fond of placing men in such predicaments.'

'And if they do not choose wisely?'

'They die.'

'Like a cat with a mouse,' muttered Tarnowski, 'and now he has cast you aside once again, as he has done with so many others. This is where we end up and our job becomes to simply stay alive, a task you might find difficult, since there are men who are here in this camp because of you.'

'No.' Pekkala shook his head. 'They are here because of the crimes they committed.'

'A distinction which is lost on them, Inspector. But I have passed the word that anyone who lays a hand on you will answer for it with his life.'

'And who will answer for the murder of Captain Ryabov?'

The muscles clenched along Tarnowski's jaw. 'Saving your life and seeking vengeance for his death are not the same thing, Inspector. So many have perished since we came to this camp, I can no longer even remember their names. It would take a hundred lifetimes to avenge them all. And even if I could, what would be the point? The desire for revenge can take over a man's life.'

'And can also be the end of it,' said Pekkala.

'As you and I have seen for ourselves.'

'We have?'

'Oh, yes, Inspector. You and I have met before.'

Pekkala was startled by the revelation. 'You mean at this camp? But I thought . . .'

Tarnowski shook his head. 'Long before that, Pekkala, on a night even colder than this, outside the Hotel Metropole.'

At the mention of that place, memories came tumbling like an avalanche out of the darkness of his mind. 'The duel!' whispered Pekkala.

He was sitting at a table in the hotel restaurant, waiting for Ilya to arrive. For his fiancée's birthday, Pekkala had promised her dinner at the finest place in St Petersburg.

Large white pillars, like relics from a temple on Olympus, held up the high ceiling in the centre of which was a huge skylight, its view of the heavens obscured by thick swirls of cigarette smoke.

From every corner of the room came laughter, the clink of cutlery on plates, and the dry clatter of footsteps on the tiled floor.

Tuxedoed and ball-gowned couples danced on a raised floor at the far end of the room, to music played by a troupe of gypsies, dressed in their traditional bright, flowing clothes. In front of the musicians stood the most famous singer in St Petersburg, Maria Nikolaevna. Her quavering voice rose above all other sounds as she sang Panina's melancholy song, 'I Do Not Speak to You'.

A high balcony skirted the large, rectangular room. Set into the walls along this balcony, and interspersed between tropical elephant-ear ferns, were rows of doors leading into private rooms known as 'Kabinets'. What went on in those cramped spaces, judging from the endless stream of waiters in short white jackets delivering blinis and caviar, as well as the scantily dressed women who flitted like ghosts between the Kabinets, was not difficult to guess.

Now and then, the warmth of the tobacco-foggy air would be disturbed by waves of cold as the double doors to the street were flung open and new customers entered, stamping pom-poms of snow from the toes of their boots and shedding huge sable coats. Immediately, they would be ushered to their tables, leaving behind a glittering dust of frost in the air, as if they had materialised from the haze of a magician's spell.

Pekkala kept his eyes on the door as he sipped a cup of smoky-tasting tea. He wondered why Ilya was late. She was normally punctual, which was perhaps to be expected from a teacher of young children. Probably, the headmistress had kept her behind again to discuss some change in the curriculum, not in spite of the fact that she must have known it was Ilya's birthday and that Pekkala had made reservations at the Metropole but precisely because of that fact. The headmistress had done things like this before and now Pekkala clenched his fist upon the tablecloth as he silently cursed the old woman.

Just when he was about to give up and go home, the door opened and this time Pekkala felt sure it must be Ilya. Instead, however, a giant of a man walked into the room, swathed in the uniform of an Imperial Cavalry Officer. The newcomer removed his cap in the manner of a cavalryman, lifting it from the back and tipping it forward off his head. Briefly, he glanced about to get his bearings, then climbed the stairs and strode along the balcony. The leaves of palm trees brushed against his shoulders, as if bowing to the giant as he passed. He came to a stop outside one of the Kabinets, knocked once and entered.

Late for the party, guessed Pekkala, and for a moment, he went back to thinking about Ilya – whether she would like the present he had bought her: a silver dragonfly necklace made by the St Petersburg jeweller Nijinsky. The necklace had been very expens-

118

ive, and quietly it galled Pekkala to pay so much for something so utterly impractical.

The wanderings of Pekkala's mind were halted by the sound of the door to the Kabinet opening again. This time, two men emerged; the giant cavalry officer again and a man Pekkala recognised as Colonel Kolchak.

Kolchak was fastening the buttons on his tunic as he descended from the balcony and made his way towards the exit. Glancing across the sea of guests, he caught Pekkala's eye.

The two men nodded in greeting.

Kolchak's expression was grim and angry. He muttered something in the ear of the cavalry officer, who then crossed the dining room, sidestepping in the narrow space between tables with an agility surprising for such a heavyset man. He arrived at Pekkala's table, clicked his heels and jolted his head forward in a hasty bow. 'I am the Colonel's aide-de-camp. He requires your help, Inspector.'

Immediately Pekkala rose to his feet, dropping his napkin on the table. 'What is it about?'

'Colonel Kolchak needs you to be his second.'

'His second what?'

'His second in a duel.'

The word took Pekkala's breath away. 'A duel? When? Where?'

'Outside. Now.'

Pekkala hesitated. Although the fighting of duels was legal, as far as he knew, it had been years since one had taken place in the streets of St Petersburg. In order to make the duel legal, a second was required for each man, and these seconds, if asked, were required by law to witness the event.

'If you don't mind my asking, Lieutenant, why aren't you his second in this matter?'

'Because the Colonel asked for you, Inspector. Now if you will kindly follow me . . .'

Out in the street, it was snowing. Horse-drawn carriages passed by, wheels purring through the slush.

A staff car, which Pekkala recognised as belonging to Colonel Kolchak, was pulled up on to the kerb.

In the road stood a man Pekkala had never seen before. He was of medium height, with short, dark hair parted down the middle and a neatly trimmed moustache. The man was in the process of taking off his jacket, which he handed to another man standing beside him.

This second man was gaunt and narrow-lipped, with a sheepskin cap perched high upon his head.

Opposite these two, about twenty paces away, stood Colonel Kolchak. Weaving on his feet, the Colonel was obviously drunk. 'Let's get this over with!' he shouted.

'Kolchak,' said Pekkala, 'let us talk this through. I beg you to reconsider the challenge you have brought against this man.'

Kolchak turned to him and laughed. 'You are talking to the wrong man, Pekkala. I am not the one who asked to fight a duel.'

'But what is this about?'

Kolchak shook his head and spat into the snow. 'Nothing that matters to me.'

Realising this was the only answer he was going to get, Pekkala approached the other men.

The gaunt figure in the sheepskin cap came out to meet him. 'I am Polivanov,' he said.

'And who is he?' Pekkala nodded towards the gentleman with the moustache.

'That is Maxim Alexeyevich Radom,' answered Polivanov. 'It is he who has brought the challenge against Colonel Kolchak.'

'But why?'

'It is a point of honour,' Polivanov replied. 'I am acting as second on behalf of Maxim Radom. Am I to understand that you are the second for Colonel Kolchak?'

'I . . .' began Pekkala. 'Yes, I am but . . .'

From the pockets of his coat, Polivanov removed two revolvers. Holding them by the barrels, he held the weapons out towards Pekkala. 'Choose, please.'

'What?'

Polivanov leaned towards Pekkala and lowered his voice. 'You must select a gun, sir.'

'Are you sure this can't be stopped?' pleaded Pekkala.

'I am quite sure,' replied Polivanov.

Hesitantly, Pekkala reached out and took one of the pistols. He could tell from the weight that it was fully loaded.

Polivanov measured out twelve paces. At each end he drew a line with his heel in the wet snow.

Maxim Radom walked forward to the line which had been drawn for him. Clasped in one hand was a crumpled piece of paper. Wearing only a shirt above his waist, Radom shuddered with the cold.

Now Kolchak advanced to his line. He held out his hand to Pekkala. 'Give me the gun,' he ordered.

Reluctantly, Pekkala handed him the weapon. 'Colonel, I beg you to reconsider. What honour can there be in gunning down another man?'

Kolchak did not reply. Instead he opened the cylinder, cocked the revolver and peered down the barrel at his opponent. Then he spun the cylinder, holding it up to his ear, like a burglar listening to the tumblers of a safe. With a jerk of his wrist, Kolchak closed the cylinder: 'Stand aside,' he told Pekkala, and suddenly he did not sound drunk any more.

Once more Pekkala turned to face the two strangers, still convinced that there might be a way to end this without bloodshed. But there was something about the way they stood, and the grim formality of their expressions, which made Pekkala realise that he was part of something he could not prevent.

Radom unfolded the piece of paper in his hand. 'Colonel Kolchak,' he announced in a loud but shaking voice, 'I will read the charge against you.'

'Go to hell!' snarled Kolchak. 'Do you want to kill me or don't you?'

Radom flinched, as if the Colonel had just spat in his face. With trembling fingers, he attempted to fold up the paper again, but instead, he dropped it in the snow. For a moment, he stared at it, seemingly contemplating whether there was more dignity in bending down to retrieve the note, or in leaving the paper where it lay.

Before he could make up his mind, Kolchak's voice thundered once more through the darkness. 'Who's first?'

'The choice is yours,' answered Radom.

In that moment, Pekkala no longer felt the freezing air blowing in off the Neva River. Nor could he hear the sound of laughter and music from inside the Metropole. Even the drifting snowflakes seemed to pause in their descent.

Kolchak examined the revolver in his hand. He turned it one

way and then another and the glimmer of the street lamps winked off its blued steel barrel. Then, casually, he raised the gun and pulled the trigger.

The sound was flat and brittle, like that of someone breaking a dry stick across their knee.

Maxim Alexeyevich Radom stood perfectly still.

Kolchak missed, thought Pekkala. Thank God, the man is too drunk to shoot straight. Now surely they will call the whole thing off.

Another moment passed before Pekkala realised that he was mistaken.

Radom's neat, dark hair stuck up on one side, like a shard of black glass. Slowly, the man raised his arms out to the side, like someone about to set out across a tightrope. He took one careful step backwards, then fell into the slush, the gun tumbling out of his hand.

Pekkala and Polivanov both ran to help the injured man, but there was nothing they could do.

Radom had been shot just above the left eye. His skull had been cracked open, and the scalp folded back upon itself. Steam drifted from the hole in his head.

Radom was still alive but his breathing had become a deep, guttural snore.

It was a sound Pekkala had heard before, and he knew that the man had only minutes left to live.

At that moment, the double doors of the Metropole flew open and a woman ran out into the street. Her hair was a dark, tangled mass. She was wearing only a silk negligee, and as she passed through the lamplight, the gossamer fabric seemed to disappear like smoke, leaving her naked in the freezing air.

Stumbling barefoot through the snow, she made her way to where Radom had collapsed. With a wail she sank down next to him, pressing her hands against his bloody face.

Kolchak had not moved since he fired the revolver. Now he shook his head and tossed the gun away.

The Lieutenant emerged from where he had been waiting in the shadows and the two men climbed into Kolchak's car.

That was when Pekkala caught sight of Ilya coming down the road.

He ran to meet her.

'Why is that man lying here?' Her cheeks were rosy in the cold.

'We should go.' Gently he took her by the arm.

'What about the Metropole? What about our dinner?'

'Some other time,' Pekkala replied.

'What happened?' She was staring at the woman in the negligee.

'Please,' whispered Pekkala. 'I promise I will tell you later.'

Sitting behind the wheel, the Lieutenant started up the car.

Hearing the noise of the engine, the woman in the negligee raised her head. She caught sight of Kolchak in the back seat of the car and let out a scream of sadness and rage.

The car pulled out into the road and drove past, showering them all with icy water.

Pekkala glimpsed a match flaring in the car as Kolchak lit himself a cigarette.

As they passed, the driver turned towards Pekkala. That man was Lieutenant Tarnowski.

Their eyes locked, and then the car was gone, and the glittering frost which filled the air seemed to close up around it, as if it had never been there.

Kolchak's duel was the last one ever fought in St Petersburg. Two days later, the Tsar outlawed this barbaric ritual.

After Tarnowski, there were no more visitors.

It was hunger that preoccupied Pekkala now, no matter how hard he tried to steer it from his mind.

On his fifth day in solitary, Pekkala spotted a cockroach scuttling across the floor. The thumb-sized, amber-coloured insect reached the far wall and began to move along it.

Without another thought, Pekkala lunged across the floor and caught it. With nausea rising in his throat, he crushed the cockroach in his fist and ate the mash of legs and shell and innards, mixed with the grey-brown silt, like the ashes from a crematory oven, which he had clawed up from the floor along with the insect.

Pekkala felt no revulsion, knowing that, in the gulags, only those who were prepared to set aside all pretence of dignity would go on living.

To take his mind off the fact that he was starving, he focused his thoughts on the murder of Ryabov. Since arriving at the camp, he had been presented with several possibilities, all of which appeared to circle around the truth. But none of them, as far as Pekkala was concerned, pointed directly at it. Commandant Klenovkin was convinced that the killing had been carried out by the Comitati. Melekov blamed Sergeant Gramotin. The Comitati themselves seemed resigned to their gradual extinction in this place, at the hands of whoever dared to challenge them. For Tarnowski, the killer and his reasons hardly seemed to matter any more. The only thing they had left to believe in was that their leader would one day return to set them free.

Pekkala admired the Comitati for the depth of their faith, but for that same reason, he also pitied them. Even if Kolchak had promised to return some day, Pekkala did not believe that the Colonel would keep his word. Although Pekkala had not been well acquainted with Kolchak, he knew precisely the kind of man the Tsar would have chosen for such an important task. Kolchak may have selected the men under his command for their loyalty to him, but the Tsar had picked Kolchak for his ability to carry out the mission, no matter what the cost in human life. That mission was to transport the gold. For such a task, cold blood, not compassion, was required. Once his soldiers had fallen into captivity, Kolchak would have weighed the risks of trying to free them and realised that the odds were too great. What the men under Kolchak's command had never been able to accept was that they were, in the eyes of their leader, expendable.

The mission had failed. The gold had fallen into the hands of the enemy. The Tsar was dead. The war was over. For Colonel Kolchak, these bitter truths would have been harder to accept than the loss of his soldiers.

One thing continued to puzzle Pekkala more than anything else. After holding out for so many years, why had Captain Ryabov suddenly approached the Commandant in order to bargain for his freedom with information too old to be of any probable use? Even if he did possess some scrap of useful knowledge, why would he choose this time to betray the Colonel?

Perhaps Commandant Klenovkin was right, and the Captain had finally grown tired of waiting. But what Pekkala did not believe was Klenovkin's claim that time and hardship had simply caused Ryabov to crack. Something specific had pushed Ryabov over the edge, perhaps a horror he had glimpsed on the horizon or else an event from his past which had finally caught up with him. If the latter was true, then the answer might lie in the contents of Ryabov's file – if only the missing pages could be found.

The time had come to bring Kirov on to the case. All Pekkala had to do now was wait until they let him out of this cell.

At dawn on the seventh day, Gramotin and Platov came to fetch him. In their heavy greatcoats, they were sweating by the time they had trudged up the hill.

Pekkala was sitting with his back against the wall, his knees drawn up to his chest, clinging to the tiny pocket of warmth he had created under the threadbare blanket.

'Get up,' ordered Gramotin.

'Time to get back to work,' added Platov.

Stiffly, Pekkala rose to his feet, and the two guards walked him down towards the camp.

Halfway there, Platov tripped Pekkala, sending him sprawling on the muddy path.

Rolling over on to his back, Pekkala found himself staring down the muzzle of Gramotin's rifle.

'We heard about you,' Gramotin said.

'Heard you were a detective,' Platov chimed in.

'That's right.' Pekkala tried to stand but Gramotin swung his rifle butt into Pekkala's shin and knocked him down again.

'We also heard that the Comitati want you to stay in one piece,' continued Gramotin. 'We have learned, over the years, to get along with those gentlemen, which sometimes means granting them a wish or two, but the next time you see a fight, Inspector, you stay out of it. If I have to come all this way again to fetch you down from solitary, no matter what the Comitati want, I swear you'll never make it to the bottom of the hill. Understand?'

Pekkala nodded, gritting his teeth from the pain in his bruised shin.

By the time they reached the camp, a large truck had arrived in the compound.

The canvas flaps had been thrown back and a group of hawk-eyed women were climbing down into the slush. Even more than their gender, it was the colours of their clothes that set them apart from the dreary world of Borodok. To Pekkala, they looked like tropical birds which had been blown off course from their migrations, and ended up in a place where their survival would depend on a miracle.

'Hello, my darlings!' Gramotin called to them.

'I'll see you later,' said a woman with a tobacco-husky voice. As she spoke, she drew apart the lapels of her heavy coat and swayed her hips from side to side.

'I love it when the whores come by.' Platov was grinning. 'But look at the line already.'

At the camp hospital, the queue of men stretched halfway round the building. The hospital windows, lacking glass, were made from opaque panels of pressed fish-skin, and they wept with condensation. Out of the back door of the hospital, the sick were being moved to other parts of the camp. Two hospital orderlies carried out one man on a stretcher. The sick man's face was grey with fever. He seemed oblivious to what was happening, as the orderlies parked his stretcher in the woodshed beside the main building. Even though he did not fit inside the shed, the orderlies left him there, bare feet jutting out into the snow.

The two guards walked Pekkala to the kitchen.

Melekov met Pekkala in the doorway. With arms folded across his chest and a large wooden spoon clasped in each fist, he eyed Pekkala disapprovingly.

As soon as they were both inside the kitchen, Melekov launched into a scolding. 'What did you think you were doing getting involved in a fight with the Comitati? If you want to get yourself killed, there are much simpler ways of going about it.' As if to emphasise his point, Melekov walked over to his cutting board. The huge slab of wood had been worn down smoothly in the middle, like a rock pool formed by centuries of dripping water. Melekov scrubbed it at the end of each shift and treated the wood twice a month with special almond oil which he kept just for that purpose.

Pekkala thought it was one of the most accidentally beautiful things he had ever seen.

Heaped on the board now was the skinned leg of a goat, pale and bloodless, filmed with a strange shimmer of colours that reminded Pekkala of opals. 'Much easier ways to die!' Melekov shouted, cleaving through sinew and gristle with his monstrous carving knife. 'Well, don't just stand there, convict. You have to bring the Commandant his breakfast.' He nodded towards a tray which had been covered by a dish towel.

Pekkala went over to pick it up.

'Wait!' Melekov shouted.

Pekkala froze in his tracks.

Melekov stabbed a piece of goat meat with his butcher knife and raised it to his lips. With cruel precision, his pasty white tongue slithered out. Goat blood trickled down his wrists.

Pekkala watched in pleading silence.

Just before the meat disappeared into Melekov's mouth, he gave the blade a sudden flick, which sent the little cube flying across the room. It bounced off Pekkala's forehead, falling to the dirty, concrete floor. With a speed that surprised even himself, Pekkala dropped to his knees. Snatching up the meat, he swallowed it without chewing. By the time the gristly knot of flesh had made its way down his throat, his eyes were watering. 'Thank you,' he managed to whisper.

*

Carrying the tray, Pekkala walked across the compound. Inside Klenovkin's office, he laid the breakfast tray before the Commandant.

'There is only so much I can do for you,' Klenovkin barked at him. 'If you will insist on breaking the rules of this camp and getting yourself thrown into solitary . . .'

Pekkala didn't let him finish. 'I need to send a telegram to Moscow.'

Klenovkin snatched up a piece of paper and one of his needle-sharp pencils, then slid them both across the desk. 'Get on with it,' he muttered.

Pekkala scribbled out a message –

FIND MISSING CONTENTS OF RYABOV FILE STOP SEARCH
ARCHIVE 17 STOP PEKKALA

He handed the paper to Klenovkin. 'This should go out straight away.'

Klenovkin took the piece of paper and stared at it. 'But why is this even necessary? I told you the Comitati were responsible. As far as I'm concerned, the only reason you're here is to pick out which one of them did it. Now what I suggest you do is arrest them all and be done with it. The only telegram you should be sending to Moscow is to announce that the case has been closed.'

'I do not share your certainty, Commandant.'

'But they are the only ones who stand to benefit from Ryabov's death!'

'On the contrary. You have made no secret of your hatred for these men. What better way to be rid of them than to kill one man and blame the others for his murder? In a single act, you could sweep all of them away.'

Klenovkin smashed his fist down on the table. 'I will not stand to be accused!'

As if propelled by some invisible current of air, the pencil Pekkala had been using began to roll.

Both of them watched it gathering speed until it tipped off the end of the desk and fell with a rattle to the floor.

Deliberately, Pekkala bent down, picked up the pencil and placed it back where it had been before. 'I have not accused you of anything. I am merely showing you that the situation is more complicated than you imagine. I am beginning to think that the reason for his death might lie outside this camp.'

'And you hope to find the answer in this Archive 17?'

'With your permission, Commandant.'

'Very well,' he replied gruffly. 'I will allow it to go through.'

When Pekkala had gone, Klenovkin sank back into his chair. His heart was beating so quickly that he felt as if he were being rhythmically punched in the throat.

Sergeant Gramotin poked his head around the door. 'I heard shouting. Is everything all right? Has that prisoner been causing any trouble?'

Klenovkin grunted. '*Any* trouble? At the moment, he is causing *all* the trouble.'

'I can take care of that, Commandant.'

Klenovkin sighed and shook his head. 'Patience, Gramotin. The bastard is protected. At least, he is for now.'

*

Returning to the kitchen, Pekkala set to work delivering the thin vegetable broth known as *balanda*, which was served to the miners for their midday break.

The soup was carried in buckets which fastened with a wooden lid and a toggle on a piece of string; Pekkala hauled the buckets on a cart that was made out of rough planks, its wheels yawed on gap-toothed hubs. A horse that used to pull the kitchen cart had died of exhaustion one week before Pekkala arrived at the camp. Without another animal to take its place, Pekkala strapped himself into the leather harness and struggled across the compound, his sweat mixing with the sweat of the horse whose bones had long since been sucked hollow by the camp inmates.

Arriving at the entrance to the mine, Pekkala called into the darkness and listened to his voice shout back to him. Then he waited, hypnotised by the tiny swaying flames of lanterns along the tunnel wall.

*

'A message!' Poskrebyshev burst into Stalin's office, brandishing a telegram. 'A message from Borodok!'

Stalin held out his hand. 'Give it to me.' He snatched the telegram from Poskrebyshev, placed it carefully on the desk in front of him and stared at the piece of paper. 'Archive 17,' he muttered.

'What exactly is in Archive 17, Comrade Stalin?'

'Old files, misplaced files, files out of order, files incomplete. Archive 17 is the graveyard of Soviet bureaucracy. The question is what does Pekkala hope to find there?'

'He is looking for the file on a man named Ryabov,' said Poskrebyshev, trying to be helpful.

'I know what he is looking for!' Stalin shouted. 'I mean what he hopes to find on Ryabov, assuming anything can be located. The question was rhetorical. Do you know what rhetorical means, Poskrebyshev?'

Poskrebyshev did not answer directly, in case that question might also have been rhetorical. The discovery that Kolchak might still be alive seemed to have disrupted the order of Stalin's universe in ways that even the outbreak of war had not achieved. It was as if Stalin had remained locked in a private war with the Tsar, even though Nicholas II had been dead for years. He would not rest until every last vestige of that defunct civilisation had been trampled into dust. Of the old guard, only

Pekkala had escaped Stalin's wrath, but for how much longer, Poskrebyshev did not dare to guess, as long as the case remained unsolved.

*

There was a thunderous knocking on the door of Kirov's office.

Kirov stood up from his desk and strode across the room. Opening the door, he found himself looking at a corporal of the NKVD, smartly dressed in an olive tunic, deep blue trousers and black boots. The man's cap was tucked under his left arm. He saluted and held out a brown envelope. 'Telegram for you, Major.'

'All right,' said Kirov, taking the envelope and haphazardly returning the salute.

'Have you taken over from Inspector Pekkala, Comrade Major?' asked the corporal.

'Of course not!' replied Kirov. 'What are you talking about?'

'It's just that you're wearing his coat.'

Kirov glanced at his sleeve and then down at his chest, as if he could not figure out how he had come to be wearing Pekkala's overcoat. He had only tried it on to see how it felt, just for a minute, to see if it was comfortable. Kirov had often made fun of this coat, along with every other piece of Pekkala's clothing. None of it was remotely in style, not surprising since Pekkala bought his clothes from a place just down the road called Linsky's. Its shop window boasted mannequins with mismatched limbs, lopsided, grassy wigs and haughty stares which seemed to follow people in the street. Kirov had known people who not only wouldn't shop there but crossed the road rather than catch the eye of one of Linsky's mannequins.

Linsky's prided itself on the durability of its clothing. The sign above their door read – 'The Last Suit You'll Ever Need'. This was an unfortunate choice of words, since Linsky's was best known for providing clothes for bodies at funeral viewings. 'Linsky's!' Kirov used to announce with mock solemnity, before adding the slogan, 'Clothes for Dead People!'

But when he actually tried on the coat, Kirov could not help admiring its construction. The tightly woven wool was so thick it seemed almost bullet-proof. The pockets had been lined with moleskin for warmth and there were other, strangely shaped pockets on the inside, whose existence Kirov had not known about and whose purpose remained a mystery to him.

'What makes you think this is Pekkala's?' demanded Kirov.

The corporal pointed hesitantly at the collar of the coat.

Kirov's hand drifted up to the place. Unsure where to keep Pekkala's badge of office, he had simply returned the emerald eye to its original place beneath the lapel. 'You can go now,' muttered Kirov.

Hurriedly, the man saluted and left, steel-shod boots clattering away down the stairs.

Back in the office, Kirov opened the telegram. 'Archive 17? What the hell is that?' Immediately, he sat down at his desk, picked up the phone and dialled a number. 'Hello? Yes. Hello. This is Major Kirov from Inspector Pekkala's office. Yes, I am looking for the file of a man named Ryabov. Captain Isaac Ryabov. File number is 4995-R-G. Good. Yes. I'll stay on the line.' Kirov breathed out slowly while he waited, allowing the black receiver's mouthpiece to slide under his chin. He tilted back in the chair and put his heels up on Pekkala's desk.

A moment later, a voice came back on the line.

'I know, I have the file,' said Kirov. 'I'm looking at it now, but it contains only one page!' He picked up the sheet and wagged it in the air. 'There must be something missing. According to this file, there is no record of a Captain Ryabov before March of 1917. In other words, as far as we know, he did not exist before the Tsar stepped down from power. Well, I know that can't be right. I've been told it might be in Archive 17, so if you could just connect me with them . . . What? Are you serious? There isn't even a telephone? Yes, I could fill out a written request, but how long would it take to process? I don't think you understand. I don't have a month to get this done. I could see to it myself? Today? Very well. Where is it located? I didn't know there was a government building on Zelionka Street. I thought those were all abandoned warehouses. Yes, I'll be there when it opens.' With a dry click, the line disconnected.

A few minutes later, wearing his uniform, complete with polished boots, dress cap and Tokarev automatic in a holster at his belt, Major Kirov set off to find Archive 17. Tucked under his arm was the file of Captain Ryabov.

In order to save time, he took a short cut across the sprawling Bolotnia Market, where old women in muddy-hemmed dresses hawked jars of gooseberry jam, and gap-toothed men with bloodhound eyes chanted the price of potatoes.

He stopped to ask directions from a young boy in a floppy, short-brimmed cap, who sat behind a table on which a pile of dead rabbits lay stretched as if stolen from their lives in the moment of leaping to freedom.

'Zelionka Street? There's nothing but ghosts in those old buildings.'

'Nevertheless,' replied Kirov, 'it is where I need to be.'

The boy pointed in the direction Kirov was headed.

Kirov nodded thanks, took one step, then stopped and turned to face the boy again. 'Why aren't you in school?' he asked.

The boy laughed. 'And why are you looking for ghosts, Comrade Major of the NKVD?' With that, the boy picked up one of the dead rabbits and, taking hold of one paw, flapped it up and down to say goodbye.

Still clutching the file, Kirov arrived at Archive 17 of Internal Security just as the clerk was unlocking the door to a dingy, windowless and flat-roofed building which stood between two empty warehouses.

The clerk was a small, aggressive-looking man with a thin moustache and narrow shoulders. He wore an overcoat with a scarf neatly tied around his neck and an old-fashioned round-topped hat, the likes of which Kirov had not seen since before the Revolution. Although the man was obviously aware of Kirov's presence, he ignored the major while he unlocked the door. Finally, just before he disappeared inside, he turned and spoke to the Major. 'Wherever you think you are, I can assure you this is the wrong place.'

'Archive 17,' Kirov said quickly, to avoid having the door shut in his face. The clerk seemed ready to barricade himself inside the building.

'You have come to the right place,' the man replied abruptly, 'but these archives are reserved for Internal Security. A person like you can't come in here.'

'I am Major Kirov, with Special Operations.'

'Oh,' muttered the clerk. 'Then I suppose you can come in, after all. I am Professor Braninko, the guardian of Archive 17.' Reluctantly, he motioned for Kirov to enter.

Inside the archive, Kirov was startled to see, among the hundreds of wooden filing cabinets lining the walls, statues of soldiers in outdated military uniforms, as well as busts of men with gruff faces and wide, unseeing eyes. In the centre of the room lay a huge severed hand, held out as if waiting for giant coins to be placed in its palm.

'This place used to be a sculpture studio,' Braninko explained. 'Some of these have been here since the Revolution. When they moved me in here fifteen years ago, they couldn't be bothered to clear out the statues.'

'Couldn't you get rid of them yourself?'

Braninko laughed. 'Young man, they are made of bronze! It would take a dozen men to lift any one of these statues. Besides, I have grown used to them.'

Kirov stopped before a larger-than-life statue of a man wearing the cocked hat of an admiral. 'Do you know who they are?'

'No idea,' replied Braninko. 'To me, these statues are like the bones of dinosaurs. They may once have ruled the earth, but all that remains of them now are harmless, empty shells.' He hung his overcoat upon the outstretched finger of the hand, exchanging it for a heavy, grey shawl-collared sweater which fastened with wooden toggles up the front. 'Of course, a day might come when the titans of our own generation are hidden from the light in dusty rooms. Until that time, these relics will be my companions.'

'It smells of smoke in here,' remarked Kirov.

'Yes. Those are the Okhrana files. During the Revolution, the Headquarters of the Tsar's Secret Police was burned by . . . by . . .' He seemed to have lost his train of thought.

'By revolutionaries?' suggested Kirov, hoping to steer the man back on course.

'You can call them that if you want to!' blustered Braninko. 'Vandals are what I call them! Hoodlums! Destroying a place of records is inexcusable. Information does not care whose side it's on. Information is what helps us to make sense of the world. It points us to the truth. Without it, we are at the mercy of every self-serving liar who comes along. Believe me, Comrade Major, when you find yourself talking to a man who keeps the truth from you and tells you it's for your own good, you are dealing with a common criminal! Fortunately, they destroyed only a portion of the files. Those that could be salvaged were brought here to Archive 17, still smelling of smoke, I'm afraid.'

'I am looking for the file on Captain Isaac Ryabov, of the Imperial Cavalry. Is it possible that his documents survived the fire?'

'I'm afraid not, Major. Everything from the letter K onwards in the Okhrana files was destroyed. But I see you already have a file on this man.'

Kirov handed it over.

'Only one page?' asked Braninko, when he had looked inside the folder.

'There's no information on Captain Ryabov from before the Revolution. I thought it might simply be missing from the file, and I was informed that I might find the information here.'

'As I said, Major, everything beyond the letter K went up in smoke.' Braninko continued to study the contents of the folder. 'I see here that Captain Ryabov was transferred to Borodok.'

'Yes, that is correct.'

Braninko cleared his throat. 'Major, I don't know how familiar you are with the gulag system, but I can tell you that Ryabov won't be coming back from there.'

'You are quite right, Professor. Captain Ryabov has been murdered.'

'Ah,' Braninko went back to studying the sheet.

'Is there nothing you can do to help?'

The professor shook his head. 'I'm sorry, Major.'

Kirov sighed with disappointment.

'Unless,' said Braninko.

'Unless what?'

'There are some other documents.' The professor spoke quietly, as if afraid the statues might be listening.

'Well, what are we waiting for? May I see them?'

'No. That's the problem. You may not.'

'But why not?'

'There exists a set of papers known as the Blue File.'

'I have never heard of it.'

'Few people have. The contents of the file are secret. Even the existence of the file is classified information.'

'What's so special about it?'

'The Blue File contains the names of spies who operated within the Okhrana.'

'But that doesn't make any sense,' protested Kirov. 'Back then all Russian spies operated within the Okhrana. They were part of the Tsar's Secret Service. They answered to the Okhrana.'

'You misunderstand me, Comrade Major. The Blue File does not contain the names of Russian agents who spied *for* the Okhrana. These were agents who spied *on* the Okhrana.'

Kirov blinked. 'You mean to tell me there were agents who spied on our own Secret Service?'

Braninko nodded.

'But the Secret Service controlled all spying operations!' protested Kirov. 'Who would these agents answer to?'

'To the Tsar,' replied Braninko, 'and only to the Tsar.'

Kirov was stunned. 'And the Okhrana did not know about this?'

'That is correct. Even the great Chief Inspector Vassileyev was unaware of it.'

'Then why was the file discovered at Okhrana headquarters?'

'It wasn't,' Braninko explained. 'This file was found in a locked desk in the Tsar's study. In the chaos of the Revolution, he forgot to dispose of the documents. Either that, or he could not bring himself to destroy them.'

'Why is it called the Blue File?'

'The entries are written in blue pencil. It is the Tsar's own writing.'

'And who else knows about this file?'

'Let me put it this way, Major – I have taken a great risk by even informing you of its existence.'

'But Ryabov might be in there!'

'Once again, Major, there is that possibility, but let me ask you something. What is it exactly that you need to know?'

'I'm not sure,' replied Kirov. 'If Inspector Pekkala were here . . .'

Braninko breathed in sharply. 'Pekkala?'

'Yes,' answered Kirov. 'He and I work together.'

Braninko's head tilted a little to the side, like that of a curious dog. 'You work with the Inspector?'

'I am also an inspector, you know.'

'I didn't say an inspector,' replied Braninko. 'I said *the* Inspector.'

'All right, then,' muttered Kirov. 'I work with *the* Inspector, and if he were here . . .'

'Why isn't he here?' interrupted Braninko. '*He* would be allowed to see the Blue File.'

'Why would you let him see it and not me?'

Braninko paused before he spoke. 'Do you remember what I said about men who hide the truth?'

'You called them common criminals.'

'Correct, and the only defence against them is men like Inspector Pekkala. No matter what the regulations called for, I would never do anything to hinder one of his investigations.'

'Comrade Braninko, this *is* his investigation.' Kirov went on to explain Pekkala's mission to Borodok. 'Now can you help me or not?' he asked when he had finished.

'Follow me,' replied Braninko.

At the back of the old sculpture studio, a massive safe stood in the corner of an otherwise empty room. After opening the safe, Braninko took out a drawer which had been removed from a desk. The drawer was made from some exotic wood, inlaid with ornate flower patterns done in ebony and mother-of-pearl.

'As you see,' Braninko told Kirov, 'they took it straight from the Tsar's study. These documents have never been integrated with those of our own Intelligence Service.' Turning to the file, Braninko began sifting through the documents. 'Here it is!' he exclaimed, hauling out an envelope. 'Ryabov, Isaac; assigned to the Kolchak Expedition.'

Kirov felt his heart jolt. 'Now we can find out what this man was doing before the Revolution.'

'It won't be that easy, Major. There is a good reason NKVD have so little information on this man. Isaac Ryabov is a cover name. Unlike in Okhrana and NKVD archives, the real identities of agents working secretly for the Tsar were never written down. When Nicholas II died, the names of these men died with him. All we have left are the clues remaining in the Blue File, but if there is anyone on earth who could make sense of them, it would be Inspector Pekkala.'

Kirov stared at the Tsar's handwriting, precise and ornate. The faded blue pencil resembled the veins in an old person's hand. 'May I borrow this, Professor?'

'For Inspector Pekkala, of course.' Braninko handed him the time-brittled paper.

The two men walked out into the sculpture studio.

Once more, Kirov breathed in the smell of that long-extinguished fire which had consumed Okhrana headquarters.

Braninko sat down on the huge severed hand, looking like some tiny helpless creature resting in the palm of a capricious god, as he waited for his fate to be decided.

'There is something I don't understand,' Kirov told him. 'Why does our government choose to keep the Blue File secret? The Okhrana is gone forever. The men whose names are in that file are either dead or in exile. The information it contains should no longer be considered classified.'

Braninko smiled, raising his hands and resting them upon the fingertips of the great bronze hand. 'My dear Comrade Major,' he said, 'the reason for keeping the Blue File secret has nothing to do with what it contains. The very fact that there was once a group of men who spied upon those whose job it was to spy on others is, in itself, a dangerous thing. It might lead people to wonder if there is another such file kept, perhaps, by our own government and hidden away in the desk of some untouchable man. The best secret, Comrade Major, is not one whose answer is hidden from us by the strongest lock and key. The best secret is one which nobody even knows exists.'

As soon as he was outside the archive, Kirov ducked into one of the abandoned warehouse buildings. With his back against a cold brick wall, he opened the Kolchak Expedition file. It contained three sheets of paper. Each was embossed with the double-headed eagle of the Romanovs.

From the Tsar's handwritten notes, Kirov learned that an Okhrana agent had been wounded in an attack on a house in St Petersburg, where a convicted murderer had been hiding. The murderer, whose name was Grodek, had been a notorious terrorist before the Revolution.

Kirov had learned about this mission from Pekkala, who had been a part of it. But what Kirov read next, even Pekkala didn't know.

Rather than return the wounded agent to active duty, the Tsar had secretly ordered the man's name to be placed on the list of those who had died in the attack. In the meantime, the agent was brought to a clinic on the grounds of the Ekaterinburg estate. There he was tended to by the Tsar's own doctor until he had recovered.

The Tsar then summoned the agent, and gave him a choice. Either he could return to the ranks of the Okhrana and the report of his death would be attributed to a bureaucratic mix-up, or he could agree to work as an agent for the Tsar, and only for the Tsar, taking part in missions so secret that not even his own intelligence service would be informed.

The agent had required no persuasion. He readily agreed and, soon after, was given a new identity as a cavalry officer with the cover name of Isaac Ryabov.

There followed a list of several missions undertaken by Ryabov, ranging from payoffs made to women made pregnant by Rasputin to the assassination of a Turkish diplomat suspected of involvement in smuggling stolen Russian steam turbine technology out of the country.

The last entry in the file detailed how the Tsar had appointed Ryabov to the cavalry brigade of Colonel Kolchak, only days before the Expedition departed for Siberia. Ryabov's orders were to report back not only on the whereabouts of the brigade, but also on the location of where the Romanov gold was hidden. Ryabov had been the Tsar's insurance policy against Kolchak running off with the treasure.

Kirov had no idea whether this file would provide Pekkala with the information he was looking for, but Braninko had been right when he said that if anybody could make sense of the contents, it would be Pekkala.

Stashing the pages in the pocket of his tunic, Kirov ran back towards his office. Within the hour, he had telegraphed his findings to the Camp Commandant at Borodok.

While Pekkala was away, delivering soup to the miners, Melekov sat alone in the kitchen, on a rickety wooden chair, reading a scrap of newspaper that he had peeled off the carcass of a frozen pig which had arrived that morning on the train.

Gramotin walked in from the compound. Instead of ignoring Melekov, as he usually did, he sauntered over to the cook and slapped him on the back.

'What do you want?' asked Melekov, without looking up from his paper.

'Nothing,' replied Gramotin. 'Nothing at all.'

Which was, of course, a lie.

Ever since Gramotin's last meeting with the Camp Commandant, dark thoughts had entered the guard's mind. Klenovkin was usually upset about something or other – Dalstroy was continually demanding higher quotas, providing him with fewer guards and cutting salaries at random – but this was the first time Gramotin had seen the Commandant so unhinged by a single prisoner. And to learn that this convict Pekkala was the source of Klenovkin's distress had fixed in Gramotin's mind only one possible course of action.

He needed to get rid of Pekkala.

This decision was not made out of any particular love for Klenovkin, but rather because Gramotin had, over the years, created a fine-tuned balance between himself and the Commandant.

At the heart of this arrangement was the fact that Klenovkin could not run this camp without Gramotin's particular talent for hostility. No one could stay as permanently angry as Gramotin. It was a gift which amazed even Gramotin himself.

Klenovkin had learned to leave all matters of camp discipline entirely to Gramotin's discretion, in return for which Gramotin could do whatever he wanted without fear of repercussions.

It was the kind of life Gramotin had always dreamed of living, and the only thing that had worried him until now was that someone might see through his mask of rage to the pride he took in his work and the contentment it afforded him each day.

But if Klenovkin really did fall apart, instead of merely threatening to as he did at least once every week, Dalstroy would simply replace him. If that happened, Gramotin knew he'd have to start from scratch grooming a new Commandant. It was a task which might take years.

And suppose, Gramotin asked himself, this new man does not appreciate my particular talents? He might change things around, or even transfer me to another camp. The idea left Gramotin nauseous with anxiety.

He could not allow it to happen.

The sooner Pekkala was dead, the quicker things could go back to the way they'd been before. Besides, this prisoner made him uneasy in a way no other convict had. Looking Pekkala in the eye felt like staring down the barrel of a gun.

Killing a prisoner was easy, but disposing of Pekkala had to be done without implicating the Commandant. The safest way to accomplish that was to make sure Klenovkin knew nothing about it. At the same time, Gramotin would have to avoid bringing down a Dalstroy board of inquiry upon himself.

Someone else would need to be the instrument of Pekkala's doom. After many hours of plotting, Gramotin believed he'd found a perfect candidate.

'You don't want anything?' Melekov narrowed his eyes with suspicion. 'Then what are you doing here?'

'I just wanted to see how you are enjoying your last few days in the kitchen.'

'Last days?' Melekov laughed. 'What are you talking about?'

Gramotin shrugged. 'I hear you are going to be replaced.'

The blood drained out of Melekov's face. 'By whom?'

'That prisoner Klenovkin sent to work in here, 4745, the one who delivers his breakfast.'

'But that's ridiculous!' spat Melekov.

'Is it? Why do you think Klenovkin sent someone to work with you in the kitchen? Has he ever done that before?'

'Well, no but . . .'

'And why do you think he has that convict delivering his breakfast instead of you?'

'I don't know.'

'Well, think about it! That convict goes into his office. Every day. Did *you* ever go into his office?'

'No,' admitted Melekov.

'And they talk. I've heard them. Did *you* ever talk to Klenovkin?'

'Of course!'

'In an actual conversation?'

'Well, no, I wouldn't say that exactly.'

'Pekkala is going to replace you. And do you know why?'

Melekov shook his head. He looked miserable.

'So Klenovkin doesn't have to pay you!' announced Gramotin. 'And, of course, he doesn't have to pay the convict either. Think of how much money he will save Dalstroy. He's been after a promotion for years and this time he might just get it!'

'That bastard!' The scrap of newspaper fell from Melekov's hands. 'But what am I supposed to do?'

'That's your problem,' spat Gramotin. 'At least, it will be if that prisoner isn't stopped.'

'Stopped? What do you mean?'

Gramotin slapped him on the back of the head. 'I mean prevented from taking your job! And what could possibly prevent him?' He leaned closer and lowered his voice. 'Perhaps an accident. So many accidents can happen in a kitchen.'

'Yes,' agreed Melekov. 'Many things can go wrong.'

'And the sooner the better, my friend, before things start going wrong for you.'

*

Poskrebyshev knocked once and, without waiting for a reply, walked into Stalin's office. He held up a sheet of yellow telegraph paper. 'Major Kirov has sent a reply to Borodok.'

Stalin looked up blearily from the file he had been reading. 'When was it intercepted?'

'Less than an hour ago, by NKVD signals headquarters in Omsk.'

Stalin held out his arm and snapped his fingers. 'Give it to me.'

Poskrebyshev handed over the transcript, then stood back while Stalin squinted at the tiny print.

'The Blue File!' he bellowed. 'Of course! I should have known.'

'What is the Blue File, Comrade Stalin?'

For the moment, Stalin ignored him. 'How did Pekkala know to look in Archive 17?' he wondered aloud. 'How did he know that the Blue File had even survived?'

Poskrebyshev did not reply, fearing another lecture on the word 'rhetorical'.

'This Captain Ryabov must have been a special agent of the Tsar. That proves he did not trust Kolchak. And he was right! In such a situation, no one can be trusted.' Resting one elbow on the desk, Stalin placed his forehead against his palm. 'I should never have sent Pekkala back to Borodok. He must have known all along what this was really about.'

'Is Pekkala in danger, Comrade Stalin?'

Stalin brushed away the words as if they were flies buzzing around his head.

'What about Savushkin, the bodyguard you sent to protect him?'

'Pekkala might have won him over,' answered Stalin, still talking more to himself than to Poskrebyshev. 'After all, Savushkin volunteered to work with Pekkala. I should have taken that into consideration.'

'Won him over? But why, Comrade Stalin, and with what?'

'Threats. Bribes. Some act of Finnish sorcery! And as for why, perhaps Pekkala's loyalties to the past are stronger than I thought. I see now that Pekkala has been hiding. All this time, he has concealed himself in a disguise of incorruptibility. They were good at disguises, those agents of the Tsar. Vassileyev taught them well. But now I see Pekkala as he really is. He can no longer hide from me!'

'Comrade Stalin,' Poskrebyshev pleaded with him, 'there is no evidence to suggest that what you are saying is true.'

'Evidence!' roared Stalin. 'The evidence was right under our noses the whole time, hidden away in Archive 17. And that is where it should have stayed. Who is in charge there? Who is responsible for releasing the information?'

'That would be Professor Braninko.'

'Get me Kornfeld. Tell him he has work to do.'

*

Pekkala stood at the entrance to the mine, waiting to deliver the soup ration.

At last, a man appeared, ghoulish in his coating of radium. When he caught sight of Pekkala, he raised his hand in greeting.

'I brought you soup,' said Pekkala.

'Don't you recognise me?' asked the stranger.

'I'm sorry, Zeka, I do not,' replied Pekkala, using the common name by which prisoners addressed each other. The stranger's face was so caked in yellowy powder that it reminded Pekkala of masks he once saw used by a troupe of Japanese kabuki actors at the Aksyonov Theatre in St Petersburg.

'It's me!' The prisoner slapped his hands against his chest, sending puffs of yellow dust into the air. 'Savushkin!'

Pekkala leaned forward, squinting. 'Savushkin?' The man who stood before him now bore no resemblance to the friend he had made on the journey to Siberia. Savushkin's shirt was open at the neck, revealing a collarbone stretched so tightly against the flesh it looked as if the slightest movement would cause his skin to tear like wet paper.

The smile on Savushkin's face faltered. He gathered up a bucket in each hand. The wire-bale handles dug into his raw, chapped skin. 'I know my task is to protect you, Inspector, but they are making it very difficult. I'm trying. Believe me, I'm still trying.'

Overcome, Pekkala reached out and set his hands on Savushkin's shoulders. 'Don't worry about me. Look after yourself. I'll do what I can to get you transferred from the mine.'

'No.' Savushkin shook his head. 'People will only get suspicious. Solve the case, Inspector, as quickly as you can. Then we can both get out of here.' Carrying the buckets, he disappeared into the tunnel, his shadow lumbering across the walls, giant and grotesque in the lamplight.

Pekkala looked at his hands. His palms and fingertips were chalky white where they had touched Savushkin's jacket. Shaken, he made his way back across the compound.

Outside the kitchen, Gramotin was waiting for him. 'The Commandant wants to see you.'

Pekkala nodded.

'I'm watching you, convict,' said Gramotin.

'I know,' replied Pekkala.

*

'This just arrived for you,' said Klenovkin, holding out a telegram.

It was from Kirov.

Pekkala studied the faint grey letters fanned out across the flimsy sheet of paper.

RYABOV COVER NAME FOR AGENT LISTED IN BLUE FILE AS KILLED DURING ARREST OF GRODEK BUT SURVIVED STOP

Pekkala stopped reading. The Blue File. This was the first time he had heard a mention of it since before the Revolution. He hadn't even known the Blue File was still in existence, although it didn't surprise him to learn that the Tsar had failed to destroy it, as he should have done, in those final days of his captivity at Tsarskoye Selo. The Tsar had been such a meticulous keeper of records that getting rid of anything he'd written down would have gone against every instinct he possessed.

Pekkala gave a quiet grunt of admiration that Kirov had managed to track down this information in the labyrinth of Archive 17, especially since that meant dealing with Professor Braninko, its notoriously uncooperative curator.

Even more astonishing than the mention of Grodek was the fact that one of the Okhrana agents on that mission had survived. Until now, he had believed they were all dead.

'What's the matter?' asked Klenovkin. 'You look as if you've seen a ghost.'

On a clear winter's day, a car filled with heavily armed Okhrana agents raced through the streets of St Petersburg.

Pekkala was crammed in beside a young officer whom he had never met before. The task of the Okhrana agents was to clear the ground floor, not thought to be occupied, and make their way swiftly up to the apartment rented by Grodek and his mistress.

'Do you think he will come quietly?' asked the officer.

'No,' replied Pekkala. He did not believe it would be possible to arrest Grodek without sustaining casualties. Neither did he believe that Grodek would allow himself to be taken alive.

As they spoke, the young officer was loading his Nagant pistol. When the wheels of their car bounced over a pothole, a bullet slipped from the officer's fingers and fell into the seat well below. The men were too closely packed for him to bend down and retrieve it. The Okhrana agent swore quietly at his own clumsiness. Then he glanced across at Pekkala.

'Last year,' the officer explained, 'one of my colleagues closed a car door on my fingers.' He held up his hand as proof.

Pekkala could see that the man's thumb and index finger had been deformed by the bone not setting straight.

'The doctors tell me I have nerve damage,' continued the officer. 'Sometimes I can't help dropping things.'

'I see,' said Pekkala.

'To tell you the truth, Inspector, I am also a little nervous.'

Before Pekkala could reply, they rounded a corner and Grodek's house slid into view.

The officer closed the cylinder of the revolver and placed it in the holster strapped under his armpit. 'Well,' he told Pekkala, 'I will see you on the other side.'

The three cars screeched to a halt outside Grodek's house. The Okhrana agents immediately piled out and began battering down the door.

As they had planned in advance, Pekkala moved around to the rear of the building, in case Grodek tried to escape along the canal path. He took cover behind a stack of crates containing salt used for preserving fish which were caught in the summer months at the mouth of the Neva River. In winter, due to the ice, none of the boats could get up the river. At that time of year, the whole wharf was deserted.

Once the agents were inside, they raced up the stairs to Grodek's apartment on the second floor.

From his hiding place, Pekkala heard a heavy, muffled thump inside the building. The windows seemed to ripple. This was followed a fraction of a second later by a concussion which threw him off his feet. Jets of fire belched out of the windows. Glass sprayed over the street. Dazed and lying on his back, Pekkala watched a door sail over his head and into the canal.

Grodek had planted a bomb. Only seconds before the blast, he and his mistress, Maria Balka, had managed to escape through a side window.

By the time Pekkala got back on his feet, the two fugitives were already running away down the street.

After a chase, Pekkala caught up with Grodek and arrested him, but not before Maria Balka met her death in the icy waters of the Moika canal. She'd been killed by her own lover, so as not to let her fall into captivity.

Having witnessed the devastation caused by the bomb blast, Pekkala did not even consider that any of the Okhrana agents could have survived the explosion. When Chief Inspector Vassileyev confirmed that all of the agents had perished, he was only reporting what Pekkala already knew. Or thought he knew.

The agents who died that day were all strangers to Pekkala. All except the young officer, whose name he'd never learned. And afterwards, Pekkala had done what Vassileyev had taught him to do with memories of the dead. He had filed them away in the great archive deep in the labyrinth of his mind, and left them there to fade away, like photographs abandoned in the sun.

Now Pekkala wondered if the young officer had died, after all.

'I need to see Ryabov's body again,' he told Klenovkin.

'What? Now?'

'Yes!'

'But what if Melekov is still in the kitchen?'

'He won't be. Melekov goes back to bed as soon as his shift is finished.'

Klenovkin's eyebrows bobbed up in surprise. 'Back to bed? He's not allowed to do that in the middle of the day!'

'Nevertheless . . .'

'That lazy Siberian piece of...'

'Please, Commandant. It is crucial that I see the body immediately.'

Leaving Kirov's telegram on the desk, the two men made their way to the kitchen.

Klenovkin opened the freezer with his master key.

Inside, at the back, Pekkala pushed aside the wall of vodka crates. Ryabov's corpse was still there, lying on the floor under a tarpaulin.

Crouching down, Pekkala pulled back the tarp, whose ice-encrusted contours retained the shape of Ryabov's face.

The shadows made it difficult to see.

'Do you have a match?' Pekkala asked.

Klenovkin pulled a box from his pocket and handed it down.

Pekkala struck a match and held it close to Ryabov's hand. In the quivering light, he glimpsed the crookedly healed thumb and index finger of the Okhrana officer he had met years ago, on their way to the Moika Canal. As a pawn in this game of trust between Kolchak and the Tsar, Agent Ryabov had played his role to the end.

For a long time, Pekkala stared into the dead man's face – the alabaster skin, sunken eyes and blue-black lips. He could not shake the feeling that he was staring at himself. 'See you on the other side,' he murmured, and his breath uncoiled like silk into the still and frozen air.

'What?' asked Klenovkin. 'What did you say?'

'I knew this man,' replied Pekkala. 'I thought he had died long ago.'

'Well, he's dead now, anyway.' Klenovkin tapped Pekkala on the shoulder. 'Come on, let's get the hell out of here.'

On their way back to Klenovkin's office, Pekkala tried to fathom why on earth Vassileyev would have lied to him about this officer having survived the blast.

The answer soon became clear when Pekkala read the remainder of the telegram.

RYABOV COMMISSIONED BY TSAR TO MONITOR KOL-CHAK EXPEDITION STOP ACTIVITY OF AGENT RYABOV NOT DISCLOSED TO OKHRANA STOP

The reason Vassileyev had not told Pekkala that there were survivors from the bomb at Grodek's house was that he did not know of any. But the Tsar had not only lied to his own Director of Intelligence. He had lied to Pekkala as well.

The Tsar's story had been very specific. He had told Pekkala that the precise location of the gold would be known only to Colonel Kolchak and his uncle, Admiral Alexander Kolchak of the Tsar's Pacific fleet in Vladivostok. Even the Tsar himself was not to be told. There was good reason for this. Although the Tsar was confident that Kolchak could evade any attempt at capture by the Red Guards, the Tsar was equally certain that he himself would soon fall into captivity. And the first thing his captors would want to know was the location of the Imperial Reserves. Unless the Bolsheviks could be convinced that the Tsar didn't know the whereabouts of his gold, they would resort to whatever means necessary to acquire that information.

For the Tsar, the trick would be in persuading these captors of his ignorance before they even asked the question.

Now an idea began to surface in Pekkala's mind. At first, it seemed so sinister that he felt sure this couldn't be the answer. But the more Pekkala thought about this, the more convinced he became that it was true. The Tsar must have known that if Pekkala were arrested, he would be interrogated using whatever means the Bolshevik Security Service, known as the Cheka, thought necessary. For a man like Pekkala, in the hands of the Cheka, torture was a guarantee. The Bolsheviks would realise, as they beat and starved and questioned him, that Pekkala was telling the truth when he said that neither he nor the Tsar was aware of the gold's hiding place.

Except it wasn't the truth. It was a lie, but one that Pekkala had believed.

There was only one catch. For the Tsar's plan to work, Pekkala would have to be caught.

It was the Tsar who had provided Pekkala with the means

of escaping the country – forged papers, rail tickets, even the route he should take to avoid capture. But Pekkala never made it. At a small railway station on the Russo-Finnish border, with freedom almost within his grasp, Pekkala had been hauled off a crowded train by Bolshevik Revolutionary Guards. From there, he had begun his journey to Butyrka prison, and eventually to Borodok.

He had always wondered how the Revolutionary Guards singled him out so effectively. Now he knew.

The only way the Tsar could have guaranteed that Pekkala would be arrested was by revealing the information of his escape route to the enemy.

In this way the Tsar and his family would be spared the same fate as Pekkala. There would be no point in interrogating the Romanovs for information which they didn't have.

The facts were inescapable.

The Tsar had betrayed him, his most trusted servant, who in return had trusted the Tsar with a devotion far beyond the value of his life.

It was an ingenious and intricate plan. Not surprisingly, the Tsar had calculated almost every detail, but the one thing he had not anticipated was that Kolchak might actually be caught. Or that the members of the Romanov family might be herded to the city of Ekaterinburg and, on a sultry August night in 1918, butchered in the basement of the Ipatiev House.

The knowledge that the Tsar had, in those final days of their acquaintance, offered him up as a sacrifice, struck Pekkala like a hammer to his skull.

'Well,' demanded Klenovkin, 'do you have your answer?'

'I have an answer,' replied Pekkala. 'But it was not the one I'd been expecting.'

As soon as Pekkala had left the room, Klenovkin began to pace around the room, like a cat trapped in a cage. He had read the telegram as soon as it came through but wasn't able to make head or tail of it. And what did Pekkala mean, wondered the Commandant, when he said it wasn't the answer he'd been expecting? Klenovkin could not help but fear the worst. Pekkala was refusing to accept his theory about the Comitati. 'And who else is there to accuse, but me?' he asked himself. Already, in feverish dreams, he had found himself before a board of inquiry, accused of Ryabov's murder. To this imaginary jury, he had pleaded his case, but was always found guilty.

'It's time I took matters into my own hands,' he muttered to himself. Seating himself at his desk, Klenovkin took out a piece of paper and furiously scribbled down a note.

*

Professor Braninko had fallen asleep as he sat at his desk, consolidating dusty files for the archives.

A banging on the metal door startled him awake. He breathed in sharply, rose stiffly to his feet and straightened his tie as he walked towards the door.

The knocking came again.

Braninko knew who it was. Major Kirov had come to return the file he borrowed. In the brief time he'd spent with Kirov, Braninko had been impressed by the young officer's willingness to listen to the outbursts of an old man who had no one else to talk to except the unblinking statues of old generals and politicians. Before Kirov, there had been no visitors for several weeks and, after he left, there were unlikely to be others for a while.

As he made his way towards the door, the knocking continued.

'I heard you the first time,' muttered Braninko, but he was not angry. In fact, he was looking forward to seeing Kirov again. Of course, it would not be appropriate to appear too enthusiastic. He would maintain his usual reserve, but this time, he decided, he might at least offer the Major a cup of tea. He had a kettle in the back room, and a few old tin cups, which he hoped were clean enough to use. As he opened the door, Braninko was trying to remember if he had any sugar left to sweeten the tea. He had just enough time to realise that the person outside was not Kirov before the air seemed to catch fire all around him.

The next thing Braninko knew, he was lying on his back, staring up at the ceiling of the archive. Someone had seized his ankles and was dragging him across the floor towards the back of the building. He could not understand what was happening. The only clear thought in the old professor's head was that it felt undignified to be hauled around like this. With a feeble, barely conscious gesture, he reached up to adjust his tie, which suddenly felt too tight around his throat.

The man who was dragging him wore a dark hat and a coat which came down below his knees. Both were civilian garments. It occurred to Braninko to inform him that only government personnel were allowed in Archive 17.

What is wrong with me? Braninko wondered. His stomach felt strangely empty and he experienced a terrible thirst, as if he were lost in a desert.

At last, the dragging stopped. The man let go of Braninko's feet and the professor's heels struck the floor hard.

Braninko was relieved to be lying still. He felt dizzy and sick. He glanced at his palm and realised he was covered with blood. Only now did it dawn on him that he had been shot. Tugging at the buttons of his vest, he pulled the cloth away and saw the deep red marks of two bullet holes punched through the fabric of his shirt.

The man turned around and looked at Braninko. He was narrow-faced, with a black moustache tinged grey along the edges. He wore thick corduroy trousers and a short double-breasted wool coat.

Although such clothes were common in the streets of Moscow, Braninko had no difficulty identifying this man as a member of NKVD. It was not the clothes, but how the stranger wore them; with no regard for comfort, all the buttons fastened, and the lapels stitched into place, rather than being allowed to rest naturally against the collarbone.

'Who are you?' As the professor spoke, a thread of bloody saliva trickled from his mouth.

'My name is Kornfeld,' replied the man. Removing a handkerchief from his pocket, he wiped the perspiration from his cheeks. 'You are heavier than you look, old man.'

'Why have you done this to me?'

'It is my job.'

'But what have I done to deserve it?' Braninko had trouble breathing, as if someone were kneeling on his chest.

'The only thing I can tell you is that you have upset someone very important.'

'The Blue File,' whispered Braninko. 'Is that what this is about?'

'I told you, I don't know.'

'I was helping with an investigation.'

'I have no interest in what you were doing.'

'The man I was helping is Inspector Pekkala, and you will answer to him for what you've done to me; you and whoever sent you on this butcher's errand.'

From the pocket of his coat, Kornfeld removed a Browning automatic pistol. 'You may be right, Professor, but he will have to find me first.'

'Oh, he will find you,' Braninko replied angrily, 'and sooner than you think. By the time you leave this building, the Emerald Eye will be upon you.'

Kornfeld did not appear to be listening. Instead, he busied himself with checking the number of rounds in the Browning's magazine.

Observing the casual efficiency of his executioner, Braninko abandoned all hope. The old man gazed around the room, his eyes flickering across the faces of the statues which had kept him company all these years. He thought about the papers on his desk, which still needed sorting, and of his cat, on the windowsill at home, watching for him to return, and of all the important and unfinished business of his life which swirled around him like a cloud of tiny insects, then suddenly scattered and lost all meaning. Reaching into the blood-drenched pocket of his vest, Braninko removed a spindly iron key and held it out towards the man who was about to kill him. 'Please lock the door on your way out.'

Kornfeld took the key from Braninko's outstretched hand.

'Of course,' he said. Then he shot the old man twice in the head and left his body lying on the floor.

On his way out, Kornfeld locked the door behind him. With unhurried steps, he crossed the street, pausing only to drop the key down a storm drain before he disappeared into the chaos of the Bolotnia market.

*

That morning before dawn, one of the camp's generators had caught fire, sending a cloud of thick, oily smoke unravelling into the sky. The snow that fell from the clouds that morning was tinged with soot, adding to the sense of desolation hanging over the valley of Krasnagolyana.

Arriving at the kitchen, Pekkala discovered that Melekov had left the freezer door open. Pekkala called Melekov's name, but there was no reply.

He must have gone to watch the generator burn, thought Pekkala.

Knowing that Melekov would soon return, and unable to resist the temptation of helping himself to the best food in the camp, Pekkala slipped into the freezer.

By the light of the single bulb, hanging like a polyp from the metal ceiling of the freezer, Pekkala surveyed the bowls of offal, like coils of slippery orange rope, the white bricks of tallow fat, and the huge and severed tongues of cows. At the back of the freezer, four pig carcasses hung from gaff hooks, their skin like pink granite and glittering with frost.

At that moment Pekkala heard someone enter the kitchen –

166

the creak of the spring on the outer door and then the gunshot slam of the inner door being closed.

Realising he was trapped, he darted to the end of the freezer and hid behind the pig carcasses. On his way he yanked the dirty pull-string of the light. The freezer was plunged into a coffin-like darkness but, seconds later, the sharp glare of a torch burst like an explosion in the cramped space.

Pekkala glimpsed the unmistakable silhouette of Melekov. Immediately he began to calculate how much trouble he might actually be in. He hadn't actually eaten anything, so perhaps Melekov would let him off. He could say he found the door open and went in to see if any food had been taken. It was a flimsy excuse, but the only one he could come up with. It would all depend of what mood Melekov was in. He might laugh it off, or he might decide to make life difficult.

Knowing there was still a chance he could escape detection, Pekkala remained silent, while Melekov's footsteps scuffed slowly across the concrete floor and the torch beam played across the carcasses, making them seem to twitch as if there was still life in them.

Pekkala's lungs grew hot as the air in them became exhausted. He could only last a few more seconds before breathing out, at which point Melekov would surely see his breath condensing in the cold.

He heard another footstep, then another. Just when Pekkala had made up his mind to step out into the open and surrender, he heard a dull thump and, in the same moment, the blade of a long butcher knife pierced the meat of the carcass next to him. The point jammed to a halt against the pig's ribs, only a hand's width from Pekkala's throat. Then the knife disappeared again, back the way it came, like a metal tongue sliding into a mouth.

'Melekov!' shouted Pekkala, still blinded by the torchlight and holding up his hands to shield himself. 'It's me!'

'You walked into my trap,' snarled Melekov.

'This was a trap? For me? But why?'

Melekov's only reply was a bestial roar. He raised the butcher knife, ready to strike again.

Pekkala jumped to the side, crashing into a shelf, as the blade glanced off the wall, leaving a long silver stripe through the frost. Bowls of food tumbled from the racks. Jars of pickled beets smashed in eruptions of ruby-coloured juice and cans of army-issue Tushonka stew clattered across the floor.

Snatching up one of the heavy cans, he hurled it at the silhouette.

Melekov howled with pain as the can struck him full in the face. The torch fell from his grasp.

Pekkala dived to grab it, turning the beam on his attacker.

With one hand, Melekov covered his face. Blood poured in ribbons from between the fingers. His other hand still gripped the knife.

Intent on disarming the cook, Pekkala grabbed a frozen pig's heart off the shelf and pitched it as hard as he could.

The rock-hard knot of meat bounced off Melekov's face. With a wail of pain, he tumbled back among the bowls of guts and dropped the knife.

By the time Melekov hit the ground, Pekkala had already snatched up the weapon. 'Why on earth are you trying to kill me?' he demanded.

'I figured it out,' groaned Melekov.

'Figured out what?' demanded Pekkala.

Melekov clambered up until he was resting on his knees. Dazed from the fight, his head bowed forward, as if he were a supplicant before the slaughtered pigs. 'Klenovkin is going to give you my job.'

'I don't want your damned job!'

'It doesn't matter what you want or do not want. In this camp, Klenovkin decides our fates. And where will I be if he throws me out? This isn't like Moscow, where a man who loses his job can walk across the road and find another. There are no other jobs for me here. I'm too old to be a guard. I have no training for the hospital. If Klenovkin wants to replace me, I'll have no place to go.'

'Even if I did want the job, did you ever stop to think that Klenovkin could never hand it to a prisoner? Dalstroy wouldn't let him. The company would never trust a convict with their food.'

'I didn't think of that.' Melekov raised his head sharply. 'None of this was my idea.'

Pekkala threw the knife away across the floor. 'Just get up!'

Gingerly, Melekov dabbed his fingers against his nostrils. 'I think you broke my nose,' he muttered bitterly.

'Whose idea was this, Melekov?'

Reluctantly, the cook shook his head. 'If I tell you . . .'

'Give me the name,' growled Pekkala.

'Gramotin,' he replied in a whisper.

Pekkala breathed out slowly. 'Did he say why?'

Melekov shrugged. 'It doesn't matter. From now on, my life's worth even less than yours, and yours wasn't worth much to begin with.'

Pekkala realised that the time was fast approaching when he would either have to leave this camp or risk becoming the subject of his own murder investigation.

In the meantime, Ryabov's death remained unsolved.

That thought sent a familiar shudder through his bones.

This was not the first time Pekkala had failed to close a case.

Pekkala and the Tsar stood on a balcony outside the Alexander Palace. It was an early summer day, the sky powder blue, and pollen lying luminous and green upon the puddles of a rain storm from the night before.

'A man has been found dead,' said the Tsar. 'He was a courier for the Turkish Embassy.'

'Where was the body found?' asked Pekkala.

'It was pulled from the water just beneath a bridge over the Novokislaevsk River, north of Moscow.

'Their Ambassador asked for you by name. Given the value of our relationship with that country, I could hardly refuse.'

'I will begin immediately.'

'Of course, but do not exhaust yourself with this inquiry.'

Pekkala glanced at the Tsar, trying to fathom the meaning of his words.

'What I am telling you,' explained the Tsar, 'is that this is ultimately a matter for the Turks to unravel. It is not our job to oversee their diplomats. Look around, see what you can find, and then move on.'

Pekkala's preliminary inspection of the body revealed no marks which would suggest a violent death. The dead man was fully clothed, but did not appear to have drowned. Pekkala quickly ruled out suicide, since the drop would not have killed, or even injured him.

Every day, during that first week of the investigation, Pekkala returned to the bridge and stood looking down into the water as he attempted to compose in his mind not only the reason for this man's death but the questions which might lead him to the answer.

He stood among fishermen, who dangled bamboo poles above the water, smoked their pipes and talked about the body. They had been the first to find it and barraged Pekkala with questions about the case.

But Pekkala had questions of his own. 'Could the body have drifted here from somewhere upstream?' he asked.

'This is a lazy old river,' one of them replied. 'Somebody threw him off the bridge. Where he fell is where he sank and where he sank is where we found him.'

'Do you fish here every day?'

'This time of year we do. Carp, pike, dace. They're all down there in those weeds.'

'Then they knew you would find him. In fact, somebody wanted you to find him.'

'Unless,' suggested another fisherman, 'they didn't know the area and were just getting rid of the body.'

Pekkala shook his head. 'This was done by a professional. The dead man is a message. But about what? And to whom?'

'That would be your job, Inspector,' said the fisherman.

After one week, without explanation, the Tsar called Pekkala off the case and did not assign a new investigator to take over.

Ever since, Pekkala had been haunted by his failure to arrest the killer. He felt an obligation to the victim, as if they'd formed a partnership between the living and the dead. Since that day, like

stones in his pockets, he had carried the unanswered questions of
that murder.

The next day, Melekov showed up at the kitchen with a bandage on his face and two black eyes.

The two men did not speak about what had happened the day before.

Pekkala was just finishing his breakfast duties, when Tarnowski, Lavrenov and Sedov barged into the kitchen.

Melekov, with a mound of fresh dough balanced in his hands, stood paralysed with fear.

Tarnowski grabbed the cook and pushed him to his knees. The dough fell with a splat on to the floor.

At the same time, Lavrenov produced a leather cord from his sleeve, looped it around Melekov's neck and began to strangle him.

Melekov's face turned purple. His eyes bulged. Feebly, he clawed at the leather cord which had sunk into the soft flesh of his throat.

'Enough!' Pekkala shouted.

Lavrenov, his teeth bared with the effort of strangling Melekov, glanced first at Pekkala and then towards Tarnowski.

Tarnowski jerked his chin.

Lavrenov let go of the cord.

With a gasp, Melekov collapsed on to the floor.

'We weren't going to kill him,' explained Sedov.

'Just teach him a lesson is all,' said Lavrenov.

Tarnowski went to Melekov and rolled the man over with his boot. 'I told you to leave him alone.'

Melekov nodded weakly, his hands pressed to his throat.

'Now get out,' Tarnowski ordered the cook. 'Come back in half an hour.'

Crawling on his hands and knees, Melekov departed from the kitchen.

'You didn't need to do that,' Pekkala told them. 'We had already made our peace.'

'With him, perhaps,' replied Tarnowski, 'but what about the next one? And the one after that? Because, believe me, there will be more, which is why I have come here to make you an offer.'

'What kind of offer?'

'The chance to save your life.'

'How?'

'By getting out of here,' said Taranowski.

'You mean escape? What makes you think I'd stand a better chance than anybody else who's tried to leave this place?'

'Because we are coming with you,' replied Sedov.

Lavrenov nodded in agreement. 'We have a plan. If it works, we'll soon be living like kings.'

'That doesn't sound like a plan,' answered Pekkala. 'It sounds more like a fantasy.'

'It is indeed a fantasy, but one a man can bring to life with pockets filled with gold, agreed.'

'What gold?' demanded Pekkala.

'The last of the Imperial Reserves,' whispered Lavrenov.

Pekkala stared at the men with a look of pity on his face. 'I am sorry to be the one to tell you this, but the Imperial

175

Reserves are gone. The Czechs handed them over to the Bolsheviks at Irkutsk, in exchange for being allowed to pass through the Lake Baikal tunnels, which the Reds would have destroyed otherwise. By the time this occurred, you were already in prison. Perhaps nobody ever told you.'

'We know about the Czechs,' Sedov interrupted. 'We know how they betrayed us and that they gave everything they had to the Bolsheviks.'

'The thing is,' said Lavrenov, 'they didn't have it all.'

'That is a secret we have kept for many years,' continued Tarnowski, 'but the time has come for you to know the truth.'

It was Sedov who spoke first. 'Colonel Kolchak had told us that the safest place for the gold was in the hands of his uncle, Admiral Alexander Kolchak, who had gathered together an army of anti-Bolshevik forces. Getting to them meant crossing the entire length of Russia, but if we could do it, not only would the gold be safe, but we would also be out of danger. You see, we made that journey as much for ourselves as for the Tsar. By the time we reached the city of Kazan, we had crossed almost half the country, but the Red Cavalry were catching up with us. We knew we'd never make it if we tried to hold on to the gold.'

Lavrenov picked up the story. 'We made the decision to hide the Imperial Reserves in Kazan. The Czech Legion was behind us, but moving along the same route and heading in the same direction. They were a much stronger force than our own, over 30,000 men. If only we could have linked up with them, we would have been safe from the Reds, but the Reds had positioned themselves between our two forces. If we had stayed where we were and waited for the Czechs to catch up with us, the Reds would have finished us off long before the Czechs arrived to help. We managed to get word through to the Czechs about where the gold was hidden and they picked it up when they passed through Kazan.'

'You say they didn't have it all. What happened? Did you spend it along the way?'

'Some of it,' admitted Tarnowski. 'At almost every town we came to, the locals demanded bribes or tried to overcharge us for food or feed for our horses. We had used up three crates of gold by the time Colonel Kolchak declared that from then on, we would simply take what we wanted. But those three cases were only a fraction of what was missing from the Imperial Reserves that the Czechs handed over at Irkutsk.'

'You mean they just left the rest of the gold behind in Kazan? Is that it?'

Tarnowski shook his head. 'What happened was that, at the last minute, the Colonel decided we should take some of the gold with us. His uncle was expecting that gold and Kolchak was afraid to come to him empty-handed. We were moving more quickly when we pulled out of Kazan, but still not quickly enough. The Reds caught up with us. What happened after that was a slaughter.'

'But how did you manage to prevent them from capturing it?' asked Pekkala.

'When we realised the Reds were only a day or two behind us,' continued Lavrenov, 'we sent Colonel Kolchak on ahead. At first, he did not want to go, but we knew what would happen if the Bolsheviks got hold of him. We begged the Colonel to save himself and finally, he agreed.'

'Before he left,' said Sedov, 'he swore that he would not

abandon us, and in return each man who stayed behind took an oath that we would never give up the location of the gold. That night, once we were sure that the Colonel had got away safely, we buried the crates in the woods beside the railroad, not two days' march from this camp.'

'How can you be certain it's still there?'

'If it had been found,' replied Lavrenov, 'word would have reached us by now.'

Pekkala realised he was right. If that gold had been discovered, Stalin would have made sure that the whole country knew about his final triumph over the Tsar. He also knew the area where the Comitati had buried those crates. It was as wild and inhospitable a place as any he had seen. Once the gold was underground, no one would have stumbled upon it by accident, even if trains passed by not more than a stone's throw away.

During his years as a tree marker in the valley of Krasnagolyana, the railroad had marked the northern boundary of the Borodok timber-cutting region. Beyond it lay a region assigned to another camp, a notorious place called Mamlin 3, where experiments were conducted on human subjects. To be caught outside this region meant certain death.

If the wind was right, Pekkala could hear the sound of the Trans-Siberian Express passing through the forest. Sometimes, overcome by loneliness, he would trudge through the woods on his home-made snowshoes until he reached the tracks. There, standing at the edge of his world, he waited for the train to go by, just to catch a glimpse of another human being.

The railway guards on board the train would shoot at Pekkala if they saw him, whether on orders or for sport, he did not know, so he always stayed hidden, eyes fixed on the stutter-ing images of passengers, staring bleary-eyed out at the impen-etrable wilderness of Siberia, unaware that the wilderness was staring back at them.

'The next day,' said Tarnowski, 'the Reds attacked. The battle took place almost within sight of this valley. We held out for three days, but they outnumbered us by four to one. We knew we couldn't win, but still we made them pay for every inch of ground. By the time it was over, of the two hundred men in the Expedition, there were only seventy of us left. The Reds marched us straight to Borodok and we have been here ever since. Since the Bolsheviks found no gold, they concluded that we must have left it all with the Czechs.'

'And now your idea is to reclaim it?'

'Exactly,' replied Sedov.

'But this time,' said Lavrenov, 'we are keeping it for ourselves.'

'That gold belongs to us now,' muttered Sedov. 'God knows, we have earned it.'

'A hundred times over,' agreed Lavrenov.

'Where will you go once you've escaped,' asked Pekkala, 'as-suming you can even make it through the gates alive?'

'The border with China isn't far from here,' Sedov told him. 'Once we cross over, we'll be safe.'

'But until then, you'll be in the country of the Ostyaks. How do you plan to get past them when no other prisoner has ever succeeded before?'

'The Colonel will take care of us,' Sedov answered. 'We have waited many years but at last the day of our deliverance is near.'

'Are you insane?' stammered Pekkala. 'Now listen to me,

for the sake of your lives. I admire your loyalty to Colonel Kolchak. No one could have asked from you more than you have already given. But that loyalty has not been repaid. The Colonel is gone. He has been gone for a long time. Even if he's still alive, a fact of which I am by no means certain, whatever special powers you have granted him will not persuade the Ostyaks. Those men out there will kill you. They do not care about your faith, in God or anyone else. They care about the bread and salt Klenovkin gives them in exchange for your frozen corpses.'

Sedov only smiled and shook his head.

'Soon you'll understand,' said Lavrenov. 'Just wait until you see the gold.'

'I already have,' said Pekkala.

It was a Sunday afternoon in August.

Pekkala had been sitting at his kitchen table, trying to read the newspaper. On either side of him lay large bowls filled with ice. In spite of this effort to cool himself down, he was still drenched in sweat. The newspaper stuck to his damp fingers. The ticking of the clock in the next room, which, under normal circumstances, he only ever noticed if it stopped, now seemed to be growing louder, as if a woodpecker was tapping against his skull.

At the moment when it seemed as if his mood could not get any worse, he received a summons to the Alexander Palace. The message was delivered by a horseman from the Royal Stables. Dressed in a white tunic with red piped collar and cuffs, the rider appeared so dazzling in the glare of sun off the crushed stone pathway, that Pekkala wondered if he might be hallucinating.

The summons caught Pekkala by surprise, since he had thought the Romanovs were away at their hunting lodge in Poland until the end of the following week. They seemed to have perfectly anticipated the heatwave, which had clamped down on St Petersburg less than a day after the royal train departed for the west.

'The royal family has returned from Spala?' he asked the horseman.

'Only the Tsar, he came back early.'

'Any idea what this is about?'

The man shook his head, then saluted and rode away. Horse

181

and rider seemed to merge in the heat haze, until they appeared to have transformed into a single creature.

Pekkala did not keep a horse, nor did he own a car, so he walked to the Alexander Palace. The route took him along the edge of the Alexander Park. There was no shade along this stretch, since the trees originally planted here obscured the Tsarina's view of the park from the room where she took breakfast every morning, so she'd had them all cut down.

Head bowed in the heat, Pekkala resembled a man who had lost something small on the ground and was retracing his steps to find it. The blood pounded behind his ears as he walked, stamping out a rhythm in his brain. Pekkala thought of stories he had heard about birds in the city of Florence which, driven mad in the summer heat, flew straight into the ground and killed themselves. He knew exactly how they felt.

When, at last, Pekkala reached the Alexander Palace, he paused beside the Tsukanov fountain, mesmerised by the glittering cascade of water.

The Tsarina had commissioned it from the architect Felix Tsukanov, who specialised in fountains and had been making the rounds of royal enclaves in Europe. These days it was no longer fashionable to have a palace without one of his creations.

The centrepiece was a large, tulip-shaped structure, from which the water spouted in three directions at once, falling into a waist-deep basin decorated with mosaics of Koi fish.

The Tsar had confided in Pekkala that he hated the fountain. It was noisy and garish. 'And what is a fountain for, anyway?' the Tsar had declared in exasperation. 'The horses won't even drink from it!'

Pekkala stood at the edge of the fountain, droplets splashing against his shirt and face. If he had given any thought to what he did next, he never would have done it. Before he knew what was happening, he had climbed into the fountain, without pausing to remove his clothes. He even kept his shoes on. As if compelled by forces beyond his control, he lowered himself into the water until he was sitting on the bottom, and the water rippled above his head.

He remained there, eyes open, a pearl necklace of bubbles slowly escaping from his lips. It occurred to him that he had discovered the real purpose of this fountain.

There was no time to return to his cottage, change clothes and make his way back to the palace. A summons from the Tsar required immediate action. And the Tsar, being the Tsar, had probably calculated exactly how long it should take Pekkala to walk the distance.

With as much dignity as he could manage, Pekkala clambered out of the fountain and made his way up the staircase to the palace balcony. With each footstep, water squelched from his shoes.

It was only when Pekkala reached the top of the stairs that he realised the Tsar was sitting on the balcony overlooking the front courtyard and must have witnessed the whole thing.

Pekkala walked over to the table where the Tsar was sipping tea in the shade of a large umbrella. He had been out on his horse and still wore tan riding breeches, along with brown knee-length leather boots. The Tsar had taken off his riding coat, revealing maroon suspenders that stretched over the shoulders of his white, collarless shirt. He seemed completely untroubled by the heat.

'Majesty,' said Pekkala, and bowed his head in greeting.

'Good afternoon, Pekkala. I would offer you something to drink, but you seem to have taken care of that all by yourself.'

In the moment of silence that followed, Pekkala heard the faint tap-tapping of water as it dripped from his sleeves and splashed on the yellowish-white stone of the balcony. The droplets sank into the stone, as if even the rock was thirsty in this heat.

'*What brings you back from Spala, Majesty?*'

*The Tsar smiled mischievously. '*Lena has brought me back.*'*

*Pekkala had never heard of anyone named Lena before, at least in connection with the Tsar. As far as he knew, the only woman besides his wife for whom the Tsar harboured any affection was the prima ballerina of the royal ballet, Mathilde Kschessinska. '*I look forward to meeting her, Majesty.*'*

*The Tsar, who had been sipping his tea, burst out laughing. The delicate porcelain cup slipped from his fingers, fell to the ground and shattered musically on the stones. '*Lena is not a woman!*' said the Tsar. He glanced at the smashed cup and seemed to be contemplating whether or not to bend down and pick it up.*

Pekkala knew that the smashed cup would be swept up by the palace staff and deposited on a garbage heap near the gardener's compost pile, close by the palace but hidden from view by a line of tall juniper bushes. No matter how slight the chip or blemish, any piece of imperfect crockery from the royal household was immediately taken out of circulation and could never be used again, by the Romanovs or anyone else. It was one of the quirks of the Tsarina that such a policy had gone into effect. To Pekkala, it seemed wasteful, but even if he had been offered any of these slightly damaged saucers, bowls or plates, he would not have wanted them, preferring wooden bowls and metal enamelware cups.

The same was not true of Mr Gibbs, the English tutor of the Romanov children, who had been discovered one night, sitting in the middle of the crockery pile and hunting for pieces he could repair and use.

'If Lena is not a woman...' began Pekkala.

'Lena is a place!' explained the Tsar, rising to his feet. 'Come with me and I will show you.'

Mystified, Pekkala followed the Tsar down the long central hallway of the palace.

One of the housekeepers stuck her head out of the doorway of the kitchen, stared at the wet footprints on the polished wooden floor and glared, beady-eyed, at Pekkala.

Arriving at the door to his gun room, the Tsar fished out a key and unlocked it. Unlike those of the other rooms in the palace, the gun-room door was double-thick and reinforced with metal panels.

Inside, the walls were covered with rifles held in place by velvet-padded racks. Some of the guns dated back to the sixteenth century, while others were modern hunting rifles equipped with telescopic sights. The room had no windows, only a table in the centre, covered with green felt, where the Tsar laid out and inspected his weapons before putting them to use on hunting trips or in clay-pigeon tournaments.

The Tsar closed the door behind them, locked it from the inside, then turned and winked at Pekkala. 'Almost there,' he said. Advancing to the centre of the room, he grasped one corner of the table and motioned with his chin for Pekkala to pick up the other end. Together, they moved the table aside.

Then the Tsar rolled up the carpet which lay beneath the table, revealing a trapdoor in the floor.

'Lena is down there?' asked Pekkala.

'No,' replied the Tsar, 'but what is down there came from Lena.'

Then, suddenly, Pekkala understood. The Tsar was talking about the Lena mines. It was one of the richest sources of gold in the country, and notorious for the harsh conditions under which the miners worked. In 1912 the workers had gone on strike, demanding better conditions. Rather than give in to their demands, the Tsar had sent in a regiment of Cossacks. By the time the strike was finally called off, hundreds of miners had been cut down by the Cossacks' swords.

Pulling on a brass ring set flush into the floor, the Tsar opened the trapdoor and led Pekkala down a tightly spiralled stone staircase, lit by small electric bulbs. The air was cool and damp and hard to breathe. At last, deep underground, they arrived at an unpainted metal door set straight into the rock.

There was no lock on this last door, only a metal bolt, which the Tsar slid back with a dull clank. Then he pushed the door open, revealing a chamber of darkness so complete it felt to Pekkala like a patch of blindness in his eye. The Tsar gestured for Pekkala to enter. 'After you,' he said.

Pekkala froze. He could not bear confined spaces, especially when they were unlit.

'Go on!' urged the Tsar.

Hesitantly, Pekkala stepped into the black. His breathing became shallow. It felt to him as if the floor was crumbling away beneath his feet.

At that moment, the Tsar flipped a switch and the room was suddenly flooded in light.

Pekkala found himself in a chamber ten paces wide by twenty paces long. The ceiling was so low that he could touch it easily by raising his hand above his head. The floor was dirt and the walls themselves were chipped out of the bedrock on which the palace had been built. Of this space, only a small fraction remained empty. The rest, from floor to ceiling, was completely filled with gold. Reflected in the glow of light bulbs hanging from the ceiling, the air itself seemed filled with a trembling fire.

The gold had been moulded into large ingots, each one roughly the length of a man's forearm. The only variation was in the finish of the metal. Some were polished smooth and brilliant, while others looked as if they had been wrapped in yellow velvet. All of the ingots were stamped with the double-headed Romanov eagle, in addition to weight and purity marks and the letter L in a circle, denoting its source as the Lena goldfields.

Pekkala noticed that each stack of gold contained exactly the same number of ingots and that the ingots themselves had been placed, one on top of the other, with a precision that reminded him of pictures he had seen of ancient Peruvian stonework, fitted together so closely that not even a sheet of paper could be slid between them.

'Another shipment arrived today,' the Tsar told him. 'That's why I came back from Spala. I needed to be here to meet it.'

Pekkala turned and looked at him. The sight of this fortune, scraped from the darkness of the earth by slaves and returned to that same darkness by an emperor, filled him with profound uneasiness.

'Few people have set eyes on this treasure,' the Tsar confided. 'Few people ever will.'

Pekkala spread his arms, taking in the contents of the room. 'But Excellency, how much gold does one man really need? What do you intend to do with it?'

'Do with it?' This question caught the Tsar by surprise. 'I possess it. That is what you do with treasure.' Seeing the lack of comprehension in Pekkala's face, he tried a different tack. 'Think of it as my insurance against a world of instability. Say something were to happen to this country, a disaster of biblical proportions. This gold would help to see me through. And my family. And you, of course,' he added hastily and smiled. 'What would I do without my Emerald Eye?'

'And the people of Russia?' asked Pekkala. 'What are they to do when this disaster hits?'

The Tsar rested his hand upon the shelf of gold. The feel of the metal seemed to comfort him. 'As my wife is fond of saying: on the Day of Judgement, only the chosen will be saved.'

Listening to the Comitati speak of their deliverance, Pekkala began to think Klenovkin might have been right. The years in prison had worn through the fabric of their collective sanity. And even if the gold was real, Pekkala felt sure these men would never live to see it.

He thought of a prophet named Wovoka: a Paiute Indian of the American West who, faced with the annihilation of his way of life, began to speak of a day when all the whites would disappear and the Indians' shattered civilisation would be made whole again if only they would take part in the Ghost Dance. The prophesy spread quickly from tribe to tribe. Wearing buckskin clothes decorated with the most powerful symbols of their tribe, the dancers assured themselves that even bullets could not penetrate their sacred ghost shirts. But when, in the winter of 1899, soldiers of the 7th Cavalry unleashed their Gatling guns upon the Sioux at a place called Wounded Knee, the dead fell in heaps upon the frozen ground.

Pekkala wondered if Kolchak had become, for the last remaining men he had abandoned in this camp, an illusion which would lead them to their deaths, as it already had done, Pekkala now felt certain, with the murdered Captain Ryabov.

*

The next day, at noon, Pekkala made his way across the compound, struggling under the weight of soup rations as he carried them up to the mine.

Arriving at the entrance, he called into the dark and waited.

A cold and musty breeze blew past him from the gullet of the mine, smelling of metal, dirt and sweat.

Eventually, he heard footsteps. Then a man appeared out of the shadows, a pickaxe slung on his shoulder. It was Lavrenov.

'Put down those buckets,' he said, 'and follow me.'

'In there?' Pekkala hesitated. 'Why?'

'You ask a lot of questions, Inspector; too many, as far as I'm concerned. Now some of them are going to be answered.'

With his eyes on the huge, arcing blade of the pickaxe, and certain, by now, that Lavrenov was unwilling to take no for an answer, Pekkala placed the soup cans beside the wall of the tunnel and followed him into the darkness. He felt like an insect which had strayed into a spider's lair.

The entrance to the mine was lit by kerosene lamps, but further in, the light source came from bulbs strung like Christmas lights along a sagging electrical cable.

The deeper they travelled into the mine, the narrower the tunnel became. The dirt floor angled downwards into the earth, spliced with puddles and tiny streams that glimmered eerily when their footsteps broke the surface.

Pekkala struggled to understand why the Comitati would bring him to this place. What strange rituals, he wondered, do these men perform down in the bowels of the earth?

In spite of the cold, Pekkala began to sweat. His breathing grew shallow and fast. He thought of the mountain of rock above him. Unable to shake from his head the thought of it all collapsing on top of him, he stopped and lurched against the wall, as if the ground had suddenly shifted.

Lavrenov went on a few paces, then halted. 'What is the matter with you?'

'Give me a second.' Claustrophobia swirled inside Pekkala's brain. He felt as if he were choking.

'Keep going,' ordered Lavrenov.

They passed intersections in the tunnel system, from which new passageways branched off at angles, some climbing and some descending. Handcarts filled with chalky slabs of radium ore stood parked against the walls. In the distance Pekkala could hear the sound of rusty wheels turning and the clink of metal on stone. Now and then he caught a glimpse of silhouettes, as men moved about in the shadows.

They reached a place where the tunnel was blocked by wooden pallets and metal-reinforced buttresses which propped up the ceiling.

Lavrenov twisted his body around the barricade of pallets and slithered into the darkness. 'This way!' his voice hissed out of the black.

'Why is the passage blocked?'

'Last month, this tunnel caved in. It leads to the part of the mine where they dig out Siberian Red.'

'What's to stop the tunnel from caving in again?'

'Nothing.'

Forcing himself onward, Pekkala angled past the crooked beams.

Just ahead the tunnel turned sharply to the right. As soon as they rounded the corner, Pekkala noticed a faint glow, which seemed to be coming out of the wall.

Suddenly, Pekkala realised why Lavrenov had brought him here. They must have dug a way out, he told himself. Even if it took years, these men are stubborn enough to have done it.

Lavrenov came to a halt and Pekkala found himself opposite a small opening which led into a naturally formed cave. The space inside was large, more than twice the height of a man, and filled with ancient pillars formed out of sediment drips coming down from the ceiling. Pillowed hummocks of stone bristled with crystals of Siberian Red. Some were short and sharp, like barnacles on the hull of a shipwreck. Others resembled bouquets of glass flowers. All of them were tinted the colour of fresh blood. The space had lately served as a storage room for handcarts which had broken down. Inside, a few of the wrecked contraptions stood against the wall. Scattered on the ground were the shattered tusks of stalactites and stalagmites which had been broken to make room for them. Against the far side of this strange temple, perched upon a tongue of stone as pale as alabaster, a battered miner's lamp illuminated the chamber.

Now another possibility occurred to Pekkala. Perhaps the prisoners had not dug their way out, after all. Maybe they didn't need to. Is it possible, he wondered, that in their years of toiling in the bowels of the earth, the Comitati had discovered some naturally occurring cave network which provided them with an exit into the forest, somewhere outside the walls of Borodok? Pekkala remembered stories he had heard about the caves of Altamira in northern Spain where, in 1879, a girl walking her dog had stumbled upon the entrance to a system of connecting caverns that stretched deep beneath the ground. In the largest of these caves, she'd found paintings of animals – bison and ibex – which, like those who painted them, had vanished from that countryside millennia before.

Lavrenov gestured into the cave. 'After you, Inspector.'

Ducking his head, Pekkala stepped into the room. The lamplight shuddered. The air smelled rank. Shadows writhed like snakes across the floor.

Turning back, he saw that Lavrenov was not behind him.

His heart slammed into his throat.

In that moment, he heard a voice whisper his name.

'Who's there?' asked Pekkala.

A hand reached out and brushed against his leg.

Pekkala shouted with alarm. Stepping back, he noticed a figure sitting in an alcove formed inside the stone.

The presence of this huddled shape reminded him of tales he had heard about ancient and mummified corpses, discovered in caves such as this, creatures whose careless wanderings had brought them here to die before their species ever dared to rule the earth.

Pekkala's eyes darted among the scaffolding of pillars. He was certain now that he'd been led into an ambush. In his terror, he glimpsed his own desiccated body, sleeping through millennia.

'Tarnowski?' he called. 'Sedov, is that you?'

The figure emerged from its hiding place in the wall, as if the rock itself had come to life. Even through the matted beard and filthy clothes, Pekkala recognised a man he had long since consigned to oblivion.

It was Colonel Kolchak himself.

Kolchak spread his arms and smiled, revealing strong white teeth.

'You!' Pekkala finally managed to say and suddenly all the years since the night outside his cottage, when he had last set eyes on Kolchak, crumpled together like the folds of an accordion, so that it seemed as if no time had passed between that moment and this.

'I told you we would meet again some day,' said Kolchak. 'Many times, during my long exile in Shanghai, I imagined this reunion. I had hoped it would be in more luxurious surroundings, but this will have to do, at least for now.'

'But how did you get here?' asked Pekkala, still completely overwhelmed. 'Is there a tunnel to the forest?'

The Colonel laughed. 'There is nothing beyond this cave but solid rock. If there had been a way in or out of here other than the main entrance to the mine, I would have made use of it by now. I have been down here for almost a month, eating stale bread from your kitchen and drinking your pine-needle soup.'

'A month?'

'That was not my intention,' admitted Kolchak. 'I had arranged to spend only a few days inside the camp while we made final preparations for the escape. It almost never happened. Then one of my own men betrayed me. At least, he tried to. There was a price to pay for that.' To emphasise his words, Kolchak drew a long, stag-handled knife from under his jacket. Its massive Bowie blade glimmered in the lantern light.

'You killed Ryabov?' gasped Pekkala. 'Your own Captain?'

'I had no choice.'

'But why would he have betrayed you?'

'What does it matter now? He is dead.'

'It matters a great deal,' insisted Pekkala, 'to me and to your men.'

'He went over to the enemy. That is all you need to know. My friend,' a tone of warning had entered Kolchak's voice, 'just be glad you're coming with us.'

From the tone of those words, Pekkala realised it was the only answer he was going to get. 'What caused the delay in your plan?' he asked.

'After Ryabov's body was found,' Kolchak replied, 'the camp was locked down. Guards were doubled. Curfews were put in place. And then, when I learned you had returned to Borodok, I did not dare to make a move until I knew why you were here. Now the time has finally come for us to break out of this place.'

'Break *out*? I am still trying to understand how you broke *in*!'

'The Ostyaks arranged it. They have agreed to help us get across the border into China.'

'But the Ostyaks have never helped convicts before.'

'That is because no prisoner has ever been able to offer them a decent bribe, something better than the bags of salt and army bread paid out by the Camp Commandant for delivering the bodies of those who attempted escape.'

'What did you offer?'

'A share of the gold,' Kolchak answered. 'Which we will pick up from its hiding place on our way to the border. Of course, before any of this could happen, they first had to get me inside the camp, so that I could organise the breakout of however many men remained from the expedition. I had no idea there were so few. I wish I could have come sooner, but it took me many years to find out where the men were being held and longer still to lay out the plans for escape. I am glad their days of suffering at Borodok will soon be at an end, along with yours.'

'How did you manage to get inside the camp?'

'The only time the Ostyaks come to Borodok is to deliver the dead to Klenovkin's door and to pick up their payment for each body. They had noticed that the men who took away the corpses all had tattoos of a pine tree on their hands, just as I have on mine. Since that is the symbol we chose for our journey to Siberia, I knew those men must be survivors of the expedition. Just before you arrived at the camp, a group of men had tried to escape. Before long, like all the others, they had perished in the forest. When the Ostyaks found some of the corpses, they brought them to the camp and unloaded them at the feet of the Comitati, who were waiting to take them away. Except one of those bodies was still breathing.' Kolchak tapped a finger against his chest. 'As soon as Tarnowski and the others realised what was happening, they carried me out of sight to the generator shed, where the bodies of the dead are stored. That night, after dark, they brought me to the safety of this mine. I have been here ever since, waiting for the right moment to escape.'

'But how will the Ostyaks know when you are ready?'

'They have been watching this camp from the forest. That fire in the generator shed yesterday morning was the signal that we are ready to go.'

'I was sure you had been killed,' said Pekkala. 'When I learned that you might be still alive, I thought I must be dreaming.'

'Survival has been difficult for both of us,' replied Kolchak, 'and we are not yet out of danger. We have much to discuss, old friend, but it will have to wait until we're safe.'

'And how long will that be?'

'We leave tomorrow at first light. When the moment arrives, you will know, but you will have to move quickly in order not to be left behind. If you are delayed, we can't afford to wait for you.'

As the shock of seeing Kolchak began to wear off, Pekkala's thoughts turned back towards the gold. Stalin must have known all along about the missing Imperial Reserves, he told himself. That's why he sent me here. He knew that my acquaintance with Kolchak from before the Revolution would lure the Colonel out into the open. Once Kolchak had been found, the gold would not be far away. Ryabov was not the pawn in this game, thought Pekkala. I was.

Bile spilled into the back of his throat as he realised he had been played by Stalin, just as the Tsar had used him, and both times because of this gold.

Pekkala suddenly remembered a conversation he'd had with Rasputin many years before. He sometimes had difficulty in deciphering the musings of the Siberian holy man and even when Rasputin did manage to make himself understood, Pekkala often found it hard to take him seriously. But this time Pekkala wished he had listened more closely.

It was evening.

He was walking along a tree-lined boulevard on the outskirts of St Petersburg. Heat from that summer day still lingered in the air.

Following the odour of frying garlic, Pekkala made his way to a club known as the Villa Rode.

Pekkala was looking for Rasputin, who could be found at this place almost every evening. He did not normally seek out the Siberian mystic. In fact, Pekkala usually went out of his way to avoid Rasputin, but he was the only person that Pekkala knew he could talk to about what he'd seen earlier that day.

The Villa Rode was popular with the St Petersburg elite because it did not close until dawn. When the famous Streilna restaurant, which resembled a miniature palace made of ice in the middle of Petrovsky Park, shut its doors at 2 a.m., followed by the Koupeschesky casino club at 3 a.m., those who were still conscious and had money in their pockets paid a visit to the Villa Rode.

The building's wooden plank exterior was badly in need of paint. Inside, the rooms were cramped, the tables small and rickety, and the acoustics notoriously strange. It was sometimes possible to hear the whispered conversation of a couple on the other side of the room while having to almost shout to be understood by someone sitting at the same table.

Through the open windows of the Villa Rode came the sounds

of laughter and piano music. A deep and slightly drunken voice crooned out Sorokin's song: 'As long as I can see the flame, out there in the darkness, I know that I am still alive.'

The Villa Rode had become Rasputin's favourite haunt for the simple reason that he never had to pay for anything when he was there. His bill was handled by the Tsarina Alexandra from an account set up specially to pay for his food and drink, as well as to cover the costs of the broken chairs, tables, china and windows, which were often the result of his evening entertainment.

Rasputin had been thrown out of so many places that restaurant owners were given a special number to call if they needed him removed from their premises. Once the call had been made, an unmarked car would be dispatched and Rasputin would be hauled away by agents of the Okhrana, operating under the direct orders of the Tsarina. Fetching Rasputin was said to be one of the worst duties an Okhrana agent could be assigned. Chief Inspector Vassileyev, head of the Petersburg Bureau, reserved it for those men under his command who required an extra dose of humiliation.

Just when it seemed as if the city might be running out of places for Rasputin to disgrace himself, the owner of the Villa Rode, a sombre-looking man named Gorokhin, hit upon a brilliant plan, which assured him a steady source of income from the coffers of the Romanovs, as well as the gratitude of the Tsarina.

Gorokhin offered to build an extension on to the Villa Rode. This extra room would be for Rasputin alone. It could not be accessed by regular patrons, nor would Rasputin ever be asked to leave the extension, no matter what he did inside it.

No sooner had Gorokhin made his offer than a team of builders arrived from the palace of Tsarskoye Selo to begin construction of the extension. It was completed in forty-eight hours and, since then, Rasputin had made it his own.

Gorokhin recognised Pekkala at once, and correctly guessed that he had come to see Rasputin. He led Pekkala out the back of the restaurant, passing through a neglected garden thick with tangled bushes. The air was heavy with the smell of lavender and honeysuckle. At last, they arrived at a plain, low-roofed hut which adjoined the Villa Rode.

No noise came from behind the pinewood door. Nor was there any light glimmering through the shuttered windows.

'Are you sure he's here?' asked Pekkala.

'He kicked the door down on his way in this morning,' replied Gorokhin. 'I had to put up this new one. There have been several visitors since then, but Rasputin himself has not emerged.'

'Is he alone?'

'I doubt it.'

'Thank you,' said Pekkala.

Gorokhin nodded and left.

Pekkala opened the door and walked inside. The air was thick with the smell of sweat and alcohol and the ash of coarse Khorizki tobacco, which Rasputin preferred to the more expensive Balkan cigarettes smoked by his benefactor, the Empress.

The only light came from a single candle melted on to the head of a small brass Buddha. The melted wax had trickled down, coating the belly of the statue.

Searching the gloom, Pekkala could make out a large couch and a low table strewn with bottles. On an upholstered stool sat a man who was definitely not Rasputin. This stranger wore a black wool coat with velvet collar, and clutched a round-topped Homburg hat. His thin-soled shoes were narrow in the toe and highly polished. The man did not glance up at Pekkala, but only stared at the floor with a grim expression on his face.

Pekkala had seen that look before, from people who had been caught red-handed at some illegal activity but were too dignified, or too afraid, to run away.

Opposite the man, slumped on a couch with legs spread and bare feet resting on the table, was Rasputin. He wore a silk robe with a Japanese kimono pattern and a belt like a bell-ringer's rope. 'Pekkala,' he said, and the name seemed to crack from his lips like a tiny spark of electricity. Haphazardly, Rasputin began to rearrange his clothes. 'Has Chief Inspector Vassileyev finally sent you to arrest me or else,' he gestured vaguely at the man huddled across the table, 'is it this gentleman you've come to put in chains?'

The man still refused to look up, as if by remaining motionless, he might escape detection.

'I am not here to arrest either of you.'

'Thank God for that,' sighed the man in the black coat.

Rasputin lifted one finger and wagged it at the man. 'You can go now and be sure to thank God for that, as well.'

Obediently, the man stood. From the inside pocket of his coat, he removed an envelope and placed it on the table between Rasputin's large and hairy feet. 'So we have an understanding?'

Rasputin laughed. 'I understand you, but that does not mean we understand each other. Come back tomorrow. Bring another envelope.'

'Not without some kind of guarantee,' protested the man. 'I wouldn't dream of it.'

'You will,' Rasputin told him, 'and that is all you'll dream about.'

Too indignant to reply, the man stormed out of the room.

The candle flame shuddered as he passed by and the face of the little Buddha appeared to be laughing at him.

'What was that about?' Pekkala asked Rasputin.

'He is a representative for a jeweller in Petersburg. He is hoping to have a royal warrant bestowed upon his company.'

'And why is he asking you for that?'

'Because he can't ask anyone else! Least of all the Romanovs.'

'I don't understand.'

'And that is why I love you, Pekkala.' Rasputin sat forward, lifting his bare feet from the table and planting them firmly on the floor. He picked up the bribe, index finger shuffling through the bills as he counted them. Then he tossed the money back on to the table. 'You see, Pekkala, you can't just ask for the royal warrant. You have to be given it. If you do ask for it, there's no chance at all of receiving one. Instead, you must give the impression that you would accept it if offered, but that, in the meantime, you do not expect anything. That's the way things work.'

Pekkala did not know much about royal warrants, but the strange logic of wanting but not daring to show the want, or not asking in the hopes of receiving was familiar to him from other aspects of the royal family. It was the way that they maintained their grip upon those levels of Russian society which fanned out around the Romanovs like ripples from a stone thrown in a pond.

'He wants me to convince the Tsarina,' continued Rasputin.

'And you think you could?'

Rasputin breathed out sharply through his nose. 'Please, Pekkala. Of course I could! The question is, will I?'

'And what is the answer?'

'I don't know yet, and that is what infuriates him.'

'He would be even more infuriated if he knew you will be giving away his money to the next sad face that walks into the room.'

Rasputin laughed. 'I give away my money because it buys me something far more valuable than cash.'

'And what is that?'

'Loyalty. Affection. Information. Everything I would have spent it on, except this way I also earn friends. That's something he will never figure out.'

'Did you really think I had come to arrest you?'

'Of course not! I can't be arrested. Not in here. And probably not anywhere. Not even by you.'

'I would not put that to the test.' Pekkala went over to the table, found another candle, this one jammed into a wicker-covered Chianti bottle, and lit it.

With enough light now to see around the room, he looked at the flimsy sheets of silk which had been draped across the walls, the mud-caked Berber carpet on the floor and what he at first thought was broken glass but which, he realised, was actually money. There were shiny coins everywhere, tossed like offerings to a fountain in every corner of the room.

'Why are you here, Pekkala?' asked Rasputin, and as he spoke he stretched out one leg, nudging aside the bottles on the table with a big yellow-nailed toe, searching for one that might have some drink left in it. 'Has something caused the Emerald Eye to blink? What could it be? Not the sight of blood. You have already seen too much of that. It would not be threats. Those do not seem to bother you. No. It is something for which you were unprepared.'

'The Tsar sent for me today. There is a room beneath the palace . . .'

Before Pekkala could finish, Rasputin clapped his hands and

roared with laughter. 'Of course! I should have guessed. The Tsar has been worshipping his gold again, and it was your turn to take part in the ceremony.'

'Ceremony? What do you mean?'

Rasputin's smile revealed a mixture of pity and amusement. 'Poor Pekkala! Without me here to guide you, how would you ever understand? You see, the Tsar has already exhausted all the solitary pleasure he can take from his horde of treasure. What he needs is an audience. What satisfies him now is the look on the face of someone setting eyes for the first time on those bars of gold. What he wants, what he needs, Pekkala, is to see the flash of envy in their gaze. It destroys them. It ruins their lives. They never recover from the shock of that longing. And no matter how much they beg him for another glimpse of that gold, and believe me they do beg, those doors will remain closed to them forever.'

'I do not envy him because of what I saw today.'

'Of course you don't! You are not like the others. The Tsar has failed to tempt you with his Fabergé eggs, his Amber Room and the art work on his walls. So now he has laid down his trump card, the thing which never fails.'

'But it has failed. When I looked at that pile of gold, all I could think about was the suffering of those miners. He sent in the Cossacks to kill them!' Pekkala's voice rose in anger. 'All those men wanted was the chance to work in safety, and he would not even give them that.'

Rasputin's eyes seemed to flicker in the candlelight. 'But many things are valuable precisely because they are the product of pain. Think of the pearl. It begins as a grain of sand. Imagine the agony of the oyster as that tiny piece of stone digs into the soft flesh of the creature, like a knife stabbing into your brain! So the oyster surrounds the pearl with its own living shell until at last it becomes what we value, enough to kill the oyster for it – anyway, the same way the Tsar is prepared to kill his miners. The truth, Pekkala, is that beauty on this earth is set aside for the enjoyment of the few and comes at the cost of the suffering of the many. That is true for many things besides gold and pearls. It is true for the Tsarina, for example, although most of that suffering is her husband's. Your eyes have been opened, Pekkala. You used to see the Tsar as a victim of circumstance, secretly longing to be like any other man, like a god who wishes to be mortal. You blamed the world of extravagance into which he had been born. You blamed the need of all rulers to appear larger than life, in their manner, in their wealth, in their surroundings. You even blamed his wife, I expect. Everybody else does. But the one person you could not bring yourself to blame was the Tsar himself, and so I say again – it has not failed.'

'You can be very cruel, Grigori.'

'Not as cruel as the Tsar,' he replied. 'He knew that the one thing you would respect in him was the secret disregard for all his wealth, because that was the only way for you to see yourself in him. And why else would you agree to serve a man unless you held the same things to be sacred? What the Tsar did today was to show you his true face, and in that moment, the man you thought you knew turned out to be a stranger.' Rasputin levelled a long, bony finger at Pekkala. 'I warn you, my friend, that treasure is cursed. Even those you trust with your own life will betray you if you come between them and that gold.'

'Have you seen it?' asked Pekkala.

'Of course!' Rasputin lifted his hands and let them fall again upon the couch, sending up tiny puffs of dust from the crushed velvet. 'I enjoyed the experience immensely, because I have discovered *that my greatest source of pleasure is neither money, nor the wo-men who traipse into my life and get exactly what they're looking for and who will one day swear they've never met me.'*

'Then what is it, Rasputin?'

'What this twisted brain of mine can no longer do without', *Rasputin tapped a finger against his forehead, 'is to stand at the edge of the abyss, not knowing which way I will fall.'*

Six months later, the St Petersburg police pulled Rasputin's body from the freezing waters of the Neva River. At the spot where he had touched his forehead on that night Pekkala came to see him, Rasputin's murderers had put a bullet through his skull.

There was a scuffling in the tunnel outside, followed by a shout and a strange crunching sound, like someone biting into an apple.

Kolchak moved over to the entrance, the knife still in his hand. 'Lavrenov, what's happening?'

'I found someone prowling around.'

Kolchak and Pekkala stepped into the tunnel.

In the middle of the narrow passageway, a man lay on his back, nailed to the earth by Lavrenov's pickaxe. The man was still alive, spluttering as he struggled for breath. Blood leaked from the corners of his mouth.

'He must have followed us,' said Lavrenov.

Kolchak fetched the lantern from the cave.

Pekkala stifled a gasp as the light touched the dying man's face.

It was Savushkin, his bodyguard. Helplessly, the man stared at Pekkala.

Knowing there was nothing he could do, Pekkala struggled to contain his emotions as he watched Savushkin's last breath trail out.

'Bury him,' ordered Kolchak.

'Yes, Colonel.' Lavrenov set his foot against Savushkin's chest, and wrenched out the pickaxe blade.

Kolchak turned to Pekkala. 'Go now,' he said gently, 'before anyone notices you've been gone. And do not worry, my friend. It is all in motion now.'

*

'Kornfeld says the target has been liquidated.'

Without looking up from his paperwork, Stalin grunted in acknowledgement.

'There is something else, Comrade Stalin – a new development at Borodok.'

The paper shuffling came to an abrupt halt.

'Another telegram has arrived,' continued Poskrebyshev.

'From Kirov or Pekkala?'

'Neither. It's from the Camp Commandant, Klenovkin, and addressed to you, Comrade Stalin.' Poskrebyshev handed over the message.

BEG TO REPORT INSPECTOR PEKKALA OVERHEARD DE-
NOUNCING COMMUNIST PARTY AND MAKING THREATS
AGAINST COMRADE STALIN STOP BELIEVE PEKKALA PLAN-
NING UPRISING IN CAMP STOP HAS FALSELY ACCUSED ME
OF INVOLVEMENT IN CRIME STOP LONG LIVE THE PARTY
STOP LONG LIVE COMRADE STALIN STOP KLENOVKIN COM-
MANDANT BORODOK

Stalin sat back heavily in his chair. 'Denouncing me? An up-rising?'

'Has this been confirmed?' asked Poskrebyshev.

'There is no time to waste on confirmations,' barked Stalin. 'The prisoners will flock to him. The uprising could spread to other camps. If Pekkala isn't stopped, this could turn into a national emergency.' He sat forward, wrote something on a pad of yellow notepaper and handed the note to Poskrebyshev. 'Send this to Klenovkin. Tell him to carry out the order and to report back to me immediately afterwards.'

Poskrebyshev blinked in surprise when he saw what Stalin had written. 'Do you not wish to verify the Camp Commandant's message before such drastic action is taken?'

'What reason could this man Klenovkin have for sending me a pack of lies?' demanded Stalin.

'And what could Pekkala possibly have to gain by turning on you now?'

'More than you know! More than you could possibly realise!' With wild eyes, Stalin glared at Poskrebyshev. 'Now send the message and, another time, when I want your opinion, I'll ask for it.'

Poskrebyshev lowered his head in surrender, as if it was his own doom, and not Pekkala's, which had just been sealed. 'Yes, Comrade Stalin,' he whispered.

When Poskrebyshev had gone, Stalin walked to the window. He lit himself a cigarette and looked out over the city. As smoke flooded into his lungs, smoothing out the ragged edges of his mind, the memory of Pekkala was already fading from his thoughts.

*

Ever since sending the telegram, detailing Pekkala's non-existent threats against Stalin, Klenovkin had been poised over the telegraph, waiting for a reply. He waited for so long that he had dozed off. When the device finally sprang to life, the Commandant was so startled that he backed away from it as if a growling dog had crept into the room.

As soon as Klenovkin read the telegram, he sent for Gramotin.

While he waited, Klenovkin paced around his study, rubbing his hands together in satisfaction. For the first time in as long as he could remember, something was going his way. This would, he knew, be the springboard to greater things. The meteoric rise he had always imagined he would make through the ranks of the Dalstroy Company had finally begun.

At last, Gramotin appeared.

'Read this.'

'Liq . . .' The telegram trembled between Gramotin's fingers as he struggled to pronounce the words. 'Liquiday. Liquidate.'

'Idiot!' Klenovkin snatched the message back and read it out himself. 'Now,' he said, when he had finished, 'do you understand what must be done?'

'Yes, Comrade Klenovkin. First thing in the morning?'

Klenovkin paused. 'On second thoughts, wait until he has finished his breakfast duties.'

'So we can keep him working to the very end.'

'My thoughts, exactly, Sergeant.'

Gramotin nodded, impressed. 'Dalstroy will be proud of you.'

'Indeed they will,' agreed Klenovkin, 'and it's about time, too.'

*

The old guard, Larchenko, sat in his chair by the door, chin on his chest, lost in sleep. His rifle stood propped against the wall.

Nearby, Pekkala lay in his bunk, haunted by the death of Savushkin. He inhaled the musty, used-up air of dreaming men and listened to the patient rhythm of their breathing.

Unable to sleep, Pekkala climbed out of his bunk and walked over to the window. His felt boots made no sound as they glided across the worn floorboards. With the heel of his palm, he rubbed away the frost that had gathered on the inside of the glass.

Soon it would be dawn.

Pekkala had made up his mind to lie low when the breakout began. As Kolchak had said, they would not wait for him if he was delayed in the confusion.

There had been no time to reflect upon his brief meeting with the Colonel. He continued to be baffled by the Colonel's choice to return, in spite of the overwhelming risks involved. At the same time, Pekkala felt a surge of guilt that his own faith in this man had not matched that of the soldiers he had left behind in Siberia. Pekkala was glad that the magnitude of the Comitati's endurance would at last be repaid with their freedom.

And as for Stalin, he decided, the payment for his treachery would be the knowledge that Kolchak had slipped from his grasp yet again, along with the last of the Imperial Gold reserves. When the time came, Pekkala decided, he would simply deny that he had known anything about Kolchak's plans.

Although Pekkala had solved the murder of Ryabov, it troubled him that he had never learned the motive for Ryabov's betrayal of the Colonel. He realised now that he might never know. Whatever Ryabov's purpose, he had taken his reasons to the grave.

With shark-grey clouds hanging on the red horizon, Pekkala made his way over to the kitchen as usual in order to prepare the breakfast. It was so quiet out on the compound that Pekkala began to wonder if the escape had already taken place. The oven was on and the bread was baking inside. Melekov was nowhere to be seen. He often went back to his quarters for an extra half-hour of sleep, leaving to Pekkala the job of removing the loaves just before the kitchen opened for breakfast. When the bread was done, Pekkala took the pans from the oven and tipped the *paika* rations out into the battered aluminium tubs from which they would be served.

He had just completed this task when Melekov burst into the kitchen. 'You have to get out of here!' he hissed. 'They're going to kill you.'

'Who is?' demanded Pekkala.

'On Klenovkin's orders, you are to be shot, as soon as the prisoners have gone to work this morning.'

Pekkala wondered if Klenovkin had found out about the escape. If that was true, he would not be the only one to die. 'Who told you this?' he asked.

'Gramotin did. Only a few minutes ago.'

'Damn it, Melekov! Did you not stop to wonder if this might just be another of his lies?'

'He said that orders had come in from Moscow last night. Klenovkin even showed him the telegram. Stalin himself wants you dead!' Pekkala's mind was racing. If Stalin had indeed ordered the execution, his only hope of survival would be to escape with the Comitati. Even if the telegram was just a story concocted by Gramotin, Pekkala knew he would be dead before the lie had been discovered. It took him only a second to realise he had no choice except to run.

'Why are you telling me this?' he asked Melekov. 'If what you say is true, do you realise what your life would be worth if they found out I'd heard it from you?'

'You could have killed me, that day in the kitchen. Maybe you should have, but you didn't. I pay my debts, Pekkala, and this one is paid. Now move quickly. I know a place where you can hide.' The cook beckoned for Pekkala to follow, spun around and found himself face to face with Tarnowski, who had appeared in the doorway to the kitchen.

Before Melekov had a chance to react, Tarnowski laid him out with a fist to the side of the head. Melekov sprawled unconscious on the floor.

'Don't kill him,' said Pekkala.

'I don't have time to kill him,' replied Tarnowski. 'We are getting out of here.'

Suddenly, a wall of darkness seemed to rise from the entrance to the camp. A tremor passed through Pekkala, the ground shook under his feet. Then a flash as bright as molten copper burst through the narrow gap between the gates, which tore loose from their iron hinges, scattering the links of chain which had held them shut.

'Head straight through the entrance,' ordered Tarnowski. 'Don't stop for anything. I'll meet you on the other side.'

Without a word, Pekkala set off running across the compound. In between clouds of smoke, he glimpsed the Ostyaks milling about just outside the gates. They had brought sledges, four that Pekkala could see, each one harnessed to a single caribou.

Guards spilled out of the watchtowers. None of them made any attempt to open fire on the Ostyaks. Instead, they scrambled down their ladders and bolted for the safety of the guardhouse.

On the other side of the compound, Pekkala caught sight of Lavrenov. Kneeling in front of him was one of the guards, whom Pekkala recognised as Platov, the man they called Gramotin's puppet. On his way to the guardhouse, Platov had slipped on the ice, dropping his rifle in the process.

Before Platov could get back on his feet, Lavrenov had snatched up the gun, with its long, cruciform bayonet, and now aimed it squarely at the guard. 'Which god are you praying to now?' screamed Lavrenov, as Platov raised his hands to shield his face. 'Haven't you abolished all of them?'

Pekkala lost sight of the two men as he ran past the bronze statue. At that moment, he spotted a guard up on the walkway between the towers. This one had not fled like the others. Instead he took aim at Pekkala. As the man raised the gun to his shoulder, Pekkala realised it was Gramotin.

He heard the gun go off, brittle and echoing across the compound, and then came a dull clang as the bullet struck the statue of the woman.

Then another shot rang out, this one from the other side of the compound.

Gramotin's legs slipped out from under him. He tumbled from the walkway into the ditch below.

As Pekkala sprinted through the gates, an Ostyak grabbed him by the arm. The stocky man, his wide face powdered with smoke, steered Pekkala towards one of the sledges. As Pekkala crouched down on the narrow wooden platform, he stared through the jagged teeth of splintered wood, all that remained of the gates, at men running about in the compound. Half-dressed, disoriented prisoners poured from the barracks. The Commandant's quarters looked deserted, although Pekkala knew Klenovkin must be in there somewhere.

The Ostyaks drifted in and out of the thick smoke. The fur on their coats stood up like that of angry cats. They were busily setting fire to the stockade fence, whose tar-painted logs quickly began to burn.

Now Lavrenov emerged from camp. Immediately he took his place on one of the sledges. Crouching there, he stared back at the camp, amazed to be outside the prison walls at last.

Bullets snapped over their heads. Through the windows of the guardhouse, camp guards fired blind into the haze. Pekkala heard the clunk of rounds striking the gate posts and the spitting whine of bullets as they ricocheted off stones in the road.

Sedov lurched through the smoke. He stumbled and righted himself, then stared in confusion at a tear which had appeared in his jacket, the white fluff of raw cotton spattered with his blood. A stray bullet from the guardhouse had caught him in the back, the round passing through the top of his shoulder.

Lavrenov and Pekkala helped him to a sledge.

At last, Kolchak and Tarnowski arrived, each carrying rifles they had taken from the guard towers.

Now the four Ostyaks climbed on to their sledges, stepping roughly on the men who lay clinging to the wooden platforms.

Huddled at the feet of his driver, Pekkala heard the crack of whips. As the sledge lunged forward, he dug his fingers between the boards and held on tight. Soon they were moving fast, the metal runners of the sledge hissing as they raced across the ground. Through a blur of snow dust, Pekkala could just make out the other three sledges travelling behind. The hooves of the caribou clicked as they galloped and the frost-caked harnesses shuddered with the motion of their bodies.

Pekkala's bare hands were beginning to freeze, so he tucked them inside the sleeves of his quilted jacket. Soon, he felt the burning pain in his fingertips as his nerves began to revive.

The breakout had happened so quickly that Pekkala was uncertain how much time had passed since he left the barracks, but it did not seem like more than a few minutes. The sun was up now. Ice crystals glistened in the trees.

He wondered how long it would be before Klenovkin sent out a search party. Knowing that the Ostyaks were involved, the Borodok guards would be unlikely to venture out beyond the camp any time soon.

Only now was Pekkala able to focus on Stalin's execution order. Assuming it was true, the day might never come when he would comprehend what path of twisted logic had led Stalin to turn on him without warning. Pekkala had seen things like this before, when hundreds, even thousands of men had gone to their deaths against the wall of Lubyanka prison, shouting their loyalty to the man who had ordered them shot.

Pekkala felt lucky to be alive, even if it meant he would spend the rest of his life on the run. He did not care about the things he'd leave behind – the tattered clothes and well-thumbed books, the meagre bank account. But he wondered how Kirov would do. They will tell him I was a traitor, thought Pekkala. They will never let him know the truth about my leaving. There was so much he had not yet taught the young investigator. Feelings of regret rained down upon him. I was stingy with my knowledge, Pekkala thought. I was impatient. I demanded perfection instead of excellence. I could at least have smiled a little more.

Lost in these thoughts, Pekkala was caught by surprise when the sledge turned sharply and began to follow a winding path up through the woods. The caribou struggled over the rising ground, the smell of its sweat mixed with the leather of the harness straps and the rank odour of the unwashed men.

By now, the cold had worked its way into Pekkala's feet and across his shoulder blades. He could feel the remaining warmth in his body retreating deeper inside.

The Ostyaks halted in a clearing deep inside the forest. The men jumped down from their sledges, stamping the crust of snow from their legs.

The sun had slid behind the clouds. Now it began to snow.

Pekkala heard the noise of a stream somewhere nearby, flowing underneath the ice. Chickadees sang in the branches of the trees and it was not long before the fearless, bandit-masked birds arrived to inspect the strangers. Like little clockwork toys, they hopped along the backs of the animals.

Sedov was lifted from his sledge. The silhouette of his body, outlined in blood, remained on the rough wooden planks. Pekkala and Lavrenov laid him down in the snow but he began to choke, nostrils flaring as he struggled to breathe. Instead they sat him with his back against a tree. Helplessly, they watched the wounded man, knowing that the help he required was beyond any skills they possessed.

*

Klenovkin crawled out from under his desk, a pistol clutched in his hand. When the attack began, the Commandant had been asleep in his office, head on his desk with a pile of requisition slips for a pillow. Jarred awake by the noise, he first thought was that there had been an explosion in the mine. His semi-conscious brain was already composing the damage report he would have to make to Dalstroy when, arriving in the outer office, he saw the main gates ripped from their mountings and Ostyaks waiting on the other side. At that point, Klenovkin grabbed his gun off the bookshelf, locked the door and took cover beneath the desk, determined to shoot anyone who tried to get in.

But no one did.

Now the shooting had stopped. The camp was silent again.

Zebra stripes of sunlight gleamed through the shuttered windows.

Relieved as Klenovkin was to have been left alone by the Ostyaks, he could not help a certain indignation that none of the guards had come to rescue him.

He could not fathom why the Ostyaks had mounted an assault on the camp. Nothing like this had ever happened before. He wondered what offence, conjured from their primitive and superstitious minds, had sent them on the warpath. In spite of what had happened, Klenovkin was not overly concerned. The camp guards, with their superior firepower and Sergeant Gramotin to lead them, would certainly have fought off any Ostyaks who managed to enter the camp. Nor did he worry about any prisoners attempting to escape, especially when there were Ostyaks around.

The sooner he made his way out to the compound, the fewer

questions would be raised about his actions during the attack. Anxious to give the impression that he had been in the thick of the fighting, Klenovkin removed a bullet from his gun, detached the round from the brass cartridge and poured the grey sand of gunpowder into his palm. Then he spat on the powder, stirred it into a paste with his finger and daubed the mixture on his face.

Still cautious, Klenovkin climbed to his feet and peered between the shutters. The damage was worse than he'd thought.

Pale shreds of wood, all that remained of the gates, lay scattered across the compound. The two guard towers had burned and collapsed. One of the barracks was also on fire. Tar paper blazed on its roof, shingles curling like black fists in the heat. In an effort to stop the blaze from spreading, a couple of prisoners were shovelling snow up on to the roof, which seemed to have no effect at all.

Other prisoners had gathered at the cookhouse where Melekov, refusing to alter his habits, was now handing out the breakfast rations.

In the centre of the compound, a guard was kneeling on the ground, a rifle, with bayonet attached, propped against his shoulder.

Klenovkin looked closer, and recognised Platov, that idiot lapdog of Gramotin. The first thing he would do when he embarked on his inspection tour was to tell that lazy fool to get up and go back to work. But then he noticed that the rifle wasn't resting against Platov's shoulder as he had first imagined. In fact, Platov had been stabbed through the throat with the bayonet which now protruded from the back of his neck. Platov was dead, propped up by the rifle, which had prevented him from falling.

No one had touched the body.

The spit dried up in Klenovkin's mouth. Turning from the window, he picked up the phone and dialled the guardhouse. 'This is Klenovkin. What is the situation?' Hearing the reply, he suddenly appeared to lose his balance and grabbed hold of the corner of his desk. 'They what? All of them? With the Ostyaks? And Pekkala, too? Are you certain of this? Who has gone after them? What do you mean nobody? You were waiting for my orders? Do you honestly think you need my permission to chase after escaped prisoners? I don't care if the Ostyaks were with them! Get after them now! Now!' Klenovkin slammed down the receiver.

As the full measure of this disaster became clear to him, all the strength seemed to pour from his body.

He would be held responsible. His career was finished. Dalstroy would have him replaced. And that was the least of his worries. These were not just any prisoners. These were the Comitati, and for their escape he would answer directly to Moscow. His only chance was to blame Pekkala, in the hopes of deflecting Stalin's fury.

Klenovkin slid the phone into the centre of his desk. After breathing in and out several times, like a runner preparing for a race, he dialled the Kremlin.

Time slowed to a crawl as he listened to the click and crackle of the empty line. Vaguely, he recalled the night before, when his promotion through the ranks of Dalstroy had seemed a certainty. Last night felt like a dream, borrowed out of someone else's life. Now a great, spiralling darkness appeared in front of him, and Klenovkin felt himself drawn helplessly into its vortex. Finally he heard the distant purr of the telephone ringing in Moscow.

'Kremlin!' barked Poskrebyshev.

'This is Commandant Klenovkin.'

'Who?'

'Klenovkin. Commandant of the camp at Borodok. You gave me this number.'

'Ah. Borodok. Yes. You are calling to confirm that the liquidation has been carried out.'

'Not exactly.' Klenovkin breathed in, ready to explain, but before he had the chance a new voice broke through on the line.

'Put him through,' Stalin ordered.

Klenovkin felt as if the air had been sucked out of his lungs.

Poskrebyshev pressed a button on his telephone, transferring the line to Stalin's desk. But the secretary did not hang up as he should have done. Instead, he placed the receiver gently on his desk, then bent forward until his ear was almost pressed against it. His teeth gritted with concentration, Poskrebyshev strained to hear what was being said.

'Has Pekkala been executed,' demanded Stalin, 'or hasn't he?'

Klenovkin knew that the next words out of his mouth would change his life forever. As he tried to compose himself before delivering the answer, he stared at the white cloud of a snow squall riding in over the valley in the distance. It occurred to him that, with a snowstorm coming in, all trace of the escape would be wiped clean and the prisoners would vanish forever in the taiga.

'Klenovkin? Are you there?'

'Yes, Comrade Stalin.'

'What has become of Pekkala?'

'I beg to report that the inspector escaped before I had a chance to carry out your orders.'

'Escaped? When?'

'This morning.'

'But you received my instructions *last night*! He should have been shot within five minutes of your reading the message!'

'I decided to wait until morning, Comrade Stalin.'

'And what purpose could that possibly have served?' spluttered Stalin.

Ransacking his mind, Klenovkin could no longer reconstruct the train of thought in which postponing Pekkala's execution had seemed such a good idea to him, only a few hours before. 'There is more, Comrade Stalin.'

'More?' he bellowed. 'What else have you bungled, Klenovkin?'

'The men of the Kolchak Expedition have also managed to escape.'

For the next few seconds, only a faint rustling could be heard, which neither Stalin nor Klenovkin realised was, in fact, the sound of Poskrebyshev's breathing as he eavesdropped on the conversation.

'It is all Pekkala's fault,' protested Klenovkin. 'He made threats against you, Comrade Stalin!'

'Threats.' Stalin echoed the word. Until that moment, he'd seen no reason to doubt the Camp Commandant's words, but now suspicions were gathering, like storm clouds in his mind. 'What did he say exactly?'

Klenovkin was not prepared for this. He had assumed that

the mere mention of a threat against the leader of the country would be enough. 'What exactly?' he stammered. 'Grave threats. Serious allegations, Comrade Stalin.'

There was another long pause. 'Pekkala never made any threats, did he?'

'Why would you say such a thing?' pleaded Klenovkin.

'It occurs to me now, Klenovkin, that Pekkala has stood before me many times, wearing that English cannon he keeps strapped against his chest, and I have never had cause to fear him. If Pekkala wanted to kill me he would do it first and talk about it afterwards. It is not in his nature to make threats. In short, Commandant, I suspect you are lying to me.'

Klenovkin's whole body went numb. The thought of continuing this deception seemed beyond any willpower he possessed. It was as if Stalin were staring straight into his soul. 'There were no threats,' he confessed.

'Listen to me carefully.' Stalin sounded eerily calm. 'I want you to take out the file of Inspector Pekkala.'

Klenovkin had expected Stalin to rage at him, but the softness in his leader's voice caught him by surprise. In his desperation, he took this as a sign that he might still come through unscathed. Sliding open his desk drawer, he removed Pekkala's file. 'I have it here – Prisoner 4745.'

'Now I want you to take out his information sheet.'

'I've got it. And what next, Comrade Stalin?'

'I want you to destroy it.'

'Destroy it?' he croaked. 'But why?'

'Because as far as the rest of the world is concerned, Inspector Pekkala was never there,' Stalin's voice was rising now, 'and I will not have the Kremlin embroiled in some Dalstroy inquiry into your failure to carry out your duties! Now burn the sheet, and this time there will be no delay.'

Stunned, Klenovkin took out his cigarette lighter and set fire to the corner of the paper. The document burned quickly. Soon all that remained was a fragile curl of ash, which Klenovkin dropped into the green metal garbage can beside his desk. 'It's done,' he said.

'Good! Now . . .'

There was a sharp click. The line from Borodok went dead.

'Poskrebyshev,' said Stalin.

Poskrebyshev held his breath and said nothing.

'Poskrebyshev, I know you are listening.'

Clumsily, Poskrebyshev snatched up the receiver and fumbled as he pressed it against his ear. 'Yes, Comrade Stalin!'

'Get me Major Kirov.'

*

Klenovkin lay on the floor of his study, eyes wide and staring at the ceiling. Clutched in his fist was a pistol, smoke still leaking from the barrel. A spray of blood peppered the wall. Beneath it lay the back of Klenovkin's skull, torn loose by the impact of the bullet and looking almost exactly like the handsome onyx ashtray on his desk, presented to him by Dalstroy for his fifteen years of loyal service.

*

As Pekkala walked around the clearing, the circulation slowly returned to his frozen legs and arms. At the edge of the trees, he came across some charred wooden beams. Next he kicked up some old glass jars, twisted by the fire which had consumed the cabin that once stood here.

In that same moment, he realised that these were the ruins of his own cabin, where he had lived for years as a tree marker for the Borodok lumber operation.

These melted shards of glass had once been part of a window in his cabin. Lacking other means, he had collected pickle jars left behind by the logging crews, stacked them on their sides with the mouths facing inward and then caulked the gaps with moss.

He remembered seeing the northern lights through those makeshift panes of glass; the vast curtains of green and white and pink rippling like some sea creature in the blackness of the ocean's depths.

Where Sedov lay bleeding, Pekkala recalled lying in the shade to escape the summer heat, chewing the bitter, clover-shaped leaves of wood sorrel to slake his thirst, and how the beds of dried lichen would rustle beneath the weight of his body, with a sound like a toothless old man eating crackers.

His eyes strayed to where his storage shed had been, constructed on poles above the ground to discourage mice from devouring his meagre supplies of pine nuts, sunflower seeds, and dried strips of a fish called grayling, which he sometimes caught in the streams that flowed through this valley.

In the decade since he had been here last, a number of young trees had grown around the clearing. The skeletons of brambles lay like coils of barbed wire among the puffed and blackened logs which had been a part of his home. It had taken him weeks to clear this space, and it startled him to see how thoroughly the forest had reclaimed the ground. In a few more years, there would be little to show that this place had been the centre of Pekkala's world, each tree and stone as known to him as the freckles constellated on his arms.

On the other side of the clearing, Kolchak crouched down before Sedov. He scooped up some snow and touched it against Sedov's lips.

'I told you it wouldn't be long before we were living like kings,' whispered Sedov, 'but I didn't think I'd reach the Promised Land so soon.'

Kolchak did not reply. Gently, he patted Sedov's cheek, then stood and walked away.

Tarnowski pulled him aside and, in an urgent whisper, said, 'We can't just leave him here.'

'And we can't take him with us,' replied Kolchak. 'He would only slow us down.'

'The guards from the camp will find Sedov. You don't know what they'll do to him.'

'It doesn't matter what they do,' Kolchak snapped. 'By the time those men get here, Sedov will be dead.'

The Ostyaks beckoned them back to the sledges.

'We must leave,' said one of them. 'This is a bad place.' He pointed to the ruins of Pekkala's cabin. 'A bad place,' he repeated.

The last Pekkala saw of Sedov, he was still sitting against the tree. His head had fallen forward, chin resting on his chest. Either he was sleeping, or else he was already dead.

They did not stop again until they reached the tracks, arriving at the place where the main line of the Trans-Siberian branched off towards the Borodok railhead.

Kolchak jumped down from his sledge. 'Now let's gather what belongs to us and get out of here.'

Still carrying the rifle he had stolen from the camp, Tarnowski stood in the middle of the tracks. Nervously, he looked up and down the rails, which glowed like new lead in the dingy light. 'It's hard to say, Colonel.'

Kolchak joined him on the tracks. 'What do you mean? You told me to bring you to the place where the railroad forked down towards the camp. Here is the fork. Now where is the gold?'

Tarnowski scratched at his face like a man who had stepped into cobwebs. 'When we came around a bend in the tracks . . .'

'Keep your voice down,' hissed Kolchak. 'If those Ostyaks learn where you've hidden the gold, they'll leave us behind and steal everything for themselves.'

From then on, the two men held a muttered conversation. 'We spotted a small cliff right beside a pond,' Tarnowski continued. 'We buried the crates on the other side of that pond. I thought we would be able to see it from here, but it's been a long time, Colonel. The mind plays tricks . . .'

'You realise, Lieutenant Tarnowski, that we are almost certainly being followed, by men whose incentive for killing us is that they will lose their own lives if they fail. It will take time to dig up the gold, especially since the ground is frozen. After that, it's a race for the border. I don't need to tell you that if they catch up with us again, no one's going to spare your life this time.'

'It can't be far Colonel,' Tarnowski reassured him. 'If we send a sledge in each direction, one of them is sure find it. The rest of us can wait here.'

The Ostyaks watched and waited, knowing they were not trusted. The caribou, sensing hostility in the air, shifted nervously in their harnesses.

'All right,' said Kolchak. 'Tell the Ostyaks what we're going to do. I'll go on one sledge and you take the other. If you're the one who spots the cliff, make sure you travel past it before you order the Ostyak to turn around. Otherwise, you'll give away the location without even saying a word.'

Climbing on board a sledge, Kolchak set off to the west along the tracks. Tarnowski turned eastwards.

The snow was still falling as they headed out.

The sledges faded into the white, as if cataracts clouded the eyes of those who watched them go.

*

In the compound of the Borodok camp, the body of Platov still knelt in a puddle of blood.

To Gramotin, staring down at him, the dead man looked like a Muslim kneeling on a red prayer rug.

Gramotin's face showed a mixture of anger and disgust. He could not make up his mind whether to be angry at the man who had murdered Platov, or disgusted at Platov for dying. He rested his hand on Platov's shoulder, as if to offer consolation.

Unbalanced by the weight of Gramotin's touch, the corpse keeled over on its side.

Gramotin picked up the rifle, sliding the bayonet out of Platov's neck. He cleaned the blade by wiping it on the dead man's coat, then shouldered the weapon and made his way to the Commandant's office.

Gramotin knocked on the door, slamming his fist against the flimsy wooden panels. There was no reply. Gramotin tried the handle but it was locked. Already out of patience, he raised one boot and kicked in the door.

The first thing Gramotin saw when he walked in was a splatter of blood on the wall. The room smelled of gun smoke. Then he caught sight of Klenovkin's body, lying stretched out on the floor behind his desk. The pistol was still in his hand. It was obvious that Klenovkin had shot himself.

Gramotin thought he'd found the reason why, lying on Klenovkin's desk.

It was the empty file belonging to prisoner 4745.

'Pekkala,' muttered Gramotin. He turned his head and spat on to the floor.

He was aware that the convict had escaped, having witnessed it with his own eyes. When the attack began, Gramotin had been up in one of the guard towers. Stepping out on to the walkway, he spotted Pekkala running towards the gates. He raised his rifle and fired at the running man. The first shot missed, which did not surprise Gramotin, since he was a poor shot even on his best days, but the second time he had Pekkala square in his sights. Before he had time to shoot, a bullet had come out of nowhere and struck the butt of his rifle, knocking him off his feet. Gramotin slipped off the walkway and fell into the ditch below. Landing in a dirty heap of snow, he had not suffered any injury, but by the time he had crawled out of the ditch, Pekkala and the Comitati were gone.

Since the Comitati had never before attempted to escape, Gramotin immediately reached the conclusion that Pekkala must have engineered the breakout. To cover his tracks, the convict had even gone so far as to break into Klenovkin's office in order to steal his own file. Having discovered this, Klenovkin must have realised that the blame would fall on him. In desperation, the man had taken his own life.

Now Klenovkin would have to be replaced; the very thing Gramotin had been desperate to avoid.

Melekov had botched his attempt to kill Pekkala.

Klenovkin, too, had bungled.

Even Stalin's orders from Moscow had failed to end the bastard's life.

I will have to do the job myself, thought Gramotin. He turned to leave but then turned back. Bending down, he prised the pistol from Klenovkin's hand, tucked it into his belt and strode out of the room.

*

Kirov arrived at the Kremlin.

The message had said it was urgent.

A guard escorted him to Stalin's office.

As the outer door opened, Poskrebyshev rose to his feet, with a particular casualness he reserved for men of lesser rank than the generals who usually paraded past his desk on their way to meet with Stalin. 'He is expecting you, Major.'

'Thank you,' replied Kirov, handing Poskrebyshev his cap.

'I will require your passbook as well, Major.'

Kirov removed the booklet from the top left pocket of his tunic and placed it on the desk.

Poskrebyshev nodded towards the double doors which led into Stalin's office. 'Now you can go in.'

Stalin was sitting at a table to the side of the main window, eating a tin of sardines in tomato sauce. The smell of them filled the air, metallic and vinegary. The lid of the sardine tin had been peeled back. It looked like a clock spring, the little key still jutting from the centre of the coil. With blunt fingers, Stalin chased the slippery and headless fish out of the sauce and paked them into his mouth.

Kirov waited in silence, his eyes fixed on Stalin's jaw muscles, which flexed beneath the pockmarked skin.

Stalin sucked the oily fish scales from his fingertips. Then he wiped his hands on a brightly patterned handkerchief which lay across his knee. 'Do you know why I sent Pekkala to Siberia?'

'To investigate the murder of Captain Ryabov.'

Stalin picked a fishbone from between his teeth. 'And do you know why I took such an interest in the death of this convict?'

'He was a member of the Kolchak Expedition.'

'Correct.'

'I also know that you believed there might be a connection between this man's death and the discovery that Colonel Kolchak could still be alive.'

Stalin nodded approvingly. 'That is all true, Major, but it is only a fraction of the whole picture.'

A look of confusion drifted across Kirov's face.

'Major Kirov, what I am about to tell you is privileged information. It cannot be discussed outside this room. Do you understand?'

'Of course, Comrade Stalin.'

'The case is more important than you realise. Even Inspector

Pekkala was not made aware of its full implications. This is not merely about solving a murder, or tracking down a man I believed I had personally disposed of many years ago.'

'Then what is it about, Comrade Stalin?'

'Gold,' he replied. 'Specifically the gold that Colonel Kolchak took with him when he departed from the city of Kazan.'

'But he didn't take it with him,' protested Kirov. 'He left it behind, and then it was picked up by the Czechs and they handed it over to us!'

'The Czechs handed over thirty-seven crates at Irkutsk, but I happen to know that there were fifty cases in that convoy. Thirteen crates are still missing.'

'And how do you know this, Comrade Stalin?'

'We had an informant, one of the groundskeepers on the Imperial estate. He was the one who told us that Kolchak had departed from Tsarskoye Selo, and he even counted the number of boxes on those wagons as they rolled off the grounds of the estate.'

'And you think Kolchak held on to those thirteen crates?'

'I have always suspected it, but as of today I am virtually certain.'

'Then why did the Red Cavalry not find it when they overran the Expedition?'

'Kolchak must have hidden it somewhere along the way.'

'Exactly how much gold are we talking about, Comrade Stalin?'

'Each case contained twenty-four bars and each bar weighed one half *pood* in the old Imperial weight system.'

'How much is that by today's reckoning?'

'One half *pood* is approximately 18 pounds. Twenty-four

bars at 18 pounds each adds up to 432 pounds. Thirteen cases means over 5,600 pounds. That's two and a half tons of gold.' Stalin spouted these numbers as if he had memorised them long ago. 'Not an insignificant amount, you will agree.'

'It is more than a man like me can even dream about,' agreed Kirov, 'but why didn't you tell Pekkala any of this, Comrade Stalin?'

'Because I knew that if I sent him to investigate a murder, he would do anything to solve it. But if I sent him in search of treasure, however valuable, he would tell me to find someone else.'

'Then why didn't you find someone else, Comrade Stalin?'

'I had a hunch that solving the crime would lead Pekkala straight to Kolchak, who could then be placed under arrest. With the Colonel in custody, we would soon learn the location of the missing Imperial Reserves.'

Kirov imagined one of the Butyrka interrogation cells, its floor and walls splashed with Kolchak's blood.

'Unfortunately,' continued Stalin, 'I suspect that Pekkala has managed to find the gold on his own.'

'Then surely that is good news! You can bring him home now.'

With his thumb, Stalin pushed away the tin of sardines. 'Let me ask you, Major: if Pekkala has indeed located the gold, do you think it is possible that he might have decided to keep it for himself?'

Kirov laughed at the suggestion.

Stalin's eyes turned glassy. 'Comrade Major, do you find this a source of amusement?'

Kirov's smile vanished like the flame blown off a match.

'What I mean, Comrade Stalin, is have you seen the way Pekkala lives? That tiny apartment. The food he eats? The coat he wears? He gets his things from Linsky's! You could hand Pekkala a whole bar of gold and he'd probably just use it as a paperweight.'

Stalin studied the young major with a mixture of bemusement and respect. 'We are talking about more than a single bar of gold, Major Kirov.'

'But we are also talking about Pekkala!'

Stalin made a noise in the back of his throat. 'I see your point. Nevertheless, Major, I've just received word that Pekkala has escaped from Borodok.'

'Escaped? How can that be? He is not even a prisoner!'

'Prisoner or not, he has disappeared, along with several men who were once part of the Kolchak Expedition. I am concerned that returning to Borodok has had a greater effect on Pekkala than I anticipated. His allegiances, the old and the new, have been brought into conflict. He may not want the gold for himself but he has fallen in with people who do, one of whom, I fear, may be the Colonel himself. Pekkala's wish to deny me what is mine may be as strong as their desire to possess it.'

'You speak as if he has already betrayed you, which I refuse to believe he has done. The answer is simple, Comrade Stalin. Inspector Pekkala has been kidnapped.'

'Kidnapped?' Now it was Stalin's turn to look surprised.

'Yes, undoubtedly. And who is in charge of rescuing him?'

'Assuming you are correct, as of this moment, you are.'

'Me?' spluttered Kirov. 'But how on earth am I supposed to track him down?'

Stalin smashed his fist on the desk. 'I don't care! I want to know what happened to my gold! And when you find that Finnish sorcerer, kidnapped or otherwise, you will remind him that his duty is to the future, not the past.'

'If you truly want him found, why not send a company of soldiers? Why not a whole army? What good can I possibly do?'

'Precision is required here, Major Kirov. Sending an army after half a dozen men is like trying to remove a splinter from your eye with a pitchfork.'

'But Comrade Stalin, surely there must be people closer to the scene...'

'The reason I am sending you,' interrupted Stalin, 'is the same reason I sent Pekkala after Kolchak. He knows you. He trusts you. He will think twice before he tears your head off. And if I am right that Inspector Pekkala has chosen to forget his duties, you may be the only person on this earth who can remind him what they are. And as for an army, you may have one if you want. By the time you walk out of this room, you will be able to have anything you desire.' Stalin breathed in sharply and unleashed a deafening shout. 'Poskrebyshev!'

A moment later, the double doors opened. The bald man appeared and clicked his heels.

'Do you have Major Kirov's papers?'

Poskrebyshev held up the red identification booklet.

'Bring it to me.'

In a few strides, Poskrebyshev had crossed the room. He laid the passbook down on Stalin's desk.

'Pen,' said Stalin.

Poskrebyshev lifted one from the top pocket of his tunic and handed it over.

Stalin opened the booklet, scribbled his signature inside, then held it out to Kirov.

Kirov saw that a page had been added to his identification book. His heart stumbled in his chest as he read what was written inside.

THE PERSON IDENTIFIED IN THIS DOCUMENT IS ACTING UNDER THE DIRECT ORDERS OF COMRADE STALIN.

DO NOT QUESTION OR DETAIN HIM.

HE IS AUTHORISED TO WEAR CIVILIAN CLOTHES, TO CARRY WEAPONS, TO TRANSPORT PROHIBITED ITEMS, INCLUDING POISON, EXPLOSIVES AND FOREIGN CURRENCY.

HE MAY PASS INTO RESTRICTED AREAS AND MAY REQUISITION EQUIPMENT OF ALL TYPES, INCLUDING WEAPONS AND VEHICLES.

IF HE IS KILLED OR INJURED, IMMEDIATELY NOTIFY THE BUREAU OF SPECIAL OPERATIONS.

'Congratulations,' said Stalin. 'You are now the holder of a Shadow Pass.'

Finding himself suddenly too nervous to speak, Kirov made do with a salute and turned to leave.

'Before you go . . .'

Stalin's voice stopped Kirov in his tracks.

'Let me make one thing very clear, Major. If you fail to bring Pekkala back alive, I will not hesitate to call in others who will certainly bring him back dead. Now go, and find him quickly, any way you can.'

While they waited for the others to return, the two remaining Ostyaks drove their sledges back into the forest, out of sight of the tracks.

There, the caribou gathered beside a rocky outcrop and began to gnaw upon the brittle moss which grew in black scabs on the stone.

As Pekkala watched them eat, he remembered the taste of that moss. Only in winter, when he had completely exhausted his food supplies did he resort to eating it. Mixing the brittle flakes with snow, he boiled them down until the moss disintegrated into a gelatinous black mass. Its taste was bitter, and the consistency so slimy that he often could not keep it down. He hoped it would not be their meal tonight.

It was getting dark now and Pekkala set about gathering wood for a fire, prising dead branches from the frozen ground. The flames would act as a beacon to ensure that the returning sledges did not overshoot them in the dark. Any smoke from the fire would be hidden in the snow clouds, so they would not be spotted from the camp.

The Ostyaks, meanwhile, took up their antique flintlock rifles. Moving on large round snowshoes made from bent willow and laced with honey-coloured bands of animal gut, they vanished into the forest in search of food.

Only minutes had gone by when Pekkala heard the muffled crack of gunfire. When the Ostyaks reappeared, one of them was carrying two dead rabbits, their long ears clutched in his fist.

With the help of some gunpowder emptied from a bullet

cartridge, Pekkala soon had a fire going. Pine branches crackled and white smoke bloomed from the skeletal branches of white birch.

*

As soon as he departed from the Kremlin, Kirov drove straight to his office, gathered up a few things for the journey, then travelled to the railway junction where he had last seen Pekkala.

His hastily conceived plan was to climb aboard the first train headed east and not to stop until he reached the camp at Borodok. Once there, he would commandeer whatever men and supplies were available and set out in search of the men who had kidnapped Pekkala.

Arriving at the station, Kirov was dismayed to find no trains at the platform. At first, the whole place appeared deserted, but then the door to the guard shack opened and a man in dark blue overalls stepped out to meet him.

It was Edvard Kasinec, master of the V-4 junction.

'When is the next train leaving?' asked Kirov.

'Not for another three days,' Kasinec replied, 'but you must understand, Comrade Major; the only passengers which go through here are convicts bound for Siberia.'

'I realise that. Siberia is where I need to go.'

'Major, I assure you there are more comfortable ways to get there than in the wagons of a prison transport.'

'My destination is a prison, Borodok, to be precise.'

Kasinec's eyebrows arched with surprise. 'What could possess a man to go there of his own free will?'

Kirov was only halfway through his explanation when Kasinec, hearing Pekkala's name, ushered him into the station house.

The place was crowded with radio equipment, well-thumbed books of timetables and requisition slips impaled on long metal spikes. Kasinec went over to the far wall, where a large map showed the rail system for the entire country, the tracks laid out in red like the arteries of an animal stripped of its flesh.

Kasinec's finger traced along the line of the Trans-Siberian Railroad, through towns whose names had been smudged into illegibility by the constant jab of fingerprints, until it branched off and dead-ended just north of the border with China. 'Here,' he said, tapping his fingernail against a patch of green, surrounded by a chalky whiteness on the map. 'This is the valley of Krasnagolyana.'

For the first time, as Kirov stared at the map, he understood the enormity of the task he had been given. Stalin had demanded the impossible. 'It can't be done,' he muttered. 'I might as well give up before I start. How can I possibly track down anyone in that wilderness?'

'On the contrary,' Kasinec told him, 'these men should be easy to find. If they have escaped from Borodok, they'll naturally head towards China. Once they have crossed the border, they will be out of reach of Soviet authorities. If they head in any other direction, they will remain in Russia and it would only be a matter of time before they were recaptured.'

'So they head east,' said Kirov. 'That narrows it down, but you have not exactly pinpointed their route, stationmaster.'

'Indeed I have. These men will follow the railroad.'

'Even if they are travelling on foot? What about the other roads?'

'That's the thing, Major. In that part of the country, there are no other roads, especially at this time of the year. But the tracks of the Trans-Siberian are always kept open, no matter what the season or the weather.' Now he pointed to a red dot, which marked the next station on the eastbound route, some distance from the place where the Krasnagolyana railhead joined with the main route of the Trans-Siberian. The name of this place was Nikolsk, and it stood just to the west of a town named Chita. Here, the Trans-Siberian Railroad split in two. The north fork, which remained within the boundaries of Russia, made a wide arc through the towns of Nerchinsk, Belogorsk and Khabarovsk before dropping south again to reach the port of Vladivostok on the Pacific Ocean. The other rail line dipped into China, cutting through the town of Harbin before crossing into Russia once again and terminating, like the northern fork, at Vladivostok.

'This is not only the quickest way for them to reach China,' said Kasinec, tracing his finger along the southern branch. 'It is, for all practical purposes, the only way.'

Kirov realised that everything the stationmaster had said made sense. He was still by no means convinced that intercepting Pekkala's kidnappers could be accomplished, but the task no longer seemed to lie beyond the bounds of possibility.

'How long will it take them to reach Nikolsk?' asked Kirov.

'From Borodok? Five days, maybe, if they are travelling on foot. If they have sledges or skis, it could be only half that time.'

Kirov walked to the door and looked out over the empty railyard. 'And no train for three days.'

'That is correct, Comrade Major.'

'And three days from now, if I do climb aboard that train, how long will it take to reach Borodok?'

'A week at least, more likely two. And Borodok has its own rail line which branches off the Trans-Siberian. No trains are scheduled to arrive in Borodok for another month. The best they could do is drop you at the railhead and you could make your way on foot to the camp, although I expect you might freeze to death first.'

Kirov felt a weight settle on his heart, as if someone were kneeling on his chest. 'So it cannot be done after all.'

'I did not say that, Comrade Major.'

Kirov spun around. 'Then what are you saying?'

'I do have one idea. But what I have in mind requires knowing friends in high places.'

Kirov tapped the passbook in his chest pocket. 'If my friends were any higher, Comrade Kasinec, they would die from lack of oxygen.'

*

It was after dark when Sergeant Gramotin and the six guards he had ordered to accompany him trudged out of the camp.

'Are you sure this is a good idea?' asked one of the guards. 'Going after those savages at night?'

Gramotin did not reply. He was so disgusted with the way his men had behaved when the attack broke out that he could not bring himself to answer their stupid questions. If they had performed as Gramotin had trained them, not a single convict would have escaped and the Ostyaks would now be lying dead in a heap in the middle of the compound. Instead, his men had fled en masse to the guardhouse and barricaded themselves inside. He would have liked to execute the whole lot of them on the spot, and except for the fact that this would have required at least two of the guards to help him with the paperwork afterwards, since he could not read or write, Gramotin would have killed them all by now.

For Gramotin the only bright spot in this otherwise shameful and disastrous day was that Klenovkin had shot himself. Dead men made excellent scapegoats, and now the blame for the escape could rest entirely with Klenovkin. Had he lived, the Commandant would have wasted no time blaming someone else for the catastrophe and Gramotin knew full well that it would have been him.

Gramotin realised, however, that this did not let him off the hook entirely. As sergeant of the guard, he was obliged to account for his actions. In his mind Gramotin had already voyaged ahead to the hearing which would undoubtedly take place. The first question they would ask, those stone-faced functionaries of the Dalstroy inquiry board, would be if he had made any attempt to pursue the men who escaped. If his answer was no, the inquiry would convict him of negligence. That would be the end of his career and probably his life, as well.

This was why Gramotin had decided to set out now, even though he had serious doubts as to whether he and his men were any match for the combined force of those sunburned, reindeer-herding primitives and the tattooed Comitati, whom he despised every bit as much as they loathed him.

After an hour of marching, they came to the place where the

Ostyak sledges had turned into the woods. The snow was deeper here and the going made harder for Gramotin by the two ammunition bandoliers he carried criss-crossed over his chest. By holding a candle lamp in front of him, he was able to see the sledge tracks, even though they were now almost covered by the falling snow.

After a few dozen paces, Gramotin stopped to catch his breath. 'All right,' he wheezed, 'two minutes' rest, but no more.' It was at this point that Gramotin realised he was alone.

The other guards were still back on the road.

Gramotin raised the lantern. Shadows see-sawed through the trees, obscuring his view of the soldiers. 'What's wrong?' he shouted. 'Why have you stopped?'

'You can't expect us to chase them into the forest,' called one of the guards.

'And in the middle of the night,' another man chimed in.

'That is exactly what I expect! If we wait until morning, they'll be too far away to catch. Now then! Who is with me?'

The only reply he received was the sound of wind through the tops of the trees, like static on a radio.

Cursing wildly, Gramotin made his way back to the road and discovered, to his astonishment, that his men had disappeared. Their footsteps in the snow showed that they were already on their way back to camp. 'Bastards!' he howled into the dark.

The darkness swallowed his words.

In that moment, he realised how much he missed Platov. 'Platov would have stayed with me,' muttered Gramotin. When he thought of the dead man, kneeling in a pool of his own blood, tears flooded into Gramotin's eyes. Angrily he wiped them away with the rough wool of his glove. I will kill them for this, he decided. I will kill them all, guards and prisoners alike, starting with Inspector Pekkala.

Alone, he turned and trudged back along the trail, following the Ostyaks, the frail glow of his lamp growing fainter as the trees closed up around him.

*

Kirov's Emka skidded to a halt outside the control room of Afanasiev airport, a small installation reserved for military flights.

He had followed Stationmaster Kasinec's instructions to the nearest airfield, only five minutes' drive north of the V-4 railway station.

'I will notify the airfield you are coming!' Kasinec had shouted as Kirov got into his car. 'I'll tell them you are bound for Vladivostok!'

Out on the runway, a plane had just taxied into position, ready for takeoff. The machine was painted green, with red stars on its wings and tail. It had a long cockpit canopy to accommodate both a pilot and a navigator/gunner.

Kirov cut his engine, bolted from the car and ran inside.

The traffic controller sat behind a radio, mouse-eared by a large set of headphones. 'Are you Kirov?'

'Yes,' he gasped.

'He's waiting for you,' shouted the controller. 'Go!'

As Kirov ran out to the plane, the pilot leaned out of the cockpit and pointed to a fur-lined flying suit draped over the wing. 'Put it on and get in.'

Kirov did as he was told. The suit smelled of old tobacco

smoke, and its cuffs and elbows were tarnished black from use. He climbed into the rear seat of the plane, which faced towards the tail.

'Buckle your straps!' shouted the pilot.

The straps lay on the seat, tangled like a nest of snakes, and Kirov was still trying to figure out how they worked when the engine roared and the plane lurched forward.

Seconds later, they were climbing steeply into the night sky.

*

'Poskrebyshev!'

'Damn,' muttered the secretary. He had been almost out the door when Stalin's voice crackled through the intercom. The Boss had already made him stay late and now Poskrebyshev wondered if he would be here all night, as had happened many times before. Cautiously, he pressed the intercom button. 'Yes, Comrade Stalin?'

'How many bars of gold do you think a man could carry?'

Poskrebyshev had no idea. He had never seen a bar of gold before. He imagined them to be small and thin, like slabs of chocolate.

'Poskrebyshev!'

'I would say . . .' he paused. 'Twenty?'

'You idiot! No one can carry that much.'

Poskrebyshev tried to imagine why on earth Stalin would be asking him such a question. Most of the time, even when Stalin's ideas struck him as insane, Poskrebyshev was still able to glimpse some logic behind the insanity. This was, for Poskrebyshev, the most frightening aspect of working for Stalin – that the musings of the great man, even though they sometimes filled his mind with terror at their implications, were nonetheless easy to follow. But this Poskrebyshev could not fathom, and as innocent as the act of carrying a bar of gold might seem to be, he knew that what lay at the end of Stalin's train of thought was blood and pain and death. All he could hope for was that it might not be his own. 'Ten!' Poskrebyshev blurted out. 'I meant to say ten bars.'

A sigh drifted over the intercom. 'Go home. You are no help at all, Poskrebyshev.'

Poskrebyshev gestured rudely at the intercom. Then he went home for his supper.

*

It was after dark when Kolchak's sledge returned from the east, having found nothing that resembled the cliff Tarnowski had described.

Grim and silent, Kolchak remained on the tracks, staring into the darkness while he waited for Tarnowski to come back.

At last Tarnowski appeared. He and the Ostyak were half frozen. Together with the reindeer, they looked more like ghosts than living things under their crust of snow. Tarnowski stumbled off the sledge and collapsed by the fire, where his clothes immediately began to steam. 'I found it!' he said, the words barely decipherable through his locked jaw and chattering teeth.

For the first time Pekkala had seen, Lavrenov smiled. In that moment, the years of prison life, which had drained the blood from his face, deadened his eyes, and creased his skin like a blunt knife drawn through butter, all fell away. For a moment, he looked young again.

Kolchak pulled Tarnowski aside. 'Did you do as I told you? Did you travel past the place before you turned around?'

'Yes, just as you ordered, Colonel. The Ostyaks do not know where it is hidden.'

'All right,' he said, releasing his grip upon Tarnowski's arm. Then he nodded with approval. 'Very good, Lieutenant.'

The Ostyaks brought out the rabbits they had shot. Keeping one for themselves, they handed the other to Kolchak.

The Ostyaks skinned their rabbit. Slicing the flesh from its bones, they ate it raw, tearing at the rose-coloured meat.

Kolchak watched them with a combination of hunger and disgust.

Seeing that the Colonel was about to give up and go hungry, Pekkala borrowed a knife from one of the Ostyaks and used it to cut two wide strips of bark from a white birch tree. He curled one of them to form a cylinder and laced it together with the piece of string which served as a belt for his quilted trousers. He sewed the other piece of bark around the base to form a container and filled it with snow. Next Pekkala gathered some stones from the railroad tracks and put them in the fire. When the stones were hot, he scooped them from the flames and let them fall into the container, immediately plunging his hand into the snow to stop the skin from burning. In a couple of minutes, the snow in the container had melted. By shifting the stones back and forth from the fire to the snow, Pekkala was able to boil the water in less than half an hour. When the meat was cooked, Pekkala divided it among the four men. They sat by the fire, puffing clouds of steam as they devoured the scalding shreds of flesh.

From the other side of the fire, the Ostyaks watched and whispered to each other.

After the meal, Kolchak leaned over to Pekkala.

'You are shivering,' he said.

Pekkala nodded. Even this close to the fire, he had to clench his teeth to stop them from chattering. The quilted *telogreika* jacket he had been issued was already several generations old when he arrived at Borodok. It had been repaired so many times that there were more patches showing than the original cloth. These *telogreikas* were efficient only until they got wet. After that the only hope was to dry them over a fire or to wait for a layer of ice to form over the outer surface of the cloth, which would then act as a wind break. Pekkala's jacket was so old that neither option worked. The cotton padding had been soaked and dried so many times that it no longer retained the heat of his body. In his daily life at the camp, Pekkala had always been able to retreat to the kitchen and warm up next to the stove, but this journey had chilled him to the bone.

'Here,' said Kolchak, unbuttoning his own jacket and handing it to Pekkala. 'Take it, Inspector. It's the least I can do in exchange for a cooked meal in this wilderness.'

'That is very kind of you, but I cannot accept it.'

'Why not?'

'You'll just end up freezing instead.'

'Look!' Kolchak opened the flap of his jacket, revealing a fur vest he was wearing underneath. 'I will be fine, and I need you alive, Pekkala. There are too few of us left, as it is.'

Gratefully, Pekkala traded garments. He had not even done

up the buttons before he felt the warmth trickling through his veins.

'Don't worry, Pekkala,' said Kolchak, slapping him on the shoulder, 'it won't be long before you're wearing decent clothes again, sleeping in a bed instead of on the ground, and eating with a knife and fork, all in the company of friends.'

Pekkala nodded and smiled, but the mention of friends sent a wave of sadness through his mind as he thought of Kirov and the potted-plant jungle he had made of their office, the meals he had prepared each Friday afternoon, the pleas for Pekkala to buy his coats from any other place but Linsky's. It twisted in him like a knife that he had never been able to thank Kirov for the time they'd spent working together.

Pekkala was jolted from these thoughts by one of the Ostyaks, who approached him wearing the blood-smeared pelts of the rabbits tucked into his belt. The man squatted down beside Pekkala and picked up the container he had used for boiling the meat. 'You made this?' he asked, carefully shaping the unfamiliar words with his thin and sunburned lips.

Pekkala nodded.

'Where did you learn how?' asked the man.

'I taught myself. I had to. I used to live here.'

'Lived? In the camp?'

'No,' explained Pekkala, taking in the forest with a sweep of his arm. 'Here.'

The Ostyak smiled and shook his head. 'No,' he said. 'No man lives here.'

Pekkala pressed the flat of his hand upon the pelt he had cut from the rabbit. The he raised his arm, like a man about to take an oath, showing his palm and fingers red with the gore of the dead animal. 'Do you remember me now?' he asked. 'I used to be the man with the bloody hands.'

For a moment, the Ostyak only stared at him. Then he made a noise in his throat, got up and walked away. The Ostyak sat down amongst his friends and they began another whispered conversation, glancing now and then towards Pekkala.

He wished he could explain to them that the one man they really had to fear was nowhere near this forest.

How distant Stalin must seem to them, thought Pekkala. How safe they must feel in their hideaways out on the tundra, with only wolves and each other for company. But Stalin would learn of their betrayal, and he would bring his vengeance down upon them. Perhaps not for a year, or several years, but he would never forget. And what the Ostyaks could not fathom, even in their nightmares, was that Stalin would hunt them to extinction. He would tear their world to pieces, rather than let them go free.

At last, the exhaustion of the day began to overtake him. As Pekkala's eyes drooped shut, the last thing he saw was a gust of sparks from the fire, skittering away across the snow as if some phantom blacksmith were hammering hot steel upon an anvil.

*

All night, Gramotin marched through the forest.

It was no longer snowing. The moon appeared through shredded clouds, filling the forest with blue shadows.

When the candle burned out in Gramotin's lantern, he threw it away and pressed on, following the blurred furrows of the Ostyak sledges, which he found that he could see by moonlight.

As Gramotin scrambled through the drifts, his energy began to fade. From his pocket, he removed a *paika* ration he had taken from the kitchen the day before. Gnawing into the tough, gritty bread, he felt guilty. The truth was, although Gramotin stole these rations all the time, normally he never actually ate them. Instead, he would give them out to those convicts whose conduct irritated him less than usual on that particular day.

Gramotin's reasons for handing out the bread were complicated, even to himself. In his years as a sergeant of the guards at Borodok, he had learned that the best way to rule effectively over the prisoners was to be known as a man who could, on occasion, exhibit faint signs of humanity, instead of living as a sadist every minute of his life. These acts of generosity, small as they were, gave the inmates of Borodok hope that if they did as they were told, they might, as a bare possibility, receive treatment slightly less than barbaric.

Ruling over the guards was a more complicated proposition. Kindness did not work on them. They were like a pack of dogs who would obey Gramotin as long as they felt he was more dangerous than they were. The minute they saw any weakness in him, they would either close in for the kill, or else abandon him completely, as they had done back on the road.

It was the first time they had ever challenged his authority. Clearly, they did not expect him to return, or else they would never have taken such a risk. Gramotin knew that the only way to win back their respect was to do the one thing they refused to do themselves.

The fact that he might become lost did not bother Gramotin. Neither did he dwell upon the fact that the Comitati would probably butcher him when he finally caught up with their group. The only thing Gramotin cared about now, as he stumbled onward into the darkness, was his reputation.

*

Sedov was having a dream.

In it he was a child again, reliving the moment when his mother caught him hiding in the woodshed and eating a pot of home-made plum jam which he had stolen from the cupboard. The theft had been spontaneous and the young Sedov realised only once he got to his hiding place that he had nothing with which to eat the jam. So he used his fingers, which soon became a sticky mass of tentacles.

From the pocket of her apron, his mother whipped out the large handkerchief which she always kept ready for such occasions, licked at it ferociously and advanced upon him saying, 'You mucky boy!'

Sedov winced while his mother scraped away the jam stains around the corner of his mouth.

'Who is going to want that jam,' she shouted, 'after you have been sticking your dirty hands in it?'

'Some other mucky boy, I suppose.'

Now, in this dream, Sedov was back in the woodshed and his mother was scrubbing away at his face with her coarse spit-dampened handkerchief. 'Stop it!' he protested. 'I can wipe my own face!'

Waking with a shudder, Sedov was amazed to find himself still breathing.

It was morning. The sun had come out, glistening on the ice-sheathed branches of the trees.

A large dog was standing right in front of him. It had been licking his face. It had a shiny black nose and a long, narrow muzzle which was white around the sides and brown along the top. Its ears were thickly furred and set well back on its head. It was the eyes which most impressed Sedov. They were a warm yellow-brown and looked intelligent.

The dog seemed as startled as Sedov. It jumped back and growled at him from a safe distance.

Sedov noticed three more dogs lurking about at the edge of the clearing. Then it dawned on him that these were not dogs at all. They were wolves.

'Mother of God,' he whispered to himself.

The wolf, whose raspy tongue had translated in Sedov's dream into the handkerchief of his long-dead mother, took another step back and growled at him again, jowls quivering above its teeth.

The other wolves stepped nervously from side to side, whining as they waited to see what would happen next.

Sedov knew he did not have the strength to fight them off. He doubted he could even stand. All he could manage was to raise one hand and feebly shoo them away.

No sooner had Sedov's hand flopped back into his lap than the wolves turned and fled into the forest. In a matter of seconds, they had vanished in amongst the trees.

Sedov had not expected such a good result and, in spite of his predicament, allowed himself a moment of self-congratulation. It was then that he heard the creak of footsteps in the snow. Looking up, he glimpsed what appeared to be a snowman dressed in rags, struggling towards him with a rifle slung across its back.

The man stopped in the clearing. His gaze wandered from the ruins of Pekkala's cabin, to the hoof marks of the reindeer, to the canary-yellow patches in the snow where men and animals had relieved themselves.

When he finally noticed Sedov, the man let out a cry. As he struggled to remove his rifle, he tripped and tumbled over backwards. Instead of scrambling to his feet again, he just lay there, panting clouds of vapour, overcome with exhaustion.

'Gramotin?' croaked Sedov.

Gramotin lifted his head. Frozen breath had turned his hair into a mane of frost. 'Sedov? Is that you?'

'Yes.'

'Where are the others?'

'Gone.'

Gramotin clambered up until he was resting on his knees. 'And they left you?'

'I am wounded,' explained Sedov.

From the trees above, water dripped from melting icicles, sprinkling like diamonds upon Gramotin's head.

'They shouldn't have left you.' Gramotin's voice rose with indignation. He limped over to Sedov and flopped down beside him.

'A wolf licked my face,' remarked Sedov. 'I thought it was a dream.'

'A wolf?' Gramotin looked around nervously.

'Where are the other guards?'

Gramotin leaned over and spat. 'There are no others. Only me. The rest all ran away.'

'Cowards,' muttered Sedov.

'Looks like we've both been let down.' Although Gramotin would never have admitted it, he was glad to have run into Sedov, as opposed to any of the others. Tarnowski would either have killed him by now or would have died trying and Lavrenov would be wheedling some deal to save his life. Pekkala, being a Finn, would probably have vanished like a ghost. But Sedov was not like those men. There had always been a certain gentleness about him, which Gramotin could not help admiring, even as he despised this fatal weakness in Sedov's character. Men like Sedov did not usually last more than a few months in the camp. The ones who tended to live longest were men more like himself, who showed a minimum of compassion for those around them, and who lied and cheated and stole. If they did not arrive at Borodok that way, they soon learned how to behave that way if they wanted to survive. Sedov had been the exception. Not only had Sedov endured, but he had never lost that fundamental goodness which he brought with him to the camp. It was not in Gramotin's nature to tolerate goodness. At Borodok, it represented a useless appendage, like that of an animal doomed to extinction, and it was in Gramotin's nature to attempt to beat it out of Sedov, year after year, with a relentless cruelty that astonished even himself.

Sitting there beside this wounded man, who neither grovelled for his life, nor used up his last breath to kill another human being, Gramotin experienced remorse. This had never happened to him before and it immediately plunged him into a state of great confusion. He felt an overwhelming urge to perform some act of kindness, however small, to atone for all the suffering he had caused.

Gramotin considered apologising to Sedov, but the idea struck him as absurd. Then he toyed with the notion of abandoning his search for Pekkala and carrying Sedov back to the camp hospital. But this idea Gramotin also cast aside, knowing that even if Sedov did recover from his injury, which looked doubtful, he would be shot for attempting to escape.

As Gramotin pondered this, he pulled a loaf of *paika* bread from his pocket, broke off a piece and pressed it into Sedov's mouth. Then he bit off a slab for himself.

For a while, there was no sound except the two men chewing on the stale bread.

'I need you to do me a favour,' said Sedov.

'I just did,' mumbled Gramotin, his mouth still full of bread.

'A bigger favour.'

'What are you talking about?'

'I need you to shoot me.'

Gramotin turned and stared at Sedov.

'You've shot plenty of people before,' Sedov reasoned.

'Not like this.' Hurriedly, Gramotin stood, leaning on his rifle as if it were a walking stick. 'I have to go.'

'What if the wolves come back?'

For a moment, the permanent rage which had moulded itself into the contours of Gramotin's face completely vanished. Instead, he just looked terrified. From his pocket, he removed the gun he had taken off Klenovkin's body. Tossing it into Sedov's lap, he turned and quickly walked away. Although he knew that Sedov would not use that gun to harm him, it dawned on Gramotin that, if the positions had been reversed, he would have used whatever bullets remained in that pistol to shoot Sedov dead, wolves or no wolves. He would not have been able to help himself. This, too, was in his nature.

Gramotin had not gone far when he heard the flat crack of a pistol back in the woods. He paused, wondering whether to go back and retrieve the gun. Remembering the wolves, he decided against it and pushed on.

Three hours later, beside the Trans-Siberian Railroad, Gramotin found the Comitati encampment from the night before. They had not been gone long. Their fire was still smoking. Now that Gramotin had stopped moving, his sweat immediately began to cool. He could feel the warmth being stripped from his body, like layers peeled off an onion. Without a second thought, Gramotin threw himself down on the smouldering ground and lay there, fingers dug into the ashes, warming himself. Minutes passed. The heat fanned out across his ribs like a bird spreading its wings. Only when he could smell the wool of his coat beginning to singe did he finally get to his feet. He slapped the embers from his clothes and scrambled up the embankment to the track.

The sight of these rails brought back to Gramotin memories of the Revolution, when he had fought against the White Army of Admiral Kolchak, then against the Czech Legion, and finally against the Americans of the ill-fated Siberian Expeditionary Force. Of these three, it was the Czechs who had left him with the deepest mental scars. They had commandeered trains, fitted them with guns, blast shields and battering rams, bestowed on them heroic names, then rode the tracks to Vladivostok, destroying everything in their path. Gramotin himself had taken part in an ambush against one of these armoured convoys. Crouching with a dozen comrades in hastily dug fox-holes, he had fired an entire machine-gun belt at a Czech loco-motive, christened the *Orlik* in large white letters painted on its front, and barely left a blemish on its steel hide. And then that train, without even bothering to slow down, had turned its guns upon the place where Gramotin was hiding with his men and chopped the earth to pieces. All Gramotin could do was cower in his hole and wait for the shooting to stop. It was over in less than a minute.

For a while, the only sound was the groaning of the wounded.

Then, to his horror, Gramotin heard a shriek of brakes in the distance. The metal beast reversed until it came level with the place where the Czechs had been ambushed.

Seeing men jump down from the train, Gramotin grabbed the nearest body from among his bullet-riddled comrades and hid himself beneath the bloody corpse.

With pistols in their hands, the Czechs searched among the dead, shooting the wounded and emptying their pockets of anything that caught their eye. Gramotin trembled uncontrol-lably as one man, wearing a heavy turtleneck sweater and a sleeveless leather jerkin which came down to his knees, pulled aside the corpse under which he had been hiding.

Too terrified to run, Gramotin lay there with his face pressed against the earth, waiting for a bullet in the head.

But the bullet never came.

Ransacking the corpse, the Czech gathered up cigarettes, pa-pers of identification, a compass and a small linen bag contain-ing shreds of dried salmon, but he did not touch Gramotin.

There was no doubt in Gramotin's mind that the man could

see him breathing. He had no idea why his life had been spared. In years to come, this strange act of kindness so tormented Gramotin that there were times he wished he had been killed along with the rest.

When the Czechs finally left, Gramotin walked among the bodies and discovered he was the only survivor.

As evening fell on that day of the ambush, Gramotin glimpsed the smoke-like shadows of wolves approaching through the forest. Climbing a tall pine tree, he clung to the prickly branches, sap gluing his hands to the bark, while the wolf pack feasted on the dead.

All night, the sound of powerful jaws crunching cartilage and bone echoed in Gramotin's skull. When morning came, the wolves were gone, leaving behind an abattoir of human flesh.

Three days later, Gramotin was picked up by a band of Cossacks patrolling the tracks, by which time he had become so deranged that they had no choice except to tie him up. The Cossacks slung him over a pack horse and when they came to the nearest village, they dumped him in the middle of the street and kept on riding. Rolling in the mud, Gramotin raged and spat until at last the villagers knocked him out with a wooden mallet. It was a week before the villagers dared to untie him and another week before he spoke in any language they, or even he, could understand.

A thousand times since then, that Czech locomotive had ridden through his dreams. These days, even the sound of a train in the distance summoned from Gramotin's mind horrors so vivid that he could not tell which ones were real and which ones his crippled brain had conjured into life.

Standing on these tracks again filled Gramotin with such dread that it took all of his resolve not to turn tail and run back to camp.

The Ostyaks had been here. Gramotin could see the hoof marks of their animals. But the sledges seemed to have gone off in more than one direction. Those who had headed west, back into Russia, were none of his concern. Pekkala and the Comitati would be heading towards China and they were the ones he was after. Turning to the east, Gramotin set off walking down the tracks.

*

As the plane made its way towards Siberia, Kirov stared at moonlight glimmering off the wings.

What if I can't find Pekkala, he wondered. What if I do find him but it's too late and those bastards have killed him? What will happen to this country without the Emerald Eye? What will happen to me? Kirov's fists clenched as he thought of what a poor student he had been. I could never keep up with Pekkala's logic, he told himself. Things that made perfect sense to him were total mysteries to me. I must have been a constant disappointment. I should never have pestered him so much about those clothes he wears. Please let me find Pekkala, Kirov prayed to the outlawed gods. Please let me bring him home safe.

This wandering through the labyrinth of his mind was interrupted by the voice of the pilot, exploding through the headset as if the words had been uttered by God. 'What are you going to do when you reach Vladivostok?'

'I will commandeer a train and make my way to Nikolsk.'

'Nikolsk is west of Vladivostok,' said the pilot. 'We will fly right over it on our way there.'

'But the nearest landing field is at Vladivostok,' replied Kirov. 'At least, that's what I was told.'

'That is correct, Comrade Major. Nevertheless, you will lose valuable time.'

'I am aware of that,' snapped Kirov irritably, 'but unless you can set this thing down on the train tracks . . .'

'No, that is impossible. The landing gear would break and there are telegraph wires running alongside the tracks.'

'Then we have no choice except to head for Vladivostok!' Satisfied that they had now reached the end of this pointless conversation, Kirov let his gaze drift to the darkness below. Rivers, reflecting the moon, cut through the black like silver snakes. Far away, almost lost on the horizon, he glimpsed a tiny cluster of lights from some remote village, and they seemed so frail in that vast sea of ink that Kirov felt as if he had trespassed into a place where all that he held sacred counted for nothing any more.

'We might not have to land the plane.' The pilot's words rang crackling and metallic through the headset.

'What?'

'Do you see those straps hanging down by your seat?'

Barely able to move inside the cocoon of the sheepskin-lined flight suit, Kirov leaned forward and squinted into the seat well. 'Yes, I see them.'

'I must ask you to buckle them on.'

'Why? What are they for?'

'Your parachute,' replied the pilot, 'for when you jump out of the plane.'

Ten hours later, after two refuelling stops, the plane banked lazily to circle the railway junction of Nikolsk at an altitude of 700 feet. Kirov slid back the rear section of the cockpit canopy. With the deliberate and clumsy movements of a child just learning to walk, he climbed out on to the wing, keeping a firm grip on the rim of the canopy.

The pilot's jaunty explanation of how to bail out of a moving aircraft had done nothing to inspire confidence in Kirov. 'I can't do this!' he shouted into the wind.

'We have been over this a dozen times, Comrade Major. It's just like I told you. Wait until I tip the plane and then let go.'

'I don't care what you told me. Don't you dare tip this plane!'

'Are you ready?'

'Definitely not!'

'Remember to count to five before you pull the rip cord!'

It's simple, Kirov told himself. You just have to let go. For a moment, he thought he could do it. Then, through watering eyes, he stared past the wing to the tiny junction below him. Around it, for as far as he could see, snow-covered woods fanned out in all directions. At that moment, his courage failed him completely. 'I'm getting back in!' he shouted.

The words had not even left his mouth when the plane's right wing dipped sharply and Kirov's legs swept out from under him. For a second, his fingers maintained their grip on the cockpit rim. Then he tumbled howling into space. All around him was the roar of the plane's motor and the rushing of the air. Without counting to five, or any other number, Kirov slapped his hand against his chest, gripped the red-painted oblong metal ring and pulled it as hard as he could.

In a thunder of unravelling silk, the chute deployed.

As the canopy came taut, Kirov experienced a jolt which seemed to dislodge every vertebra in his spine.

Seconds later, he emerged into a strange and peaceful silence. Drifting through space, he had no sensation of falling.

By now, the plane was no more than a speck against the eggshell sky, droning like a mosquito as it headed on towards its next refuelling stop.

A hundred feet below him, Kirov could see the railyard of Nikolsk. There was only one building, with a tar-paper roof, a chimney in the middle and rain barrels beneath each corner gutter. Next to it stood a jumbled heap of firewood almost as big as the building itself.

The main track ran directly past the building. Opposite lay a siding, which curved in a long metal frown across a clearing littered with buckets, spare railroad ties and stacks of extra rail. At one end sat an old engine, with sides reinforced by layers of riveted steel so that it resembled a giant, sleeping tortoise. At the rear and on both sides of the train, gun turrets bulged like frogs' eyes. Painted on it, in large white letters, was the name *Orlik*. At first, the engine appeared to be nothing more than a relic, but then Kirov noticed that there was smoke coming from its stack. As he watched, a man climbed down from the engine and began to make his way across the siding.

Kirov called to the person, who spun around, searching for the source of the noise. Kirov called once more, and only then did the man raise his head, staring in amazement up into the milky sky.

Lulled by his dream-like descent, Kirov was now startled to see treetops flashing past as the ground seemed to rise up to meet him. His foot touched the roof of the station house. With long, dance-like steps, he bounded over the shingles, finally coming to a halt only an arm's length from the edge.

Kirov gave a triumphant shout, only to be swept off the roof a second later when his chute billowed past him in the breeze.

He came down hard on the ice-patched ground and lay there in a daze, the wind knocked out of him.

A face, festooned with tufts of unkempt beard, appeared above him. 'Who are you?' asked the man.

At first, Kirov did not reply. He sat up and looked around. After so many hours in the air, he found the solidity of the earth beneath his aching rear end overwhelming.

The man crouched down. Along with a set of dirty overalls, he wore a thick fur vest with the hair turned out, giving him an appearance so primitive that Kirov wondered if he had fallen not only through space but also, perhaps, through time.

'I saw the plane. Has it crashed?'

'No. I jumped.'

The man looked at his desolate surroundings, as if he might have missed something. 'But why?'

'I'll explain everything,' replied Kirov. 'Just let me get up first.'

The man helped Kirov out of his parachute harness. Then the two of them gathered the chute and, not knowing what else to do with it, stuffed the silk in one of the empty rain barrels.

'My name is Deryabin,' said the man, as they made their way towards the station house.

'Kirov. Major Kirov. Where are the others?'

'What others?'

'Is there no one else here?'

'Let me put it this way, Comrade Major; you have just doubled the population for the entire district.'

The station house was a one-room building, with bales of hay stacked three high around the outside walls for winter insulation. The shutters had been welded closed by snow whipped up from passing trains.

The air inside the station house was rank and musty. To Kirov, it smelled like the locker room of the NKVD sports facility where he had done some of his basic training.

A bunk stood at one end, its rope mattress sagging almost to the floor. Beside the stove, which dominated the centre of the room, two chairs were set out, as if the man had been expecting company. The far wall of the house was completely hidden behind a barricade of canned goods, still in their cardboard cases, with their names – peas, meat, evaporated milk – accompanied by manufacture dates more than a decade old.

The first thing Deryabin did when he entered the house was to empty his pockets on to a table beside the door. Fistfuls of what looked to Kirov like large fish scales were already heaped upon the bare wood. To these the man now added another pile. They jingled as he let them fall.

'What are those things?' asked Kirov.

'Money,' replied Deryabin.

'Doesn't look like any currency I've ever seen.'

'That's because I ran it over with the train. I take all the one-kopek coins I can get my hands on, flatten them out and the Ostyaks turn them into jewellery.'

'Ostyaks?'

'They live in the woods. Trust me, you don't want to meet them. They live to the west of here, over in District 5, where the prison camps are located. Once a month, the Ostyaks show up here with dried salmon or reindeer meat and I trade these coins for it.'

'Couldn't you just use coins to pay for the stuff?'

'They prefer to trade. For them a kopek is just a kopek. But run it over with a train and you've got yourself a work of art. I can tell you are not from Siberia.'

'No. Moscow.'

'I almost went there once,' he said thoughtfully.

They sat down by the stove. From a battered copper kettle, Deryabin poured some tea into an even more battered aluminium cup and handed it to Kirov. 'So to what do I owe the honour of your visit, Comrade Major Kirov?'

'Several men have escaped from the Borodok camp.'

'I can't say I blame them. I've heard what goes on in that place.'

'The convicts are headed this way. They have a hostage with them. I must try to intercept these men before they cross the border into China. Can that train outside do anything more than roll back and forth over your wages?'

'That train', Deryabin replied indignantly, 'is the most famous engine on the whole Trans-Siberian Railroad! The Czechs used it to transport their men all the way from Ukraine to Vladivostok. Did you see the armour on her sides? She was a nightmare to the Bolsheviks.'

'But does it run?' demanded Kirov.

'It certainly does, thanks to me. Five years ago, the authorities in Vladivostok had it shunted out here to my station. They dropped it off and told me it was my responsibility. They didn't say why. Didn't say how long. They just dumped it and rode back to the coast. They probably thought she would just rust away to nothing, but I made sure that didn't happen. I've been looking after her ever since.'

'What about those?' asked Kirov, nodding towards the gun turrets. 'Are they still operational?'

'You could blast a platoon off the map with those,' replied Deryabin, 'and the authorities in Vladivostok kindly left me with enough ammunition to do exactly that. As for the rest of the train, I could drive the *Orlik* to Moscow. And when I got there, Comrade Major,' he levelled a finger at Kirov, 'I'd teach you Muscovites a thing or two!'

'And I look forward to that, Comrade Deryabin.' Kirov's temper was beginning to fray. 'But right now I need to borrow your train, and I need you, as well, to drive it.'

'You've got some nerve! You can't just fall out of the sky and then start ordering me around.'

'Actually, that is exactly what I can do. Falling from the sky is an experience I have no intention of repeating, but I had to get to Nikolsk as quickly as possible—'

'If you were in such a damned rush to get to Nikolsk,' Deryabin interrupted, 'why didn't you just parachute in *there*?'

Kirov felt his stomach flip. 'Are you telling me this isn't Nikolsk?'

Deryabin led Kirov over to a map identical to the one he had seen in Moscow nailed up on the wall. Deryabin pointed to a circle, some distance to the west of Nikolsk. 'Here is where we are.'

'You mean this station isn't even on the map?'

'Yes, it is.' He tapped at the black dot.

'But you drew that in yourself!'

'I had to,' replied Deryabin. 'It wasn't there before.'

'Then where the hell is this place?' shouted Kirov.

'Welcome to Deryabinsk, Comrade Major!'

Kirov shook his head in disbelief. 'You named it after yourself?'

'Why not?' Deryabin shrugged. 'I had to call it something. It didn't have a name before.'

Struggling to contain himself, Kirov returned to business. 'How far is Borodok from here?'

'I don't know exactly. It's not on the map, either, but Nikolsk is ten kilometres to the east, so you are that much closer than you thought when you dropped in here. The railhead leading into the valley of Krasnagolyana is about twenty kilometres to the west. From there, it can't be far to Borodok.'

'Good!' Kirov rose to his feet. 'There's no time to waste. Let's go!'

'Not so fast,' said Deryabin.

'There isn't much time. We must leave now.'

Deryabin folded his arms. 'Not before we have discussed my terms.'

With that, Kirov's patience disintegrated. He grabbed Deryabin by the collar of his boiler suit and dragged him out of the house. Dumping the man in a heap in the snow, Kirov fetched out his passbook, opened it and waved the Shadow Pass in Deryabin's face. 'These are my terms!' He rummaged in his pockets, fished out a handful of change and sprinkled it over the man. 'This is your compensation! Now you can stay here if you want, but I am taking that train.'

'You don't know how to drive a train!' laughed Deryabin.

'You go forwards. You go backwards. How hard can it be?'

'Very hard!' replied Deryabin, realising that Kirov was serious. 'Very hard indeed! Requiring months of training! The *Orlik* is not just any train. It has eccentricities!'

Ignoring Deryabin's pleas, Kirov set off towards the *Orlik*, whose engine chuffed patiently, as if anxious to be in motion.

Reaching the locomotive, he climbed up the short metal ladder to the driver's space. There, in the cold and oily-smelling compartment, he was faced with a bewildering array of levers, buttons and dials showing steam pressure, oil temperature and brake capacity. Hanging from the ceiling was a greasy chain with a wooden handle whose paint had been almost completely worn away. Grasping the handle, Kirov pulled down hard and a deafening hoot shook the air. Now Kirov studied the controls, wondering which to touch first. He grasped one well-worn lever and turned it.

The *Orlik* shuddered. Steam poured out from its sides, enveloping the compartment in a sweaty fog.

Hurriedly, Kirov turned the lever back to the way it had been before. Then he took hold of another lever, but before he had a chance to pull it, Deryabin had climbed aboard.

'All right! I'll drive the train! Just get out of the way Muscovite!'

Two minutes later, the *Orlik* was on the move.

Deryabin stood at the controls, adjusting levers, his hands such a blur of precision that Kirov was reminded of an orchestra conductor. From time to time, Deryabin would rest the heel of his palm upon the metal wall of the compartment, rap a knuckle on the small round window of a gauge, or brush his fingertips across the levers, as if to feel a pulse coursing beneath the steel.

Kirov stood behind him, backed up against the sooty metal wall of the compartment. Coal used to power the engine was contained in a tender attached to the back of the locomotive and its black dust glittered in the hot, damp air. On the gridded metal floor, melting snow had formed puddles which trembled with the force of the engine, making patterns in the water like damascus on a Cossack sword.

Deryabin stooped down and opened the door to the train's furnace, revealing a red blaze which looked to Kirov like the inside of a miniature volcano. Then Deryabin pushed past him and opened the gate to the tender. Nuggets of coal the size of apples rolled out on to the floor of the engine compartment.

'Let me tell you something a man like you will never understand,' shouted Deryabin. 'When you work on a machine and you live with that machine, you become a part of it and it becomes a part of you. And one day you realise that the machine is more than just the number of its parts. There is life in it! Like there is life in you!' To emphasise his words, Deryabin jabbed a finger against Kirov's chest, leaving an inky smudge against the cloth of his tunic.

Kirov swatted his hand away. 'Have you not realised yet that I am a major of the NKVD?'

'And have you not yet realised that you are in the wilderness, where a man's rank is judged by his ability to stay alive and not by the stars on his sleeve?'

Kirov was too stunned to reply.

Deryabin snatched up a shovel and handed it to Kirov. 'Make yourself useful, Comrade Major of the NKVD!'

Obediently, Kirov began shovelling coal into the furnace. Before long, he was drenched in sweat. When he leaned out of the compartment, he felt the moisture freezing into scabs of ice across his forehead.

The *Orlik* was gaining speed now, hammering along the tracks.

With a flick of his foot, Deryabin kicked the door of the furnace closed. He turned to Kirov. 'She's had enough!' He snatched the shovel from Kirov's hand and tossed it into the corner.

'Is everyone out here as crazy as you?' yelled Kirov.

'Of course,' replied Deryabin serenely. 'That's how you know you're from Siberia!'

Until now, Kirov had been completely preoccupied with getting to Pekkala before his kidnappers led him across the border into China. Now that he was finally close, the dangers that lay ahead were rapidly coming into focus. He hoped that the mere presence on the tracks of an armoured train would be enough to persuade the kidnappers to abandon their hostage, but there was no way of telling what such desperate men might do. As for the convicts, he did not care if they escaped. His only purpose now was to bring Pekkala back alive. With fear prickling his skin, Kirov took out his gun and made sure it was loaded.

*

The moment Pekkala opened his eyes he sensed that something was wrong.

Kolchak lay asleep nearby, his beard a mass of icicles.

Pekkala nudged him with his boot.

Kolchak's eyes flipped open. Breathing in sharply, he sat up and looked around. 'What is it?'

'They're gone,' whispered Pekkala.

Kolchak followed his gaze to where the Ostyaks had been sleeping. They had vanished, along with their sledges.

Both men clambered to their feet.

'They left some time ago,' said Pekkala, pointing to where snow had partially filled the indentations of their bodies.

'How is it possible we did not hear them?'

'They never make a sound except on purpose.'

'But why?' In a gesture of angry confusion, Kolchak raised his hands and let them fall again. 'I promised them *gold*! Their work was practically done. What on earth could have possessed them to vanish in the middle of the night?'

Pekkala was not sure. Perhaps they had finally realised the trouble they would bring upon themselves by helping the prisoners escape. That may have been the reason, but Pekkala couldn't help remembering the look on the Ostyak's face when he realised he'd been talking to the man with bloody hands. Klenovkin's words came back to him. 'They fear almost nothing, those Ostyaks, but believe me they were petrified of you.'

By now, the other Comitati were awake, shrugging off the cloaks of snow which had blanketed them in the night.

'What if they have gone ahead to take all the gold for themselves?' asked Lavrenov, wringing his bony hands.

Tarnowski shook his head. 'They don't know where it is. I made sure of that.'

'And what if they have gone to turn us in and collect some kind of reward?' Lavrenov seemed on the verge of panic.

'Then they'd be signing their own death warrants!' replied Tarnowski. 'Without them, we would still be in the camp! They're gone. That's all we need to know. What we have to do now is carry on without them. When we have found the gold, we will build our own sledges to transport it across the border. From here on, all we have to do is keep to the tracks. Where the line divides ahead, the south fork will bring us safely into China.' Tarnowski slapped him on the back. 'All you have to think about is how you'll spend the Ostyaks' share of the gold!'

Within minutes, they were on the move again.

The sun was out now, blazing so harshly off the snow that the men placed their hands over their eyes, peeping like terrified children through the cracks between their fingers.

Whirlwinds of snow, solemn and graceful, wandered across their path.

Not long afterwards, they found themselves in the shadow of a cliff. Beyond it, on the other side of the tracks, lay the frozen pond Tarnowski had been searching for the previous night.

'This is the place!' shouted Tarnowski. 'I told you it was here.'

All of them broke into a run, floundering out across the pond. After crashing through a forest of tall reeds, they entered a clearing where Tarnowski and Lavrenov immediately kicked aside the covering of snow and began scraping at the ground. But the soil was frozen solid. The crates might as well have been encased in stone.

Tarnowski sat back, wiping the sweat from his forehead. 'It's no use. We'll have to make a fire to soften the ground. We buried shovels on top of the crates. If we can get to those, it won't take long to get the gold out of the ground.'

'The smoke will be visible,' said Pekkala.

'We can't afford to wait for dark,' replied Kolchak. 'Everything must happen now.'

After gathering fallen branches, they heaped deadfall over the place where the crates had been buried. Using scrolls of birch bark peeled from the nearby trees, they soon had a fire burning. Then they stood back, watching nervously as the smoke climbed up into the sky.

*

Looking like a creature sculpted from ice and soot, Gramotin wandered through the forest. The trees seemed to be closing in on him. I've been out here too long, he thought. I think I am losing my mind.

In the distance, Gramotin saw what he thought at first was a cloud drifting in from the east, but soon he realised it was smoke. Why they would have stopped and made a new camp again so soon after leaving the old one, Gramotin had no idea. They must think no one is following them, he told himself. And to light a fire in broad daylight struck Gramotin as an arrogance which could not go unpunished. Encouraged, he pressed on, the weight of his rifle and ammunition bandolier dragging on his shoulder blades.

Later, when he paused to catch his breath, he noticed a pack of wolves skulking among the trees, their fur a greyish purple haze against the maze of birches. A jolt of fear passed through him, but he choked it down. Hoping they would keep their distance, he quickened his pace. After that, whenever Gramotin stopped, the wolves stopped. When he moved on, they followed. Each time, the gap between him and the wolves grew smaller.

An image barged into Gramotin's head of his old platoon, lying strewn and half-devoured on the ground. A blinding anger flared inside him. He unshouldered his rifle, hooked his left arm through the leather strap and braced his hand against the forward stock. Closing his left eye, he squinted down the notches of the gunsight and picked out the lead wolf. At this range, he thought, even a lousy shot like me can't miss. To calm himself before pulling the trigger, Gramotin breathed in the comforting smell of armoury oil sunk into the wooden stock and the familiar metallic reek of gunpowder from the breech of the Mosin-Nagant.

But then Gramotin hesitated, knowing that the men he was pursuing would be close enough to hear the gunfire. Even though the group had split up, they still outnumbered him. His only chance would be to catch them by surprise. Slowly, he lowered the gun. When the notched sights of the rifle slid away from the wolf's face, Gramotin realised the animal was staring right at him. It seemed to be mocking the Sergeant's presence, as if daring him to pull the trigger.

Gramotin reshouldered his gun and moved on.

Soon afterwards, as he rounded a bend in the tracks, a cliff rose up to his left. To his right, across a frozen pond, the smoke he had seen earlier was rising through the forest canopy. Leaving the path of the railroad, Gramotin scrabbled up the sloping ground beside the cliff until he reached a clearing near the precipice. Then he got down on his belly and crawled the rest of the way, dragging his rifle by its strap. From here, the footprints of the Comitati were clearly visible crossing the snow-covered pond. In the trees on the other side, Gramotin could just make out a group of men standing beside a fire.

As quietly as he could, Gramotin slid back the bolt of his gun.

*

Unable to wait any longer, Tarnowski waded into the flames, scattering the burning branches and emerging seconds later with two shovels. In their years beneath the ground, roots had taken hold of the handles. Now they clung like skeletal hands to the wood.

Kolchak reached out for one of the shovels.

With a smile, Tarnowski held it out of reach. 'Allow us, Colonel.'

'By all means, gentlemen!' Kolchak stepped aside.

Tarnowski and Lavrenov, each now armed with a shovel, marched into the smoke and began chiselling out clods of earth still crystallised with frost. Lavrenov's shovel, weakened by its years under the earth, broke almost immediately. But this did not slow him down. Grasping the metal blade of the shovel, he dropped to his knees and attacked the frozen ground.

Now that the two men were occupied with digging, Kolchak turned to Pekkala. 'Walk with me,' he said.

They strolled out on to the surface of the frozen pond.

'How does it feel to be free?' asked Kolchak.

'I'll tell you when I know,' said Pekkala.

'There is something else I wanted you to know as well. Even

though that gold is almost in our grasp, our work is not yet done.'

'Yes, we have to get across the border.'

'I am talking about more than that. What I mean is that you and I still have important roles to play in the shaping of our country's future.'

'Once we cross the border, this will not be our country any more.'

'That is precisely why we will be staying only as long as it takes to acquire weapons. We will then be returning to Russia and, within six months, my uncle's dream of an independent Siberia, which he died trying to fulfil, will be a reality.'

Pekkala was thunderstruck. Kolchak has gone completely mad, he thought to himself. 'An independent Siberia? With what ghost army are you planning this invasion, or are we to manage this just by ourselves?'

'Not ghosts, Pekkala. Refugees.' Kolchak's voice was trembling with energy. 'Just across that border there are over 200,000 men who fled Stalin's Russia. They are soldiers and civilians who had made lives for themselves in Siberia, but who were forced to flee into China during the Revolution, rather than surrender to the Reds. I am talking about the Izhevsk Rifle Brigade, the Votkinsk Rifle Division, the Komuch People's Army, and my uncle's own Siberian Provisional Government Troops. Some of them took their families with them.'

'And haven't they made new lives for themselves?'

'Of course, but they have kept alive the dream of returning to their native country. They all want the same thing, Pekkala – to return home to the richest land in all of Russia.'

'Even if what you say is true,' replied Pekkala, 'and these

refugees were prepared to fight, what makes you think you could defeat the Red Army?'

'The Russian military is busy in Poland. Soon, if the rumours in Shanghai are true, it will be defending its borders against Germany. They will have neither the time nor the resources to stand up to us.'

'And suppose you did take Siberia, what then?'

'Then we form an alliance with Germany. The land west of the Ural Mountains will belong to them, and everything to the east will belong to us.'

'What makes you think the Germans would agree to this?'

'They already have,' explained Kolchak. 'Their diplomatic representatives in China have promised to recognise us as a legitimate government as long as we can reclaim Siberia, which means that Japan will automatically recognise our new frontier as well.'

'And which country is providing the weapons for this adventure?'

'The men I'm speaking of are not concerned with politics.'

'You mean you are dealing with gun runners.'

'Call them whatever you want, Pekkala. Even as we speak, there are two ships moored in a cove in the Sea of Okhotsk, loaded with rifles, machine guns, even a few pieces of artillery. All we have to do is pay for them. And when we get across the border into Russia, what we do not have – more guns, food, horses, whatever the gold has not bought – we'll take from those who try to stop us.'

Even though Pekkala had now recovered from his initial shock, he was still astounded at the audacity of Kolchak's plan. Under any other circumstances, such an insurrection could not stand a chance against the massed forces of the Soviet Military, which Stalin would not hesitate to use if he felt that his power was threatened. But Kolchak's timing had placed him in the centre of a chain of events which might soon engulf the whole world. If his prediction of a German invasion was correct, Stalin might not be able to prevent a determined and organised opponent from occupying Siberia. No one would understand this better than Stalin himself, whose own party had come to power in the closing stages of the Great War, when the Tsar's army was crippled by defeats against Germany. Had the Bolsheviks chosen any other moment, their own uprising might never have succeeded, but with a combination of ruthlessness and popular support, they had taken over the whole country.

'I was right about you,' said Pekkala. 'You didn't come back for these men. You came back for the gold, and the reason they are free is because they are the only ones who knew where to find it. They believed in the oath you swore to them.'

'The oath was to the *mission*!' Kolchak howled.

'The mission failed. It's over.'

'Not yet, Pekkala. I know I can't bring back the Tsar, but I can use his treasure to build a new country, one that is not founded on the values of his enemies.'

'With yourself as Emperor?' Before Kolchak had time to answer, Pekkala continued. 'You may have calculated the cost of this new country in gold bullion, but what about the cost in human life?'

'I will not lie to you,' replied Kolchak. 'We have many scores to settle with those who fought against my uncle in the winter of 1918 when he was trying to liberate this country. Even those who stood by and did nothing will receive the punishment they deserve. Thousands will die. Maybe tens of thousands. Numbers do not matter. What matters is that they are swept aside until all that remains of them is a footnote in the history books.' He gripped Pekkala's arm. 'Blood for blood! Those are the words on which the new Siberia will be founded.'

Pekkala pointed at the trees, where Lavrenov and Tarnowski were still digging. 'What about those two men who have remained loyal to you? Have they learned about this plan of yours? All I heard them talk about was building mansions for themselves in China. Do they know you are leading them straight back into another war?'

'Not yet,' admitted Kolchak. 'After what happened when I tried to explain things to Ryabov...'

'You mean you *told* Ryabov?'

'I tried to!' Kolchak's voice rose in frustration. 'He was the senior officer among the Comitati. I thought I owed it to the man to tell him first. I had imagined that, after so many years in captivity, he would be glad to learn that the thieves who had stolen his freedom would pay for that crime with their lives.'

'What happened instead?'

'He told me he wouldn't go through with it. He didn't even hesitate. I explained that he could stay behind in China. I said I didn't care whether he came or not. But that wasn't enough for Ryabov. He insisted that enough lives had been lost on account of the gold. I told him it was about more than treasure. It was about eliminating Stalin and the Communists. If there is one thing I have learned in my years of exile it is that the only way to get rid of a monster is to create an even bigger monster. After that, it's just a matter of seeing who bleeds to death first.'

'And what did Ryabov say to that?'

'He said he would refuse to give up the location of the gold. After all, the Comitati were the only ones who knew where it was, since I had left before they buried it. Ryabov told me that the men in Borodok had learned to trust him. Everything they had lived through, he had also endured. Ryabov was certain they would listen to him before they listened to me.'

'And you believed him?'

'I wasn't sure, but I couldn't take the chance that he was right. That night, when he came to the mine, I thought he had come to speak with me, perhaps to try and talk me out of it. I didn't realise that he was there to meet Klenovkin. He didn't expect to find me outside that cave where I'd been hiding, deep inside the mine. Tarnowski and the others had warned me to stay put, but I couldn't stand it, cooped up in there like some animal in a cage made out of stone. So I had taken to wandering those tunnels at night, anything but stay holed up in that cave. That's when I discovered Ryabov. I could tell he was surprised to see me. I tried again to reason with him, but he told me his mind was made up. He was putting a stop to the escape. I reminded him of how long he had struggled to ensure the survival of our men so that one day they might find their way out of this camp.'

'And what was his reply?'

'He said their freedom, and his own, would not be worth the countless thousands we'd leave butchered in our path.'

At last, the mystery of Ryabov's death became clear to Pekkala. He realised he had misjudged the murdered officer.

'Pekkala, I did not want to kill him, but when he told me that Klenovkin would be there any minute, thinking perhaps

281

that I would see the situation as hopeless and surrender, I knew I didn't have any choice except to silence him for good.'

Their conversation was interrupted by a shout from the men who were digging. An arm rose from the smoke, the fist clutching a bar of gold. Tarnowski staggered out, half blinded, and laid the ingot down at Kolchak's feet. Then he turned and went back to his digging.

Slowly, Kolchak bent down and picked up the bar, whose surface was hidden by a residue of dirt, which had leached through the wooden crate over time. Kolchak rubbed it away with his thumb, revealing the double-headed eagle of the Romanovs. Then he glanced at Pekkala and smiled.

'Those men deserve to be told,' said Pekkala, nodding towards Lavrenov and Tarnowski, 'and told now.'

'They will be, as soon as they have finished.'

'Have you considered the possibility that they might not want to go through with it?'

'Of course,' replied Kolchak. 'That's why I am telling you first. These men know that you were trusted by the Tsar. If you are with me, they will be as well. Think of it, my friend. We won't just be living like kings. Kings are what we will *be*!'

But all Pekkala could think about was the lives which would be lost if he stood by and did nothing. He remembered the Tsar, driven to the brink of madness by the dead from the Khodynka Field; the men and women he believed he could have saved whirling in a ceaseless and macabre dance inside the white-walled palace of his skull.

It took both men to raise the first crate from the ground. As they lifted it, the rotten wood gave way. With dull, metallic clanks, ingots tumbled out into the snow. Other crates followed quickly, wrenched from the dirt and dragged clear of the steaming ground.

'Did it not occur to you', asked Pekkala, 'that I might agree with Ryabov?'

Kolchak laughed, certain that Pekkala must be joking. 'We are all of us entitled to vengeance, but none more than you, Pekkala.'

'Vengeance has become the purpose of *your* life, Kolchak, but not of mine.'

Kolchak's smile faded, as he grasped that Pekkala was serious. 'I trusted you! I broke you out of that prison. I gave you the coat off my back and this is how you repay me? The Tsar would be ashamed of you.'

'The Tsar is dead, Kolchak, and so is the world in which he lived. You cannot bring it back by spilling blood. If you have your way, the rivers of Siberia will soon be choked with corpses. And if Germany invades in the west, millions more people will die. By the time your vengeance has been satisfied, Russia will cease to exist. Your uncle did not die for that.'

Kolchak's eyes glazed with rage. 'But you will, Inspector Pekkala.'

Almost too late, Pekkala saw the knife. He grabbed Kolchak's wrist, as the weapon flickered past his face.

With his other hand balled into a fist, Kolchak struck Pekkala in the throat, sending him down in a heap on to the trampled snow.

While Pekkala fought for breath, Kolchak raised the blade above his head, ready to plunge it into the centre of Pekkala's chest.

When the two men emerged on to the ice, Gramotin could scarcely believe his good luck. Shielding his eyes with one dirty hand, he strained to make out who they were. Even though their faces were unclear, he could still see the numbers painted in white on their faded black jackets. One of them was 4745. 'Pekkala,' he muttered to himself. The other, he decided, must be Lavrenov, since he was neither bald nor the size of Tarnowski.

Lavrenov and Pekkala seemed to be involved in a heated conversation. Pekkala, who did most of the talking, even grabbed Lavrenov by the arm.

With trembling fingers, Gramotin slid back the bolt of his rifle and double-checked that he had a round in the breech.

Now the two men appeared to be arguing.

The next thing Gramotin saw was that Pekkala had drawn a knife. Suddenly, Pekkala struck Lavrenov, who fell in a heap in the snow. As Pekkala prepared to finish off the wounded Lavrenov, Gramotin felt a sudden rush of pity for the man, to have come this far, only to be killed by the very person who had convinced him to escape in the first place.

Without a moment's hesitation, Gramotin lined up the sight, right in the centre of Pekkala's back, and pulled the trigger. The gunstock bucked into his shoulder. After so much time spent with no other sound but his own breathing, he was deafened by the noise of the gunshot. It echoed back and forth between the forest and the cliff, as if guns were firing from all directions. For a moment, Gramotin lost sight of the men, but when he raised his head above the sights, he saw that Pekkala was down and a splash of blood darkened the snow beside the fallen man.

Lavrenov, meanwhile, had scrambled away into the trees, but Gramotin did not care. His mind was in an uproar. His whole body trembled and a cackling, nervous laugh escaped his lips. He had done it. He had killed Pekkala.

This laughter ceased abruptly as it occurred to Gramotin that he needed the Inspector's body as proof of what he had done. Without it, doubt would be cast upon his story. Determined to kill as many of the Comitati as he could, and force the rest to leave Pekkala's corpse behind, Gramotin began to fire round after round into the smoke. When the rifle's magazine was empty, he rolled over on to his back and removed a handful of bullets from his bandolier.

As he hurriedly reloaded the rifle, Gramotin heard a noise which, at first, he mistook for thunder although, in the middle of winter, that would have been unlikely. Perhaps it is an avalanche, he thought. The mysterious sound grew, filling the sky, vibrating the ground beneath his shoulder blades until, suddenly, Gramotin realised what it was. Immediately, old nightmares reared up in his mind and a choking sensation clamped down on his throat. Squinting into the distance, he spotted a train approaching from the east.

It took a moment before Gramotin was able to comprehend that, in fact, the arrival of this train was the best thing that could possibly happen to him. It meant that help was on the way. All trains on the Trans-Siberian carried a contingent of armed guards. The men would assist him in rounding up the last of the Comitati. For certain, they would be amazed to find him there, a solitary warrior, having pursued these escaped convicts across the taiga before cornering them in the forest. They, not he, would be the ones to tell the story of his heroic journey. He no longer needed to concern himself with any Dalstroy board of inquiry. They would not be punishing him. Instead, they would shower him with honours. There would be a promotion. That much was certain. Master Sergeant Gramotin. They might even make him an officer. There would also be a medal. But which one? Hero of the Soviet Union, perhaps. All he had to do was go down there and tell that train to stop.

*

When the noise of the first gunshot echoed through the trees, Pekkala had dived for cover into the frozen reeds.

Tarnowski was waiting for him on the other side, a rifle in his hand. 'The Colonel?'

Through the brittle screen of rushes, both men looked out on to the pond. Kolchak's open eyes stared blindly back at them. A round had hit him in the shoulder, leaving a gaping tear just under the right armpit as the bullet left his body.

Pekkala glimpsed a muzzle flash from the cliff, just as another round slammed into the ice on the pond, filling the air with a strange popping sound, like the cork coming out of a champagne bottle.

Pekkala and Tarnowski crawled back among the trees, where they found Lavrenov hiding in the hole from which they had dug out the crater. 'Where's the Colonel?' he asked.

'They got him with the first shot,' replied Pekkala.

Bullets hacked through the branches above them, showering the men with pine needles.

'There must be a dozen of them out there,' whimpered Lavrenov, 'to judge from all that fire.'

'But who are they?' asked Pekkala.

'Whoever they are,' Tarnowski answered, 'they're using army rifles.'

Pekkala realised that their situation was hopeless. The others knew it, too. No one had to say the words. He could see it on their faces. He looked at the gold bars, which lay strewn across the scorched and trampled ground, and thought of how close he and the Comitati had come to living out their lives as free men. Tarnowski was right. There would be no prisoners this time. There was nothing to do but fight it out until the last of them was dead.

With his eyes fixed on the lustre of the ingots, Pekkala fell backwards through time, to when he had last seen this treasure.

*

Deep beneath the Alexander Palace, hidden in the stone vault of his treasure room, the Tsar placed his hands against the neatly stacked bars of the latest gold shipment from the Lena mines.

To Pekkala, he looked like a man trying to push open a heavy door, as if that wall of gold would give way into another room, or perhaps another world.

'Excellency,' whispered Pekkala.

The Tsar turned suddenly, as if he had forgotten he was not alone. 'Yes?'

'I must he getting back.'

'Of course.' The Tsar nodded his approval. 'Be on your way, old friend.'

Pekkala began to climb the winding stone staircase which led to the ground floor of the palace. After a few steps, he paused and looked back.

The Tsar stood at the bottom of the stairs, looking up at him.

'Will you be staying, Majesty?' inquired Pekkala.

'You go on ahead, Pekkala,' said the Tsar. 'I have yet to count the shipment. Every bar must be accounted for. This is a task I trust to no one else.'

'Very well, Majesty.' Pekkala bowed his head and turned away. He continued up the narrow stone stairs. Just as he reached the main hall, he heard the Tsar's voice calling to him from the bowels of the earth.

'Remember, Pekkala! Only the chosen will be saved.'

Pekkala did not reply. Silently, he walked along the hall, where his own wet footsteps still glistened on the polished floor, and out into the pitiless heat of that August afternoon.

*

Faintly in the distance, Pekkala heard the sound of a locomotive.

Moments later, the three men glimpsed the dull grey snout of an armoured engine barely visible among the ranks of pines.

Lavrenov began to panic. 'Those men up on the cliff were only keeping our heads down until the reinforcements arrived. There's no way out of this. We're as good as dead.'

'Just try to take one with you,' ordered Tarnowski.

Both men seemed resigned to their deaths.

'You could run,' Pekkala said quietly.

'With those men after us?' Tarnowski laughed bitterly. 'How far do you think we would get?'

'Once they set eyes on the gold,' Pekkala told him, 'they won't be thinking about anything else.'

'You talk as if you aren't coming with us.' Tarnowski was staring at him.

'Stalin might be persuaded that your freedom is the price to be paid for getting his hands on the gold, but my escape brings him no such reward. If I go with you, he will pursue us to the ends of the earth.'

Lavrenov gripped Tarnowski's arm. 'Let's do what he says and get out of here now.'

'What about the gold?' For the first time, Tarnowski seemed completely overwhelmed. 'You can't expect us just to leave it all here, not after what we've been through.'

'Not all of it,' replied Pekkala. 'How much gold does one man really need?'

*

The train was close now.

Worried that he might not reach the locomotive before it passed, Gramotin lumbered down the steep slope. Half running, half falling, swamped with snow, he tumbled out at last on to the rails.

The engine slowed as it rounded a curve on the tracks. Then its motor roared, regaining speed and trailing a cloud of snow dust which rose like wings behind the train.

Gramotin raised his rifle above his head and began waving

his arms back and forth, all the while shouting at the top of his lungs to attract the attention of the driver.

The engine changed pitch suddenly. The great machine was slowing down. They had seen him. The sound of brakes filled the air with a ringing clash of steel.

As the train came to a stop, Gramotin stared in awe at the overlapping plates of armour, the heavy machine guns jutting from their turrets and the ice-encrusted battering ram mounted in front of the driver's compartment. Painted on the front of the engine, he glimpsed a name in large white letters. Even though Gramotin could barely read or write it took him only a moment to spell out the word, '*Orlik*'.

Gramotin swore he must be dreaming, but the shaking of the ground beneath his feet proved otherwise. 'No,' he mumbled. 'Not you. Not again!' He could almost hear the terrible, clanking rattle of the Czech machine guns as they strafed the foxholes where he lay with his platoon. He flinched as he recalled the whip-crack sound of bullets passing just above his head. He smelled pine sap from the gashed trees, mixing with the burnt-hair reek of cordite from the guns. He pressed his hands against his ears, trying to block out the terrible noise of bullets striking bodies, like that of a cleaver hacking into meat. Gramotin closed his eyes as tightly as he could, in a last, desperate attempt to banish these visions from his skull, but when he looked again, the train was even closer than before.

Convinced that his nightmares had finally sprung to life, the sergeant turned and fled.

*

'Go!' said Pekkala. 'There isn't much time.'

Lavrenov did not hesitate. Snatching up a gold bar in each hand, he vanished into the forest.

But Tarnowski had not moved.

'You must leave now!' urged Pekkala.

'I saw what happened,' said Tarnowski, 'out there on the pond. Kolchak was going to kill you.'

Pekkala nodded. 'If it hadn't been for that gunman on the cliff...'

'That gunman didn't shoot the Colonel. I did.'

The revelation stunned Pekkala. 'But why?' he demanded.

'I heard what he was planning to do,' explained Tarnowski. 'I don't care if Kolchak wanted a fight with Stalin. Unlike you and Captain Ryabov, I have no love for Russia or mankind. This whole country can go up in flames as far as I'm concerned.'

'Then why did you ever become a soldier?'

'Because I was good at it! War was my job, just as police work was yours, and I expected to be paid for doing it. I am owed, Pekkala, not only for the Expedition but for every day I spent at Borodok, especially since we should never have been there! If the Colonel hadn't insisted on bringing an entire wag-onload of treasure with us when we departed from the city of Kazan, instead of leaving all three wagons behind as we should have done, we could have outrun the Bolsheviks. At least we would have saved ourselves. Instead, I ended up in Borodok, along with the rest of Kolchak's men. My share of the gold is fair wages for spending half my life in that hellhole. And I'll be damned if Kolchak was going to spend it on another war.'

'Then take what you can and go now!' pleaded Pekkala.

Tarnowski nodded once. 'Very well, Inspector, and thank you. Perhaps, one day, I'll see you on the other side.'

Without another word, Pekkala turned and set out across the frozen pond toward the tracks. Behind him, hidden in the canopy of pines, he heard the dull ring of gold bars knocking together. After that came silence.

The train had stopped beside the cliff. The locomotive stamped and snorted, like a bull getting ready to charge. Then it belched out a cloud of steam as the driver released pressure from the engine.

Twenty paces away, Pekkala stood on the tracks, waiting to see what they'd do.

Now a man emerged from the haze. He was tall and thin, with a particular loping stride.

Only when the Major stood right in front of him did Pekkala believe his eyes. 'Kirov!' he shouted.

'Inspector,' said Kirov, trying to hide his astonishment at the sight of Pekkala's filthy clothes, the scruff of his beard, and uncombed hair. 'Where are the kidnappers?'

'Kidnappers?'

'The men who took you hostage when they escaped from the camp.'

'Ah, yes,' Pekkala replied hastily. 'They fled when they saw the train coming.' Now Pekkala raised his head and squinted at the top of the cliff. 'And where are the soldiers who kept them pinned down?'

'There are no soldiers, Inspector. Only me, and the driver of the train.'

'But *somebody* was shooting at us.'

'We did see a man on the tracks, but he ran away when

we slowed down. Whoever he was, the train must have scared him off.' Kirov nodded towards Kolchak, whose body still lay sprawled upon the frozen pond. 'Who is he?'

'That,' replied Pekkala, 'is Colonel Kolchak, the last casualty of a war which ended twenty years ago. And from what I hear, Stalin intends to make a casualty of me as well.'

'That will be true for both of us, Inspector, if we do not bring him the thirteen cases of gold he says are still missing from the Tsar's Imperial Reserves.'

'Thirteen?'

Kirov nodded. 'That's what he said. Five thousand pounds of it in all.'

Stalin has somehow miscalculated the amount, thought Pekkala. 'How did he come up with that number?'

'They had an informant,' explained Kirov. 'A groundskeeper at Tsarskoye Selo. He saw Colonel Kolchak departing from the estate and even managed to count the number of crates on the wagons Kolchak brought with him.'

As Pekkala thought back to that night, he suddenly grasped what must have happened. The groundskeeper had not realised that the third cart had broken down. He had only watched the first two carts departing. By the time the third had been repaired, the groundskeeper was already on his way to report what he had seen. Stalin must be under the impression that there were fifty cases in all, when in fact there were seventy-five. There were not thirteen cases missing. There were thirty-eight. Subtracting the three cases that Kolchak used for bribes along his route, that still left thirty-five cases of gold, and not 5,000 pounds but more than 13,000.

'Those cases are down there in the woods,' said Pekkala. 'I will go and fetch them now.'

'Let me help you, Inspector.'

'No.' Pekkala held up one grubby hand. 'As the Tsar once said to me, this is a task I trust to no one else.'

The poor man has been driven insane, Kirov thought to himself, but he smiled gently and rested a hand upon the shoulder of Pekkala's dirty coat. 'Very well, Inspector,' he said comfortingly. 'If you insist.'

It took Pekkala two hours to carry the ingots from the forest. In that time, he barely spoke, methodically shuffling back and forth between the train tracks and the clearing.

Kirov and Deryabin watched Pekkala struggling under the weight of the ingots, which he carried three at a time. The only assistance Pekkala accepted was for the two men to take the gold from his hands and stack it inside the train compartment.

'Why won't he let us help him?' asked Deryabin, when Pekkala had once more disappeared through the reeds and into the clearing on the other side.

'Don't ask me why he does what he does,' replied Kirov, 'because believe me I don't know. Most of the time only Pekkala knows what he is doing, but that was enough for the Tsar, and it is enough for Stalin, as well, so it will have to be enough for you and me, Comrade Deryabin.'

When the thirteen cases of gold, 312 bars in all, had been delivered to the train, Pekkala returned one last time to the frozen pond and dragged the body of Colonel Kolchak to the tracks, leaving a bloody trail through the snow. With Kirov's help, the two men laid Kolchak inside the tender where the reserves of coal were kept.

The rest of the gold, more than 500 bars, Pekkala left behind in the forest. In time, the Ostyaks would find it – a gift from the man with bloody hands.

'Inspector,' said Kirov, 'we have a long journey ahead of us, but before we go, I have a little gift for you.' From the pocket of his tunic, Kirov removed the Emerald Eye and placed it in Pekkala's hand.

For a moment, Pekkala stared at the badge, which unblinkingly returned his gaze from the safety of his grubby palm. Then, very carefully, Pekkala pinned it to the lapel of his coat.

In the engineer's compartment, Kirov sat down on the bars, which formed a low bench against the rear wall. He leaned back and folded his arms. 'Deryabin!'

'Yes?'

'It is time to go.'

'But where?'

'Still think you could teach those Muscovites a thing or two?'

'Damned right I could!'

Seated on his makeshift throne of gold, Kirov gestured casually towards the west. 'Then roll on, Engine Master. We are bound for Moscow. Show us what the *Orlik* can do.'

*

Too exhausted to go on, Gramotin stood beside the tracks, crying out in terror and confusion.

The *Orlik* had caught up with him at last.

Looking down from the engineer's compartment, Pekkala noticed what appeared to be a person in military uniform, although he could not be quite sure. This wretch's clothing appeared to be both singed and frozen at the same time. The helpless creature stood with its mouth open, caught up in a cyclone of whirling snow which vortexed around him as if it were a living thing. Whoever it was, Pekkala pitied him for having gone astray in such a wilderness.

As the train passed by, the two men locked eyes. In that moment, each one recognised the other.

'Gramotin!' exclaimed Pekkala.

The sergeant's screaming ceased abruptly as he gaped at prisoner 4745; the man he could have sworn he had just killed.

And then the train was gone.

Gramotin waited until the *Orlik* had vanished into the distance. Then, after swearing a silent oath never to mention what he had just seen, he tottered back on to the tracks and kept walking.

Six days later, the *Orlik* rolled into Moscow's Central Station.

*

High above the Kremlin, thunderhead clouds drifted across the pale blue sky.

From his office window, Stalin gazed out across the rooftops of the city. He never placed himself directly in front of the glass. Instead, he leaned into the thick folds of the red velvet curtain, preferring to remain invisible to anyone who might be looking from below.

Pekkala stood in the centre of the room, breathing in the honeyed smell of beeswax polish and the leathery reek of old tobacco smoke.

He had been there for several minutes, waiting for Stalin to acknowledge his presence.

Finally, Stalin turned away from the window. 'I realise you must be upset. I might have overreacted.'

'You mean by ordering me to be shot?'

'However!' Stalin raised one finger in the air. 'You must admit my instincts were right about the gold. Ingenious, Pekkala, allowing yourself to be taken hostage by the Comitati, in order to locate the treasure. A pity those two men managed to escape.'

'A small price to pay.'

'Yes,' Stalin muttered absent-mindedly.

'You seem restless today, Comrade Stalin.'

'I am!' he agreed. 'Every since I walked in here this morning, I've had the feeling that the world was somehow out of balance. My mind is playing tricks on me.'

'Is there anything else, Comrade Stalin?'

'What? Oh, yes. Yes, there is.' Lifting a file from the stack laid out on his green blotter, he slid it across to Pekkala. 'For the successful completion of this case, congratulations are in order. These are your award papers. You are now a Hero of the Soviet Union.'

'That will not be necessary, Comrade Stalin.'

Stalin's jaw clenched, but then he sighed with resignation. 'I knew you wouldn't take it, and yet I have a feeling you do not intend to leave here empty-handed.'

'As a matter of fact,' said Pekkala, 'I do have one request.'

'I thought as much,' growled Stalin.

'It concerns a man named Melekov.'

*

In the outer office, Poskrebyshev was relishing Stalin's discomfort.

The previous night, he had experienced an epiphany. When it came to him, he was hovering in that space between waking and sleep, when the body seems to translate itself, molecule by molecule, into that swirling dust from which the universe is made.

The idea appeared in Poskrebyshev's head so completely that it seemed to him at first as if there was someone else in the room explaining it to him. The drifting of his consciousness halted abruptly. Suddenly wide awake, Poskrebyshev sat up in bed and fumbled about in the dark for a pencil and piece of paper, afraid that if he did not write it down his plan might escape unremembered into the mysterious realm from which it had appeared.

Poskrebyshev had been thinking about the apparently limitless enjoyment Stalin took in humiliating him. He had always assumed that this was simply a thing he was required to endure. There could be no consideration of revenge. Stalin's sense of humour did not extend to laughter gleaned at his own expense. The only way Poskrebyshev could ever achieve any kind of satisfaction was if Stalin did not know a joke was being played on him.

Which is impossible, he told himself.

It was at this moment that the angels spoke to Poskrebyshev, or if they were not angels, then some other supernatural voice – Lenin, or Trotsky perhaps, calling to him from beyond the grave – since it hardly seemed possible to him that he could have come up with such a brilliant plan all on his own. In its deviousness, it even surpassed the revenge he had taken on Comrades Schwartz and Ermakov, currently residing in Archangel.

Arriving early for work the next morning, Poskrebyshev carefully rearranged the contents of Stalin's office. Chairs. Carpets. Ashtrays. Pictures on the wall.

As Poskrebyshev was well aware, Stalin liked everything to be in its proper place. He insisted upon it to such a degree of obsession that, the previous week, when a member of the Kremlin cleaning crew had switched his pipe rack from one side of the desk to the other, Stalin had the woman dismissed.

The brilliance of Poskrebyshev's revenge consisted in shifting these objects only millimetres from their original position. No one looking at them would be consciously aware that anything was out of the ordinary. Subconsciously, however, the cumulative effect would be devastating.

It would not be permanent, of course. When Stalin had gone for the day, Poskrebyshev would put everything back in its proper place. He would do this not to relieve Comrade Stalin of his suffering but to confound him even further as to the source of his anxiety.

Now, as Poskrebyshev eavesdropped on Stalin's conversation with Pekkala, he experienced a warmth of satisfaction he had never felt before and clenched his teeth to hide the sound of cackling which threatened to burst from his mouth.

A few minutes later, when Pekkala emerged from Stalin's office Poskrebyshev busied himself with paperwork. He expected Pekkala to walk straight past without acknowledging him, as most people did. Instead, the investigator paused. Reaching across Poskrebyshev's desk, he repositioned the intercom a finger's breadth to the right of where it had been before.

'What are you doing?' asked Poskrebyshev.

'Comrade Stalin seems particularly agitated today.'

Poskrebyshev looked at the ugly black box, as if by force of will he might return the object to its original position. Then, slowly, he raised his head until he was staring at Pekkala. Could he possibly have figured it out? wondered Poskrebyshev. What are you thinking? asked the voices in his head. It's Pekkala. Of course he has figured it out! A sense of imminent doom surrounded Poskrebyshev, but only for a moment, because he noticed Pekkala was smiling.

'And how is the weather in Archangel today?' asked the Inspector.

By the time Poskrebyshev remembered to breathe, Pekkala had already gone.

*

Melekov had just finished installing a new phone in the Commandant's office. His hands were sticky from the electrical tape he had used to bind the wiring. As he wiped his fingertips on his shirt, Melekov looked around the room. Most of Klenovkin's possessions had already been stolen by various guards who came to see the bullet hole, almost hidden by the peacock fan of blood which had sprayed across the wall.

Now the bullet hole had been repaired and the blood had been painted over, although, Melekov noted, both were still visible if he stared at the place for a while.

With a few minutes to spare before he had to be back at the

kitchen, Melekov sat down in Klenovkin's chair and put his feet up on the desk. Then, from his trouser pocket, he pulled out a cheese and cabbage sandwich.

Halfway through his first mouthful, the telephone rang, shattering the quiet of the room.

Caught by surprise, Melekov leaped out of his chair, which tipped over backwards and crashed to the floor.

Immediately, the phone rang again, its deafening clatter filling the air.

Melekov snatched the receiver out of its cradle and pressed it to his ear.

'Hello!' called a voice at the other end. 'Hello? Is anyone there?'

'Yes . . .'

'Who are you?' demanded the voice.

'Who are *you*?' asked Melekov.

'This is Vladimir Leonovich Poskrebyshev. I am calling from the Kremlin with a message for somebody named Melekov. Do you know him?'

'I *am* him.'

'Well, as of this moment, Comrade Melekov, you are the temporary Commandant of the Borodok Labour Camp.'

Melekov felt his heart clench, like a little half-inflated balloon grasped in the hand of an angry child. 'Commandant?'

'Temporary Commandant,' Poskrebyshev corrected him. 'Although, the way things work, it might be years before Dalstroy finds a replacement.'

'When do I begin?'

'You have already begun! The appointment is effective immediately. Congratulations. Long live the Motherland.'

'Long live . . .' Melekov began.

But Poskrebyshev had already hung up.

Melekov replaced the phone receiver. Silence had fallen once more upon the room. He placed the chair upright and sat down again at the desk. His desk. Slowly, he laid his hands flat upon the surface. With fingers spread, Melekov stretched out his arms and slid his palms across the wood, as if to anchor himself to the world.

There was a heavy knocking on the door.

Melekov waited for someone to do something and moments passed before he realised that the someone should be him. 'Come in!' he shouted.

Gramotin stuck his head into the room. 'What are you doing in here?'

'I am the new Commandant.'

'The hell you are,' said Gramotin.

Melekov nodded towards the phone. 'Go ahead. Call the Kremlin. Ask them.'

Nervously, Gramotin licked his lips. He realised Melekov must be telling the truth, for the simple reason that Melekov lacked the imagination, not to mention the audacity, to conjure a lie of such proportions. 'All right,' said Gramotin, 'then I suppose you'd better tell me what I'm to do with the body of our former Commandant.'

'Where is he now?'

'In the freezer.'

Melekov thought for a second. 'Put him in a barrel. Ship him out.'

Gramotin could not help but be impressed. 'You cold-blooded bastard,' he said.

Melekov ignored the compliment. 'And when you're finished,' he continued, 'you can take the rest of the day off.'

Gramotin nodded respectfully. This might work out after all, he thought.

'What was it like out there?' asked Melekov.

'Out where?'

'In the forest of Krasnagolyana. They say that place is haunted. You were out on your own a long time. Did you see anything?'

'Nothing at all, Commandant.'

*

A retired middle-school biology teacher was fishing for carp with a bamboo pole off a bridge over the Novokislaevsk River north of Moscow. No sooner had he begun than he snagged his hook on the bottom and had to cut the line. He tied on a new hook and, a few minutes later, snagged that one as well. When the same thing happened a third time, the teacher swore magnificently, threw down the pole and waded out into the lazy current, determined to retrieve his lost hooks.

As he reached down into the murky water, his fingers swept through the weeds and brushed against the soft pulpiness of rotten wood. It was only when his fingers touched the buttons of a coat that he realised that he had in fact been touching hair and the skin of a decomposing face.

The teacher staggered backwards out of the stream and stood dripping on the bank, wondering what to do next. He knew he ought to call the police and let them see to it, but as a teacher of biology he was curious to see for himself what he had only read about in books. After looking around to make sure he was alone, he waded back into the water and wrestled the body up on to the bank. Streams of dirty water poured from the dead man's pockets, sleeves and trouser legs.

The corpse was that of a man who appeared to have been lying in the water quite some time. His skin had turned a washed out greyish-white and his eyes had seemingly flattened out and sunk back into the skull. He was wearing a heavy black coat with wide lapels.

Crouching over the body, the professor grasped the man's jaw, opened the mouth and looked inside. Then he fetched a little stick, got down on his hands and knees and poked around in the man's ears. He touched the dead man's eye and pinched his cheek and flexed all the joints of his fingers.

His curiosity now satisfied, the teacher ran off to find a telephone and call the police, but not before he had retrieved his hooks from where they had snagged in the man's clothing.

Police identified the man as Vojislav Kornfeld, a known NKVD assassin. His body was taken to a morgue on Lominadze Street, where the doctor on duty found no signs of injury to the body. No trauma. No defensive wounds. No poison detected in his system. Although water was present in his lungs, the absence of lactic acid in his blood seemed to rule out drowning.

The cause of death was listed as 'undetermined'.

Further inquiries by the Moscow police yielded no results.

After six weeks, his body was cremated and the ashes scattered in a vacant lot behind the abandoned Skobelev hotel.

*

On a bright winter's morning at the Borodok railhead, a shipment of fifteen tons of lumber from the valley of Krasnagolyana was loaded on to flatbeds, headed for the west. Included in the shipment were a dozen oil barrels stencilled in bright green letters with the name Dalstroy.

Packed into one of these barrels was former Camp Commandant Klenovkin, hands folded on his chest and knees drawn up to his chin. Jostled by the movement of the train, Klenovkin's hair waved back and forth like seaweed in the tide of preserving fluid. Sealed in the darkness of that iron womb, the expression on his face was almost peaceful.

One week later, Klenovkin's barrel arrived at the Centre for Medical Studies of Sverdlovsk University, where it was immediately assigned to a newly arrived medical intern for use as a cadaver. Having collected the barrel from the shipping department, the intern loaded it on to a handcart and proudly wheeled it across to the laboratory where he and his classmates would soon begin dissections. He even took the long way around, so that everyone could see. The barrel was heavier than he'd expected. By the time he reached a deserted courtyard on the outskirts of the campus, the intern needed a rest. Propping the handcart against a wall, he lit himself a cigarette and sat down on an empty concrete platform, placed there many years ago for a statue which never arrived.

What Really Happened in Siberia

The struggle for domination in Siberia during and after the Russian Revolution is one of the bloodiest and most confusing chapters of military history. At the height of the struggle, more than twenty-four separate governments had been established between the Ural Mountains, which mark the western border of Siberia and Vladivostok on the Pacific coast. This was not merely a fight between Bolsheviks (Reds) and anti-Bolshevik (White) Russian forces. It also involved troops sent from the United States, Britain, France and Japan, all of whom saw heavy fighting, in some cases against the very people they had been sent to protect.

Central to this conflict was the role played by the Czechoslovakian Legion, whose extraordinary journey across the entire length of Russia is not only inspiring but almost incredible.

What were Czechs and Slovaks doing in Siberia, thousands of miles from their native country? The answer is that, prior to 1919, they didn't have a country. Instead, Czechs and Slovaks represented only two of dozens of different ethnicities which made up the Habsburg Empire, also sometimes called the Austro-Hungarian Empire, since these were the largest and most dominant nationalities.

The Habsburg Empire had been founded back in 1526, and had, for generations, served as a barricade of Christianity against the Muslim countries to the south and east. At the height of its powers in the sixteenth century, the Habsburg Empire controlled a large portion of Europe.

By 1914, at the outbreak of the First World War, the Empire was in serious decline. It was the assassination of the Archduke Ferdinand, a member of Habsburg royalty, that would propel the Austro-Hungarian Empire into a conflict which it would not survive. By the time the guns of the Great War ceased firing, at the eleventh hour of the eleventh day of the eleventh month of 1918, the ties which bound together the many countries of the Habsburgs had been permanently severed, and their Empire ceased to exist.

One of the new countries to emerge from this collapse was Czechoslovakia, which existed from 1919 until 1993, when it divided into two separate nations, Slovakia and the Czech Republic.

In 1914, although many Czechs and Slovaks wanted independence from Austria-Hungary, the chances of achieving this must have seemed remote. The First World War gave them the chance they had been waiting for. As subjects of Austria-Hungary, they were expected to fight under the banner of the Habsburgs, joining with Germany and Turkey in an alliance which became known as the Central Powers.

Knowing that their only hope of independence was the defeat of the very country for which they were expected to fight, many Czechs and Slovaks chose instead to take up arms against Austria-Hungary. The result of this was the Czechoslovakian Legion, whose soldiers fought alongside not only the Russians, but also the French and Italians.

It is, however, for the exploits of those Czechs and Slovaks fighting among the Russians that the Czechoslovakian Legion is best known.

Although the Russian Tsar, Nicholas II, did not encourage their independence, many Czech and Slovak soldiers chose to desert from the Austro-Hungarian Army in order to fight for the Russians. Another source of manpower came from those Czech and Slovak troops who had been taken prisoner by the Russians, and opted to serve in the Russian Army. A third group was made up of men who, although they lived within the boundaries of Russia, felt themselves to be ethnically Czech or Slovak.

After the March Revolution of 1917, when the Tsar officially stepped down from power, the interim government of Alexander Kerensky proved to be more sympathetic to the cause of Czechoslovakian independence.

Up until this time, Czechs and Slovaks serving in the Russian army had not been formed into a single fighting force. With Kerensky's approval, and thanks to the efforts of two men who would go on to become leaders of the Czechoslovakian movement for independence, Thomas Masaryk and Edvard Benes, the Czechoslovakian Legion was founded in the spring of 1917.

In October of that year, following the Soviet Government's 'Decree of Peace', the Legion found itself in a serious predicament. Having taken up arms against the Habsburg Empire, they could not return to their homeland, since the Central Powers had not yet been defeated. To make matters worse, the well-trained, heavily armed Legion was now perceived as a threat by both the Bolsheviks *and* the Central Powers.

Unwilling to abandon the cause of Czechoslovakian Independence, Masaryk suggested that the Legion now be placed under the nominal command of the French Army, which was still heavily engaged against Germany, the dominant partner in the Central Power Alliance.

This transfer of command was accomplished in December of 1917, but that was by no means the end of difficulties for the Legion. The greatest problem was one of geography. How were more than 30,000 men of the Czechoslovakian Legion supposed to get from Russia to France? The two countries were separated by their arch-rival, Germany.

It was then that the Czech Legion made the monumental decision to travel not west towards France but east, across the entire length of Russia, to the port of Vladivostok on the Pacific Ocean. From there, they would board ships that would take them to France, halfway round the world, so that they could continue the fight against the Central Powers.

Meanwhile, faced with the threat of renewed attacks, the Bolsheviks signed a peace accord with the Germans, known as the Treaty of Brest-Litovsk, in March of 1918. This treaty was both costly and humiliating to the Russians, and gave rise to the independence of the Baltic States (Estonia, Latvia, and Lithuania), as well as Finland and Ukraine. Czechs and Slovaks watched these developments with renewed hopes that their own independence might also be close at hand.

At this point, the Bolsheviks were as anxious to be rid of the Czech Legion as the Legion was anxious to leave Russia. With permission from Stalin to travel unhindered to Vladivostok, the Legion set out on its historic trek. For this, they followed the path of the Trans-Siberian Railroad, not only because it represented the most direct route across the country but also because the Legion obtained access to trains.

In spite of Stalin's permission, as the journey progressed, the Legion encountered many difficulties from local governments demanding bribes in order to allow the Legion to proceed through their territory. Partly as a result of this, by the time the first Czechoslovakians reached Vladivostok in May of 1918, the Legion was spread out over literally thousands of miles between Vladivostok and the city of Penza, far to the west.

This dangerous situation was made even worse by an event which occurred on May 14th, 1918, in the city of Chelyabinsk. An east-bound train loaded with Czechoslovakian Legionnaires found itself opposite a train filled with Hungarian troops heading west. These Hungarians were former POWs on their way home, having been released as part of the Brest-Litovsk Treaty.

To the Hungarians, these Czechoslovakians were nothing more than traitors to the Habsburg Empire. Amidst a torrent of verbal abuse hurled between the two trains, one Hungarian threw an iron bar at the Czechs, killing a man in the process.

The Czechs, who were not only armed but constituted a much larger force than the Hungarians, responded by attacking the Hungarians' train and lynching the man who had thrown the iron bar. They then stormed through Chelyabinsk and freed a number of Czechs who were being held prisoner there, having been arrested by the local Soviet for taking part in the attack.

The response from Moscow was swift. The diplomatic council representing Czechoslovakians, the Czech National

Council, was ordered by Leon Trotsky, then Commissar of Foreign Affairs, to lay down its guns and surrender.

Realising that this would be tantamount to suicide, the Czechs refused. In spite of Masaryk's plea for it to remain neutral, the Legion renamed itself the Czechoslovak Revolutionary Army, vowed to fight through to Vladivostok and continued with their journey.

Most regional governments were no match for the Czechs and their armoured train convoys, but they encountered increasingly fierce resistance at Irkutsk. Further to the east, Czech trains were involved in heavy fighting around Khabarovsk.

Czechs who had already reached the safety of Vladivostok stood ready to come to the assistance of their comrades, but were confused by contradictory reports about the clashes taking place, in some cases only forty miles away, and by Masaryk's continued demands that all Czechoslovakians remain neutral.

This confusion was resolved when, on June 28th, 1918, the Czechs learned that weapons being sent west by Bolsheviks in Vladivostok were being used against their countrymen. The Czechs immediately overwhelmed the Vladivostok Bolsheviks and, on July 11th, headed west to help their friends, using a spur of the Trans-Siberian Railroad which travels through China and is known as the Chinese Eastern Railway.

Caught between Czech troops advancing from both directions was the city of Ekaterinburg. Unknown to the Czech Legion at the time, the Tsar and his family were being held prisoner in Ekaterinburg, in the house of a merchant named Ipatiev.

Fearing that the Czechs would liberate Nicholas II, the order was given to execute the Tsar. The executions were carried out on the night of July 17th, 1918. The bodies were then doused with acid and buried in a nearby forest, where they remained hidden for most of the twentieth century. In 1991, when they were finally exhumed and identified using DNA from surviving members of the Romanov bloodline, including Prince Philip, Duke of Edinburgh and husband of Queen Elizabeth II.

Meanwhile, Czechoslovakian troops under the command of General Gaida succeeded in opening up the Trans-Siberian Railroad all the way from Vladivostok to Kazan, clearing the way for the remaining Czechoslovakians to reach the safety of the coast.

Elsewhere in the world, the odyssey of the Czechoslovakians had not gone unnoticed. Impressed by their phenomenal accomplishments, the governments of Britain, France and the United States urged the Czechoslovakians to remain in Russia and continue fighting the Bolsheviks.

All of these countries eventually dispatched expeditionary forces to Russia on what was optimistically referred to as a peace-keeping mission but was, in reality, designed to offer assistance in the event that the Reds could be overthrown by an uprising of anti-Bolshevik soldiers. With troops stationed near Vladivostok on the Pacific coast, as well as in the arctic port of Archangel in the west, the US and British governments failed to agree on whether to remain neutral or to intervene in the Revolution and thereby, if successful, to inspire Russians to continue the war against Germany.

In spite of the urgings of world leaders such as Woodrow Wilson to remain neutral, local Allied commanders promised assistance to the Czechoslovakians. In most cases, this assistance never materialised, although British, French and American soldiers were drawn into other clashes with the Reds, and with disastrous results.

As the situation among the anti-Bolshevik forces grew more and more confused, the Reds were gathering strength.

On September 10th, 1918, troops of the Red Guard, led by Leon Trotsky, launched an all-out attack on the Czechoslovakians. Meanwhile, far to the west, the dream of the Czechoslovakians was coming true at last. On October 28th, 1918, with the end of the Great War less than a month away, the nation of Czechoslovakia was established.

The effect on those Czechoslovakians still trapped inside Russia was dramatic. On that same day, disillusioned by Allied promises of help in combating the Bolsheviks, Czechoslovakian soldiers under the command of Colonel Josef Svec, mutinied. Despondent over the loss of his command, Svec committed suicide. Other mutinies soon followed. On October 20th, the 4th Czech Division refused an order to attack Red troops. On the 24th, the entire 1st Regiment of that Division revolted against its commander.

The reason for these mutinies was simple. The Czechoslovakians had achieved their independence. They had nothing to gain by continuing to fight against the Bolsheviks. The Czechoslovakians simply wanted to get home, but their ordeal was by no means over.

Although the Great War had officially ended, Siberia remained a battleground.

On November 18th, one week after the cessation of hostilities on the Western Front, Alexander Vassileyevich Kolchak, formerly admiral of the Tsar's Pacific fleet in Vladivostok, had established a dictatorship in Siberia, declaring himself 'Supreme Ruler of All Russia'. His 'war of liberation' came at a terrible price.

With the help of marauding bands of Cossacks, led by Atamans Semenov, Kalmykov and Rozanov, Kolchak went on the offensive.

Semenov, who gave up his horse in favour of an armed train known as *The Destroyer*, operated in the area of Lake Baikal. In October of 1920, having committed numerous atrocities, Semenov's troops fled across the border into Manchuria. Semenov himself escaped to Japan where, during the Second World War, he became an officer in the Japanese Army. Captured by the Russians in 1945, he was hanged as a war criminal in 1946.

Kalmykov, operating in the Ussuri Region, was equally guilty of atrocities, the most notable of which was the hanging of Red Cross personnel inside box cars in the city of Khabarovsk. So outrageous were Kalmykov's acts of violence that even his own Cossacks refused to carry out his orders. Kalmykov escaped to China and was shot in the early 1920s.

Rozanov, meanwhile, enacted a policy of killing a tenth of the population of every town he passed through and of wiping out entirely any town which offered resistance.

In an alliance brought about in part by the fact that Kolchak now controlled their only means of escape, the Czechoslovakian forces became merged with Kolchak's army. In recognition of the Czechoslovakians' fighting reputation, Kolchak placed Czech General Gaida in overall command of his troops.

By the summer of 1919, Kolchak's army had reached the city of Kazan. And they were not alone. The White Army of General Deniken was on the outskirts of Moscow, while the army of General Yudenich was approaching St Petersburg.

This was the moment when, had the Allies chosen to act, they might have tipped the balance against the Reds. Instead, they remained paralysed by indecision.

With increasing momentum, the Reds fought back. By the autumn of 1919, the White Armies were either destroyed or in retreat.

On November 14th, Kolchak was forced to abandon his headquarters in Omsk. He began a retreat which lasted through the winter, and cost the lives of thousands of his followers.

In an attempt to make scapegoats of the Czechoslovakians, Kolchak fired General Gaida. Adding to the already confused situation, Gaida responded by creating his own army, which he named the Siberian National Directorate. Gaida, who was by now both anti-Bolshevik and anti-Kolchak, began openly recruiting in Vladivostok, which resulted in a gun battle between his soldiers and those of General Rozanov. This culminated in a massive shoot-out at Vladivostok railway station on November 17th, 1919, bullet holes from which can still be seen today on the main station building.

In that same month, seeing that the situation was hopeless, the British garrison departed.

Faced with imminent defeat, Kolchak stepped down from power on January 4th, 1920. On the 7th, he placed himself in the protective custody of his old allies, the Czechs. The responsibility for this safeguarding fell to the 6th Rifle regiment, under the command of General Janin.

Hoping to reach the safety of the coast, where he might find asylum among the Allied expeditionary forces stationed in Vladivostok, Kolchak got as far as the city of Irkutsk before being halted by soldiers of a local government calling itself the Socialist Political Centre.

Although the Czechoslovakians, with over 13,000 men, eight field guns and an armoured train at their disposal, could easily have defeated the Irkutsk garrison, these soldiers had placed mines in tunnels through which the Czechoslovakian convoy would have to pass in order to reach the coast.

The Socialist Political Centre made the Czechoslovakians an offer – hand over Kolchak and we will let you proceed. There was one other thing they wanted, and that was the Tsar's Imperial Gold Reserves. These had been originally been hidden in the city of Kazan, but had since found their way into the safekeeping of the Czechoslovakians.

Faced with the possibility of never seeing his newly created homeland, Janin gave in to the demands of the Irkutsk garrison. On January 15th, 1920, Kolchak and the gold were handed over.

On January 30th, after a trial lasting one day, in which Kolchak was convicted of atrocities, the 'Supreme Ruler of All Russia' was shot against a brick wall in Irkutsk.

Although Kolchak's army was not the only force brought to bear against the Bolsheviks, its defeat and the execution of its leader spelled the end for any hopes of Allied intervention in the conflict. Leaving behind hundreds of dead, soldiers of the US Siberian Expeditionary Force (AEFS) departed in April of 1920. Japanese troops sent to help the Allied cause were the last to leave, in 1922. Their reputation for atrocities not only against Bolsheviks but also against civilians and even their own allies would soon be dwarfed by their actions against the Chinese in the 1930s and 40s.

By the time the last Legionnaires left Vladivostok on September 2nd, 1920, more than 35,000 Czechoslovakians had been evacuated from Russia. Although they had played a pivotal and heroic role in establishing their country, freedom for the Czechoslovakians would be short-lived and sporadic.

Eighteen years later, Germany invaded.

Another eighteen would pass before their one-time ally, Russia, sent its tanks across the border.

Unlike the beautifully maintained cemeteries of Great War dead in France, Belgium and the Dardanelles, the dead of the Siberian Campaign lie mostly in unmarked graves and all trace of their battles, except for a few bullet holes on the walls of Vladivostok station, is lost forever in the wilderness.

Also by Sam Eastland

Eye of the Red Tsar

It is the time of the Great Terror.

Inspector Pekkala – known as the Emerald Eye – was once the
most famous detective in all Russia, and the favourite
of the Tsar.

Now he is the prisoner of the men he once hunted.

Like millions of others, Inspector Pekkala has been sent to the
Gulag in Siberia. But a reprieve comes when Stalin himself
summons him to investigate a crime. His mission – to track
down the men who really killed the Tsar and his family, and
to locate the Tsar's treasure. The reward for success will be his
freedom and a second chance with the woman he loves.
The price of failure – death.

'A rollicking debut . . . it's written with flair and has plenty of
stand-out sequences.' *Guardian*

'Eastland's weaving of fact and fiction, of real and invented
characters, is brilliantly achieved, and Pekkala makes an unusual,
captivating hero. We are promised more of him. That's good news.'
The Times

'An excellent debut novel . . . Exciting, fast moving and eminently
readable.' Crimesquad.com

ff

The Red Coffin

1939: The forces of Nazi Germany are massing on Russia's border.

All Stalin's hopes for countering the Nazi threat rest on the development of the T-34 tank – a thirty-ton steel monster nicknamed the 'Red Coffin'. But the architect of the tank is found murdered and Stalin must turn to Inspector Pekkala to find the killer before the enemy invades.

But there's also an enemy within.

When Pekkala's investigation leads him to a group called The White Guild – a group of soldiers who also served the Tsar – he realises that the violence of the past still resonates in the present. Will his investigation lead him to the truth – or into a deadly trap?

'For those who like their tales told in the John Buchan style, with a shot of vodka downed and a fully loaded Webley at the ready.'
Independent on Sunday

'A vivid picture of a country still in a state of flux as the storm clouds gather . . . A page-turner of a book with enough neatly resolved twists and turns to keep any thriller fan happy.'
www.shotsmag.co.uk

ff

Faber and Faber is one of the great independent publishing houses. We were established in 1929 by Geoffrey Faber with T. S. Eliot as one of our first editors. We are proud to publish award-winning fiction and non-fiction, as well as an unrivalled list of poets and playwrights. Among our list of writers we have five Booker Prize winners and twelve Nobel Laureates, and we continue to seek out the most exciting and innovative writers at work today.

Find out more about our authors and books
faber.co.uk

Read our blog for insight and opinion on books and the arts
thethoughtfox.co.uk

Follow news and conversation
twitter.com/faberbooks

Watch readings and interviews
youtube.com/faberandfaber

Connect with other readers
facebook.com/faberandfaber

Explore our archive
flickr.com/faberandfaber